I0687137

FIRST BLOOD

The Russian Series
Book One

Charles Whiting
writing as
Klaus Konrad

SAPERE
BOOKS

FIRST BLOOD

Published by Sapere Books.

24 Trafalgar Road, Ilkley, LS29 8HH

saperebooks.com

ISBN: 978-0-85495-633-3

FIRST BLOOD

'This book is to be neither an accusation nor a confession, and least of all an adventure, for death is not an adventure to those who stand face to face with it. It will try simply to tell of a generation of men who, even though they may have escaped its shells, were destroyed by the war.'

Erich Maria Remarque, All Quiet on the Western Front (1929)

BOOK ONE: *THE REGIMENT*

'There's something about a soldier, there's something about
a soldier, which is fine, fine, fine!'
Popular English music-hall song between the wars

CHAPTER 1

Six o'clock! As the last hollow stroke ended in the little baroque church at the other end of the market place, the duty bugler's right foot stamped down hard on the gravel below. He puffed out his skinny young chest, spat into the silver mouth and blew hard.

Almost immediately the whistles of the duty NCOs started to shrill throughout the barracks. Doors banged. Windows flew open. A gruff voice shouted: '*Food orderlies outside — at the double now! Prepare to collect bread and coffee! MOVE IT!*'

They had opened the doors at the cookhouse now to admit the orderlies who would collect the morning rations for their squads, and the dawn air was suddenly full of the magic smell of freshly ground coffee and newly baked bread. Colonel von Ostermann sat by the open window of his bedroom and savoured the odours, as he did all the smells and sounds of the Regiment slowly coming to life: the crunch of the new guard's boots on the gravel, the rattle of dixies in the cookhouse, the hiss of the flag (the crooked-cross one he didn't particularly like) running up the pole, the tired clip-clop of the orderly officer's horse as he did his last rounds of a long boring night

Colonel von Ostermann had not slept well again. He had lain sleepless for hours listening to the Czech church clock strike the time, but even that could not spoil the pleasure he had always experienced listening to the Regiment coming to life at dawn. It had fascinated him right from the start when he had first joined the Regiment as a cadet back in '16. And it had done so throughout the long trivial years of the '100,000 Man Army', which the victors of Versailles had imposed on a beaten

Germany, when he had remained a lieutenant for ten years and they had exercised with wooden guns and tanks made of canvas. Even the new brown-shirted masters with their brutality and pushy aggressiveness which they had introduced into the Army had not been able to take from him the happiness of these moments before the day really started. At reveille he was always at one with the Regiment to which he had given twenty-three years of his life, no matter what the problems of the 'New Age' in which they lived.

There was a hesitant, polite knock on the door of his bedroom. It would be Thom, his soldier-servant, with his shaving water and coffee.

Colonel von Ostermann's face hardened. He looked at the little Czech calendar that his Czech predecessor had left behind the day the Regiment had marched into the eighteenth century infantry barracks and he had committed suicide in this very room. '*August 23, 1939*,' he deciphered the Czech slowly. Exactly eight days to go. He frowned and then called, '*Enter!*'

A new day had begun in the life of the 69th Infantry Regiment.

'The Bull!' Maltitz exclaimed fearfully and dropped from his top bunk near the window in a flurry of blue-and-white striped nightshirt, which flew up to reveal his skinny city dweller's legs.

'Is he coming here?' Red Rudi asked in alarm.

Everyone in the 1st Company, made up of reservists and recent recruits, knew that Sergeant-Major Bulle was trouble.

'You're not shitting,' said Maltitz, known in the company as 'Titty'. 'This morning he's going to burn our arses. I can tell it by the very way that the big bastard's marching over here.'

Now the young soldiers were sliding out of their bunks everywhere, throwing back their eiderdowns, grabbing for their

8

boots, hanging from the exercise bars placed at both ends of the long barracks room and attempting to do their pull-ups, which the Bull had introduced as a 'daily weakener' (as he called it) for every member of the 69th Infantry Regiment.

The door flew open and swung back and forth on rusty hinges, while the Bull stood there, his steel helmet almost touching the lintel, beefy shoulders filling the frame, charge-book held in his beefy right hand, a look of almost boundless contempt on his brick-red beefy face.

The activity died away to nothing, one nightshirt-clad figure hanging from the bar, muscles clenched as if he were frozen there by that baleful look for all time.

'Candycracks!' the Bull said suddenly in his thick Saxon accent. 'A bunch of candycracks!' His voice flew to an abrupt shriek. 'What are you — *you bunch of piss-pansies?*'

'*Candycracks! We're candycracks!*' they bellowed back fearfully, watching that terrible face change from brick-red to purple and from purple to a steaming awesome lobster.

The Bull slapped the charge-book against his massive right thigh so that his 'monkey swing' — his first-class shot's lanyard — trembled violently, and cried: '*Enemy plane attacking from two o'clock!*' As one, the soldiers dropped to the wooden floor and mimed firing imaginary rifles at some enemy dive-bomber zooming down on them at four hundred kilometres an hour from the west, while the Bull bellowed, 'Concentrate — concentrate!' striding up and down the room in his gleaming boots, aiming kicks at those of the reclining men whom he thought weren't taking careful enough aim.

After five minutes the Bull grew bored. He paused in the middle of the room, his big nailed boot poised in mid-air, as if he had been struck by some wonderful idea in midstride.

'Change of pace,' he cried abruptly. 'Dry fucking. Prepare to fuck! *BEGIN!*

As one the nightshirt-clad soldiers started to do press-ups, directed by Bull's insidiously slow command: 'One-two, one-two, wait for it, candycracks. Let her *tremble* for it… One-two, one-two … Oh, what lovely arses some of yer got! If I weren't straight, by the Great God and all his triangles, I'd have my heart in my mouth by now!' He kept them at the press-ups until the city boys among them found their arms and legs beginning to tremble like aspen leaves. The Bull would cause even the tougher farmhands among them to start to gasp harshly, as if their lungs might burst with the strain at any moment. Only then did he finally let them collapse into sweat-lathered, panting wrecks on the floor, saying contemptuously: 'What a bunch of cardboard figures you lot of wet-tails are! What is the 69th Infantry Regiment coming to?'

It was just about then that the Bull became aware of the snores coming from the far end of the room. It seemed to take him a long time to ascertain the source and nature of the noise, but slowly, very slowly, he began to turn, his face flushing crimson again, his bullet head worked as if on stiff steel springs.

Suddenly he exploded. In the shadows at the end of the long barracks room, a bulky shape was visible under the feather eiderdown, moving up and down rhythmically, deep in the sleep of a very contented man. 'Some shit is kipping there!'

Titty closed his eyes hastily. Next to him Red Rudi, the ex-Communist from Berlin-Wedding, threw his big paws over his ears, as if he could not bear to hear what would come next. Over the way a farmboy pissed the length of his right leg in horror.

'*Asleep!*' the Bull, breathed, more in awe, it seemed, than rage. '*Asleep — now!*'

As if his legs were burdened by great weights, the Bull moved down the length of the barracks room. Lying on the floor in their nightshirts, the men hardly dared to breathe as his massive bulk thundered past, assailing their nostrils with the smell of cheap cigars, stale beer and heavy male sweat that came from him.

The Bull stopped at the upper bunk where the rhythmic to-and-fro of the eiderdown indicated that the man hidden beneath was as yet still unaware of the terrible fate that now awaited him. Almost delicately, Bull poked his charge-book into the eiderdown. Something stirred. The eiderdown rose slightly in the air, and the awed silence was broken by a low, musical, almost joyful fart.

The Bull staggered back. His eyes rolled upwards, as if he were imploring some deity above to spare him any more shame of this kind.

'He farted,' he said in a broken voice. 'He had the audacity to fart — *on me!*'

The men lying on the floor waited in tense expectation. Titty told himself he would scream in a minute. Red Rudi bit his bottom lip, unaware of the salty taste of warm blood — his own — flooding his mouth. One of the Bavarian farmboys whispered a swift prayer and attempted to cross himself as he lay there.

'Farted on me,' the Bull repeated. Then his eyes flashed and, grabbing the eiderdown, he pulled it back with one great heave, crying so that the wooden walls trembled, 'By God, I'm gonna crack your arse, am I not? I'm gonna rip the eggs off'n you slowly, deliciously, pleasurably until —' He stopped short, mouth suddenly open stupidly, as he stared down at the undersized soldier who grinned back at him, as if he expected the crimson-faced furious NCO to give him a good-morning kiss.

'Morning, Sergeant-Major,' he said in a happy, easy-going Cologne voice, 'where's the fire?'

'FIRE!' the Bull exploded. 'WHERE'S THE FIRE? ... I'LL TELL YOU WHERE THE SHITTING FIRE IS ... UP... UP,' his rage was so great that he could hardly get out the words, 'UP ... *UP YOUR ARSE!*'

Sepp Deltgen was not impressed, nor did he seem to be worried at the sight of the huge NCO leaning over him only millimetres away, spluttering his face with angry spittle. 'Some sort of trouble?' he enquired mildly, while everyone tensed in expectation that the Bull would seize him by his skinny neck, whirl him around a couple of times, and smash his narrow Rhenish head against the nearest wall.

'*TROUBLE?*' The Bull could speak no more.

Deltgen's cunning narrow face assumed a serious expression. 'Oh that, Sarnt-Major,' he said easily, as if he had suddenly realized what all the fuss was about 'I was stick-man last night'

'ST ... STICK-MAN!' The Bull grabbed at his tight collar, gasping for breath, his tortured face twisted to one side, as if he were being strangled to death.

Deltgen sat bolt upright in his bed, skinny shoulders squared in the regulation position of sitting-to-attention. With his eyes abruptly wooden and fixed on some far horizon, he recited: 'In the year 1815 after the successful outcome of the Battle of Waterloo in which the 69th Infantry Regiment, then the Prince of Prussia's Own Grenadier Regiment, played a prominent part, the Regiment was gazetted with the British First Foot Guards. From them, the Regiment adopted the custom of allowing the smartest soldier at the guard mount — the so-called stick-man — to be released from the duty and in add —'

'TRAP!' the Bull cut in with a tremendous roar, finally finding his voice. 'I know the Regiment's history. I was in it when you were still shitting yer skivvies!' He swallowed hard and controlled himself with difficulty. There was nothing he could do: the stick-man not only was freed from guard duty, he was also allowed to sleep in on the following morning. It was part and parcel of the 69th's long historical tradition. He swung around and stared down at the quaking figures on the floor. 'All right, you bunch of slit-arsed slime-shitters, don't just lie there. Fatigues, full field pack and gas masks within five minutes. This day Sergeant-Major Bulle is really going to burn your tails. *MOVE!*'

And with that he was gone, smashing the door behind him so fiercely that the panes in the windows rattled, as if they might fall out at any moment. In the far corner Deltgen turned luxuriously in his bed and whispered, 'Don't say goodbye when you leave chaps, will you…'

'I assume you gentlemen have seen this morning's *Völkischer Beobachter*?' Lieutenant Adam von Sulzberger said, unable to repress his excitement any longer.

Eyes, some grave, others bored, the rest angry, looked up at the pink-cheeked young subaltern all along the oak table which ran the length of the officers' mess.

Von Sulzberger flushed.

'Didn't realize that the officers of the 69th read, er, newspapers?' said Doctor Schmitz ironically, smoothing back his iron-grey hair with his one hand. The doctor, also known as 'Pill', had lost the other as a young cadet at Verdun in '16 before he had gone to study medicine and had returned to the 69th on general mobilization the previous April.

Outside on the square the Bull was intoning in front of the sweating, red-faced men of One Company, as they hopped up and down, rifles held straight in front of them. 'Come on, you bunch of bunny rabbits, *hop … hop … hop…!*'

'But, Doctor, it's vitally important,' the young officer protested and held up the paper for all to see. 'Just look at that! Banner headlines — VON RIBBENTROP SIGNS NON-AGGRESSION PACT FOR GERMANY WITH SOVIET RUSSIA!'

Major Hardt, commander of the Second Battalion, a grey-haired middle-aged officer who had been passed over twice for promotion, looked up from his coffee and grunted sourly. 'And what are we supposed to do, von Sulzberger — faint?'

'Don't you see, sir…'

Von Sulzberger wasn't to be stopped, Colonel von Ostermann told himself. Just like his father, until an American sniper's bullet through the forehead stopped him for good in the Argonne Forest in '18.

'The Führer has a wonderful opportunity now to further his international policies,' continued von Sulzberger. 'This time it won't be like 1914. Germany will not be faced by a war on two fronts. The Russians are out of it.'

'So?' Hardt persisted, looking coldly at von Sulzberger's excited red face.

'So, Hardt —' another voice — dry, hard, yet neutral — broke into the discussion.

Colonel von Ostermann turned. It was Major von Dietz, the youngest and most able battalion commander in the Regiment. His mouth as always, even when relaxed, was curled up at the corners in what seemed like a bitter smile.

'I'll tell you what it means,' von Dietz continued, staring at Hardt with those strange, heavy-lidded cold-grey eyes of his. 'It means Germany can now go to war.' And with that he raised his tall skinny body from the table. '*Guten Morgen, Meine Herren*!' Then he was gone.

CHAPTER 2

'*Morgen, Soldaten!*' Major von Dietz reined his horse as he greeted the thousand men of the First Battalion drawn up in four rigid ranks across the barracks' square.

'*Morgen, Herr Major!*' The hoarse voices roared as one, and the major's horse pawed nervously at the cobbles. Expertly, von Dietz tugged the bit and stared at the men, whom he would soon lead to war.

They came from every part of the Reich, from the North Sea to the Belgium border, from Westphalia right over to East Prussia — young men between the ages of 18 and 24, untrained for the most part, with here and there a few overweight reservists and a handful of old soldiers who had been with the 69th ever since 1933. The material was good, he knew that. But it was untrained, and untrained material could easily develop into quickly expended cannon fodder. Even in the great bloody battles of France in the First War, the 69th had never had the reputation of wasting its men.

He rose slightly in his saddle so that he could see well into the rear ranks. 'Soldiers, in the 69th we say train hard, fight easy. But hard training does not mean brutalization. In the 69th we have never believed in the cadaver discipline common to other regiments. You will be worked hard — very hard. One day you will realize it has been for your own good. But I will not have you falsely ill-treated in the name of discipline.' Sternly the tall, handsome young officer looked along the ranks of his NCOs until his gaze finally came to rest on Sergeant-Major Bulle. He knew the Bull of old. He was the typical military sadist, who never missed a chance to harass some unfortunate recruit if he thought an officer wasn't looking. Von Dietz kept his eyes on the big, barrel-chested NCO until the latter's face flushed an even deeper red than normal. Then he continued. 'This morning you will run the battalion's bayonet course. You will wonder why, in these days of modern war, we still teach bayonet fighting in the 69th. I will tell you, soldiers.' He leaned over the neck of his nervous mount, purposely lowering his voice so that his listeners had to strain their ears to hear his words. 'Because, in the final instant, it is a soldier's unhappy duty to kill, to face up to an enemy who is also required to kill him. Despite the tank and the aeroplane, it is still steel against steel — as it has always been. *Kill or be killed!*'

For one long moment von Dietz crouched there, allowing them to absorb his words, his face sombre, as if he, too, were considering the full meaning of them. Then he barked, his face normal again: 'NCOs, take the battalion away!'

'When you run the course, I want you to yell,' the Bull bellowed.

'Yell your stupid heads off! *Scream*! Like this!' He threw back his own big head and screamed with all his might so that some of his listeners felt the small hairs at the back of their shaven heads grow erect with fear. 'Because if you can't beat the buggers, you can at least scare 'em to death! Here, you!' He pointed at a pale-faced Maltitz. 'Give me your bayonet'

The little soldier handed it over.

The Bull looked down at him scornfully from his great height. 'What do you think you're giving me, soldier? A shitting bunch of pansies or something? A soldier doesn't *hand* over a rifle, he throws it — like this!' He flung the rifle violently at Maltitz, nearly knocking him off his feet Fortunately the little man managed to hold on to it; for it was known throughout the battalion that if any soldier dropped his weapon, the Bull had it chained to him for twenty-four long hours, even in bed. 'Now give me your rifle, soldier!'

Maltitz threw the rifle with all his strength. The Bull caught it easily with one hand, a scornful look on his brutal crimson face.

Watching the scene, Major von Dietz sniffed and told himself he would have to keep an eye on Sergeant-Major Bulle. What had happened in W—, long buried deep within his subconscious, would not happen in the First Battalion — not as long as he commanded it.

'Use the butt — it's brass-plated — and smash in their skulls... Stick the blade right into their fat guts, deep... Twist when you lunge...' The Bull continued his little lecture at the top of his voice, twirling the bayonet to illustrate his points, as if it were a child's toy. His listener's faces grew progressively paler as he went deeper into the gory details of bayonet-fighting... 'That ensures the blade comes out easier... And if it sticks, you press yer trigger and blow yerself free.'

Five minutes later the battalion was being chased across the bayonet course, chivvied on all sides by bellowing, red-faced NCOs screaming out their instructions, as the sweat-lathered soldiers ran, plunged, swung their brass butts at the straw dummies tied to the posts on both sides of the track. 'Stick him in the neck, you asparagus Tarzan... Rip open his shitting jugular vein, you cardboard soldier... Stick him in the guts... *Yell... Yell... Yell!*' Those who survived the course without collapsing into the ditch at the side of the track, leaned against the wall at the far end, blind with fatigue, their hearts thumping crazily, every limb trembling like a leaf in a great wind.

But there was worse to come that morning. After what the Bull called the 'piss-pause' — five minutes to urinate in full view of the giggling Czech women working in the field opposite, during which time many of the younger men were too embarrassed to relieve the pressure of their bursting bladders — he chased them on the obstacle course. It was a treacherous quagmire. Earthen tunnels running everywhere like a maze, filled with dead-ends through which they crawled in semi-darkness, startled time and time again by the thunder flashes that the grinning NCOs threw down at them and choked by the semi-toxic gas pumped in at regular intervals. Out of the tunnels at last, the bruised, sweating frightened young men, some with their fatigues soiled with vomit from the gas, were confronted by a five-minute dash through a mass of barbed wire, high walls, rope ladders, ditches, hurdles, and finally a pond some six or seven metres in width.

There, at the last trap of the assault course, a grinning Bull waited for the nearly exhausted young men. The trick was to hurtle forward and dive for the slippery rope which hung above the centre of the pond. With luck the soldier, encumbered by pack, helmet and rifle, would manage to grasp the rope and swing safely to the other side. The unfortunate soldier who missed dropped three metres right into the slime-covered, evil-smelling water.

Man after man failed the jump, to emerge dripping from the pond, wiping the stinking muck of centuries from their miserable faces while the Bull rocked with laughter, enjoying himself hugely. Finally von Dietz had had enough. '*Haupt-feld!*' he commanded and crooked a finger at the big NCO.

Bull came running over to where he waited on his horse, tears running down his big broad face. '*Herr Major?*' he said, snapping to attention and puffing out his barrel chest, obviously very pleased with himself.

Von Dietz contained himself with difficulty. The Bull had not understood one word of what he had said that morning. 'I think, Sergeant-Major, we can dispense with the pond now.'

The Bull looked up at him in genuine bewilderment. 'Dispense with the pond, sir?' he stuttered. 'But, it's the real test of their … courage.'

'Courage, you call it, eh?' But irony was wasted on the Bull. 'Sticking their penknives in those dummies or crawling under the earth ain't anything, sir. That don't scare 'em. But to fall in that shitty water, laden down with their packs and everything, that really puts the wind, up them cardboard soldiers, sir.'

'Sergeant-Major, we are not training them to be scared…' von Dietz began but he realized that any logical explanation would be wasted on the big, brutal, bewildered man staring up at him. 'Cut out the pond, Sergeant-Major,' he ended, his voice icy.

Turning his mount, von Dietz cantered away, leaving the Bull staring after him, muttering furiously under his breath. But there was no more fun at the pond that particular morning.

Major von Dietz conducted the unarmed combat class personally, taking the battalion in groups of thirty, explaining to them in simple terms how they might defend themselves if they were attacked by an enemy when they were without a weapon. He deliberately kept on his tunic and cap, in spite of the burning afternoon sunshine. He wanted to convince the red-faced young men, who were mostly stripped to their trousers and jackboots, that it was easy, very easy.

'I am going to show you how to kill an enemy with *this*.' He held up his right hand, fingers clenched tightly together. 'Or *this*!' He displayed his two middle fingers, extended. 'And how to defend yourself against an enemy armed with a rifle, a knife, a club or any other weapon.' He looked at their suddenly interested faces with grave eyes. 'I hope to God you will never have to be in a position to kill one of your fellow human beings in cold blood.'

Suddenly that snowy day in the forest came back to him: sighting the rifle on the fat laughing figure squatting there in the white grass, helpless ... his finger curling round the trigger which would blast the squatting man into eternity... He swallowed hard and dismissed the terrible vision. 'But it will give you confidence in yourselves, men, the knowledge that you can still win and survive, even if you are unarmed.'

Swiftly von Dietz demonstrated to them how to strike an enemy just above the bridge of the nose to break the paper-thin bone located there and drive the splinters into the brain causing instant death ... how to chop below the nose to cause concussion ... how to clap hands to the ears to fell a man ... how to stab fingers, stiff as a dagger, into the celiac plexus, causing instant internal haemorrhage, which would well be fatal ... and a score of other terrible methods to injure or kill one's fellow-man.

Thereafter he gave his now-entranced audience a practical demonstration, picking, as he always did, the biggest man among them and ordering the soldier to rush him with a naked bayonet. With a swift practiced movement his right arm flashed up, blocking the man's bayonet arm. In the same instant his left forearm smashed into his attacker's elbow, bending the arm backwards. One second later he had the attacker's bayonet arm trapped in a vice-like grip, forcing his surprised opponent on to his knees, the bayonet falling suddenly from nerveless fingers.

Still holding his attacker, von Dietz explained that only one step more needed to be taken. 'Now you've got to finish him off. You can fall on his chest with both knees. Or you can jam your thumbs into his Adam's apple to choke him, or if you can't think of anything else, you can kick him swiftly into the eggs.' He paused for breath and noted how pale their faces had gone as they visualized, probably, that this might well happen to them too. He grinned. 'Then you can look down and admire your workmanship. But if the other man gets up, blood in his eyes, then make dust — *but quick*!'

The tension was broken and the men laughed, but not very confidently.

It was towards the end of his demonstration to the third group that the Bull joined the audience, the usual contemptuous sneer on his red brutal face, and von Dietz realized that now was as good an opportunity as any to take the bullying NCO down a peg or two in the eyes of the rank-and-file. Of course, the Bull had been through the same training and knew the drill, but von Dietz still thought he could manage him despite the NCO's having the advantage of weight and height on him.

He went through the usual theory and then repeated the old question: 'But what do you do when an armed man attacks you eh…? Perhaps,' he looked at the Bull, as if he had just become aware of his presence, 'you might like to act the role of the aggressor, Sergeant-Major?'

The Bull grinned suddenly, an unholy light starting to glow in his piglike eyes as he realized that a golden opportunity had just presented itself to make a fool of the snot-nose Dietz. It would make a damn good tale to tell his cronies at sergeants' mess tonight. 'Of course, sir, anything to please.'

Without any further ado, he pulled out his NCO's dirk and faced the waiting von Dietz.

'Now,' the officer commanded.

With surprising speed, the Bull came at him, crouched low, left foot leading, dirk held close to his side. He was expecting the usual defence, as were the students, but von Dietz gave him and them something new.

When the Bull was almost within striking distance, von Dietz sprang, feet first, directly at the Bull's big chest. The NCO lashed out with the dagger and missed. Next moment von Dietz connected and the Bull was on his back, yelping with pain, dirk tumbled to the ground. Von Dietz crouched grinning at his side, already upright again.

Solemnly he winked at the men, who were having a very hard time trying to control their glee at the hated NCO's misery, as he rolled back and forth in the grass, clutching his sorely hurt chest. Reaching down a helping hand, the officer said: 'I hope I didn't hurt you too much, Sergeant-Major. I'm afraid I just slipped.'

The Bull had not the strength to answer back, but his eyes spoke volumes.

Two days later von Dietz led the battalion personally on a day-long march. It had begun to drizzle as they marched out of the gate singing, their rifles balanced at the correct angle over their shoulders. The rain grew in intensity until, half an hour after they had left the little Czech town, it was pouring down in a miserable solid sheet.

At first they were glad of the protection afforded by their capes, but they were soon sweating profusely under the thick rubber. Ending at the level of their heavy jackboots, the capes also made a perfect funnel, channelling the rain down in streams right into their dice-beakers so that they sloshed forward, bent against the driving rain and looking like hunchbacks with their packs hidden beneath the rotten capes.

Von Dietz, as soaked and as heavily laden as the men, did not seem to notice the misery of that hard wet slog into the foothills that led to the border. He was here, there and everywhere along the whole length of column, encouraging the men, cursing at them, making jokes at his own and their expense, ending always with the same maddeningly cheerful phrase; 'March, 69th, *march*!'

The hours passed. The men slogged on mechanically, their gazes fixed on the feet of the man in front of them, the water squishing from their boots as the rain hissed down in solid grey sheets.

At midday the major ordered a halt and a line of trucks drove up. The men's faces brightened somewhat as they crouched in the wet grass, trying to find some shelter under the trees which lined the road at that spot. Here and there some of them had still strength enough to whisper, 'The old man's gonna give up. Call it off and let us go back by truck.'

They were doomed to disappointment. The drivers of the trucks, hardly daring to look at the soaked miserable soldiers crouching under the dripping trees, unloaded the midday rations and departed hastily, leaving the weary men to break open the packets of hard biscuits and the cans of greasy cold pork, running with thick yellow fat. When they moved off again, the ditches on both sides of the road were littered with uneaten cans of meat and bloody foot rags.

At two o'clock that afternoon with the rain still streaming down von Dietz ordered a halt. The men slumped to the ground, not caring that it was a sea of mud, each man alone with his gloomy thoughts, unable to raise the strength even to attempt to light a cigarette under the cover of the cape. Together with the MO, a former long-distance runner in the 1936 Olympics who himself was finding the going tough, von Dietz passed down the line of exhausted soldiers, personally lancing the blisters of those who complained they couldn't march any further, helping the grim-faced doctor to powder the bloody feet of the men whose blisters had already burst.

The MO waited till the inspection was completed, his face white, his eyes burning with anger. Then he led the major to one side and hissed, 'Major, what in three devils' names are you trying to do to the poor bastards?' Von Dietz's smile did not disappear from his rain-soaked face, but his eyes were serious and compassionate enough. 'You think I'm pushing them too hard?'

'I damn well know you are, von Dietz!' the MO exploded. 'Those men are on their last legs! Heaven, arse and cloudburst! They're just civvies in uniform, you know. They're not used to this kind of thing!'

Von Dietz put his hand restrainingly on the MO's wet sleeve. 'I know, Doc, I know. But can you imagine what they are going to have to go through soon? By making them tough like this, I'm hoping to save their lives one day.'

'Save their lives?' the MO stared at the other man's earnest face, as if he had suddenly gone mad. 'How save their lives? In what way?' he demanded. '*Eh?*'

Von Dietz removed his hand, as if he did not wish to feel the other man's reaction to what he was going to say. 'The next time they march, Doctor Schmitz,' he said very formally, 'they will be marching into battle.'

Now a cold drenched numbness had set in. The weary men became void of any feeling. Hell couldn't be worse than this, they thought, as they tramped down the slopes which led back to the little Czech town. A peasant cart trundled past them and its occupants, their heads wrapped in sacks, peered out from under the canvas, staring at the Germans marching through the streaming rain as if they were crazy.

The men started to fall out. As if possessed of boundless energy, von Dietz stopped at each straggler and tried to convince him to persevere with the march, now and again taking over the rifle of any man who volunteered to continue, icily taking the name of those who refused to do so, and then leaving them squatting at the side of the road, crying, glassy-eyed and too weary to understand what had happened to them.

The lights of the Czech town had begun to twinkle a faint yellow on the streaming horizon. The men limped on, eyes fixed on those faint lights glimpsed through the sheets of rain, as if they symbolized the entrance to Heaven itself. They began to forget their burning feet their chafed shoulders, their aching backs and all the rest of their aches and pains… They started to tell themselves, 'I can't drop out now … *I won't*.' Even the stragglers increased their pace as familiar landmarks began to appear.

Von Dietz looked at the MO who was limping so badly now that every fresh step was carried out only by a sheer effort of will. The major winked cheerfully.

'Blast your eyes, von Dietz!' he exploded.

Von Dietz smiled. 'Now that's not the way to talk to your superior officer, Doctor Schmitz!'

'Balls!' was Doctor Schmitz's highly unethical comment, but now he too was smiling wearily.

Just outside the town, von Dietz halted the column. 'NCOs,' he commanded, his voice totally military again, 'dress your columns!' While the MO watched open-mouthed, the NCOs chivvied their men into straight ranks, making them shuffle their raw and aching feet until the lines were perfect.

But von Dietz was not yet finished with them. 'Capes off,' he commanded.

In spite of the still pouring rain, the men slipped out of their capes and fixed them on their packs, their uniforms becoming soaked almost immediately.

Von Dietz, his own uniform black with rain, waited till they were finished before giving his final command. 'First Battalion 69th Infantry Regiment will march to attention, rifles at the slope, *QUICK MARCH*!'

Colonel von Ostermann saw them from the window of the mess as they marched through the barracks' gate singing, their soaked chests thrust out proudly, watched by an open-mouthed collection of clerks and cooks, among whom was Bull, silenced this once by the spectacle of these drenched young men wheeling into the courtyard like the Prussian Guard itself.

Von Dietz proceeded to inspect the battalion as if they had just completed a couple of kilometres' march, adjusting the slope of a rifle here, fastening up a button there, then dismissed them with three cheers for the 69th. Five minutes later von Ostermann was personally handing an exhausted von Dietz a drink as he slumped in one of the leather chairs of the mess, spreading a puddle of water all around him.

'*Prost!*' He raised his cognac glass in toast

'*Prost!*' Von Dietz felt the fiery spirit burn down his throat and spread a pleasant warmth over his soaked, frozen limbs.

'You're pleased with them, eh, von Dietz?'

Von Dietz looked at the colonel, who was watching him curiously.

'Yes, I suppose I am. They're very raw still, but they're improving rapidly.' He forced a tired grin. 'If the 69th is the best infantry regiment in the whole of the Wehrmacht, as you often maintain, Colonel, then undoubtedly one day the First Battalion will be the best battalion in the Regiment.'

Von Ostermann did not return his grin. Instead he refilled the young major's glass and said simply, 'There will be no time for one day.'

Von Dietz looked at him sharply, glass poised in mid-air. 'You mean *it* is on?'

'I do, von Dietz. We officers must turn the battalions over to the NCOs now for further training. We have some planning to do.'

'War?' von Dietz asked slowly, putting down his glass with exaggerated care.

'*War*,' von Ostermann answered.

The two of them sat in silence, their drinks untouched, each man preoccupied with his own thoughts until an orderly in a white jacket announced hesitantly, 'Gentlemen, dinner will be served in exactly five minutes.'

Neither of them ate much that particular night.

CHAPTER 3

Private Maltitz lounged on his bed, his stomach full of thick pea soup and sausage and sticking up in front of him bloated like a small barrage balloon. He was listening to the lazy chatter of his comrades all around, as they relaxed after the midday meal.

'It's the meat-heaven of Europe,' Deltgen was saying in his lively Rhenish sing-song. 'These Czech women really *like* the old salami. Hell, you've got to fight 'em off! When I go out of the barracks at night, they're standing there in line — with with their beds on their backs!'

His sally was greeted by a burst of lazy laughter.

Red Rudi, whose nickname came not from his carrot-red hair but from his former politics, which were straight from Moscow, said, 'But that's just sex you're talking about Sepp. They're not ladies.'

'Ladies are frigid, everybody knows that,' Deltgen snapped back, as quick as ever. 'But I did know a lady once,' and again the irrepressible skinny Rhinelander was off on one of his long tales about his prowess as the 69th's greatest swordsman.

Private Maltitz forgot the chatter all around him. He closed his eyes and felt the hot August sun streaming in through the barracks room window on to his pale swarthy face, dominated by a great hook of a nose. *He* had seen the looks the Czechs had flashed them in the evenings when they were off duty. Of course, to the German soldiers' faces they were friendliness itself, especially the innkeepers, the shop-owners and naturally the whores. After all, the men of the 69th Infantry had brought a lot of money into this God-forsaken border town, which prior to the German occupation and the closing of the frontier with Poland had lived mainly off the weekly livestock market. But he didn't need a crystal ball to interpret those looks: the Czechs hated them.

He opened his eyes suddenly and looked down at Red Rudi, who slept in the bunk below him. They were both Berliners and he trusted him, as indeed he trusted all the men in the First Company of the 69th Infantry. That was why he had *picked* the Regiment! 'Red,' he said hesitantly, 'what do you think we're here for?'

Rudi looked up at the other man, as if he were seeing him for the first time. With that great hooter of a nose and dark skin, old Titty might well have been Jewish, but that, he told himself, dismissing the thought the next moment, would hardly be possible in the Greater German Wehrmacht in the summer of 1939. 'What do you think, Titty?' he countered.

Back in Berlin-Wedding the bulls had told him, after the usual rubber-club treatment, that he'd better get his red arse into the Army before the Gestapo latched on to him. Now he was very careful.

'Well,' Titty was suddenly hesitant. 'You being a com — well, you know your political sentiments and everything. Now that Marshal Stalin and the Führer have reached an agreement, what are we doing here, a whole regiment of infantry, three thousand men strong, guarding this lot of lame-arsed Czechs?' Maltitz added the swear word to cover his own anxiety. It was the thing all the new recruits had quickly learned to do in order to hide their bewilderment and nervousness. 'Shit, Red, you tell me why!'

Red Rudi looked to left and right. The 'German look', they called it jokingly, but there was nothing funny about this business of always checking who was listening. Back in the

Reich there were informers everywhere. 'Have you got green in yer eyes, Titty?' he sneered. 'We're here … because we gonna have a go at the Polacks next.'

The two black stallions clip-clopped slowly across the cobbled market square. The two officers mounted upon them ignored the fawning '*Heil Hitler*' of the ethnic Germans and their Czech collaborators, faces set, eyes on some distant horizon, as if they could not bear to look at what occupation made of some people.

The midday meal finished, the Czechs were beginning to go back to work, pedalling out of the side streets on their ancient Skoda cycles, pulling down the wooden shutters of their shops, watering their flowers which hung limp in the hot August sun.

Out of the corner of his eye, von Ostermann watched the activity and wondered idly how this same square would look a week from then. He remembered those French squares in Lorraine back in '17 and '18 packed with horse-drawn transport, great cumbersome cannon, tired and heavily burdened men waiting to go up the line, deliberately not looking at the lines of groaning men lying on their bloodied stretchers … and above it all, the ever-present background music of the war, the sinister rumble of the barrage. Would it be the same here eight days from now?

He dismissed the thought, as they left the little town and started to walk down the sandy track that led by the sluggish, silver worm of the border river. 'Do you know, von Dietz, that on the first of September, the Regiment will celebrate its two hundredth anniversary?' He looked at his riding companion's blood-drained face and prominent eyes. More than once when he had caught von Dietz off guard, his face had looked haunted, almost anguished. In the mess of an evening, he sometimes sat hunched forward, with his arms crossed across his ribs, squeezing himself, as if he were suffering from extreme cold — or fear.

'Yes,' von Dietz answered, without taking his eyes off the horizon. 'Old Fritz raised us and we ran away in our first battle. Remember, sir, my father and his father before once commanded the 69th'

Von Ostermann smiled faintly. 'I remember.' He had been put in his place fairly and squarely. 'Though as colonel of this regiment, I do object somewhat to the phrase "ran away".' He paused. 'We made a, er, slight withdrawal — sounds better.'

For the first time von Dietz turned to his CO and returned his smile. 'My father used to say that Old Fritz himself ran away first and what the King could do, the Regiment could do as well.'

'Exactly.'

They rode on in silence for a while. Now the only sound was the muffled clip-clop of their horses' hooves in the sand, which swirled up around them, and the lazy buzz of the flies above the water. The very air seemed heavy with problems and uncertainties.

After a while von Ostermann said, 'von Dietz you play this game with your cards very close to your chest, you know.'

Dietz did not take his grey gaze off the horizon which was Poland. 'In these last six years, sir, one has learned to be wise and do so — it's safer that way.'

Von Ostermann knew exactly what the younger man meant. Even in a regiment like the 69th, which had a tradition of loyalty and service going back two centuries, one wasn't safe from the gentlemen of the Gestapo in the ankle-length coats.

But he didn't comment on the remark. Instead he said: 'And how do you see things in the next few months, Dietz.'

The tall major reined back his horse. Automatically von Ostermann did the same. 'Sir,' he said, his eyes brooding now so that he looked like a scholar or even a poet, 'in a year I shall be commanding this regiment. In two I shall be a general and then —'

'Go on,' Ostermann prompted, hardly able to believe that von Dietz was opening up in this manner.

'In three years I shall probably be dead, fallen on the battlefield…' Suddenly there was a sneer on his long pale face, 'for Folk, Fatherland *and Führer*!'

Von Ostermann flushed, the broken veins in his somewhat bulbous nose standing out suddenly. 'Now, young Dietz, what exactly do you mean by that?'

Von Dietz did not reply. Instead, his face wooden and revealing nothing again, he glanced at his wristwatch and said in the tone of a respectful subordinate officer, 'Sir, may I point out to you that it is nearly thirteen hundred hours. The river-crossing exercise starts at fourteen hundred hours precisely.'

The Bull was in charge. All along the line of men crouched in the baking reeds, swatting angrily at the mosquitos which were everywhere. The officers had relinquished actual tactical command of the infantrymen to the senior NCOs. After all, in a combat situation they would have to handle their squads of men in the confused situation that would exist in a river crossing under fire.

It was one of those tasks that Bull enjoyed best. Not only was he in charge of the men, he was also being observed by their officers; and he knew from his eight years in the Regiment that to be promoted you had to be *seen* doing the right thing. As he had often expounded his theory to his cronies of the sergeants' mess. 'Piss or get off the pot — that's the motto of the Greater German Wehrmacht. Action in other words! But make sure you have some wet-arsed second-lieutenant watching yer do yer pissing.' Now he played his role to its full advantage.

The Bull tipped up and down on his heels, boots wide apart, massive chest thrown out, beefy hands on his hips, a look of boundless contempt on his face for the men sweating in the reeds at his feet

They, for their part, stared back at him meanly silent. Like convicts oppressed by the immensity of the injustice done to them in a world that they couldn't control, their dull-red faces were full of resentment.

The Bull let them wait. He savoured this moment; then he spoke. For him, his tone was moderate, just a shade less than a roar. 'Who can't swim here?'

There was no reaction.

On the hill overlooking the river, Major von Dietz frowned; he had heard it all before.

'Come on, you wonderful girls,' the Bull humoured them. 'Don't keep your legs together like vestal virgins. Don't be shy now. Who can't swim?'

Hesitantly a hand went up here and there. Next to Sepp Deltgen, Ross, an undersized, rather effeminate boy from Bremen, raised his hand too; his chubby face, which had yet to feel a razor, suddenly went very pale.

The Bull gazed around at those who had raised their hands. 'So,' he said finally, 'we've got fifty or more non-swimmers in the Regiment, have we?' His eyes fell on Ross. 'You, too, you loverly boy. Remind me to come round to your bunk tonight after lights out — with a jar of vaseline. I'm always gentle with virgins the first time!'

Nobody laughed, not even the old heads who had served with the Bull when he had been a private. The smile vanished from the big NCO's face. 'All right, you candy-cracks, now's the time to learn to swim. This is how we're going to do it'

Swiftly and expertly, the Bull demonstrated how each soldier could make a serviceable float out of his ground-sheet and trousers, standing in front of them without his own trousers now and completely unembarrassed by the fact. 'The trick is,' he concluded, 'having enough air in the bundle.' He grinned maliciously at Ross. 'Because if you don't, you sink. Now, girls, off with those knickers — and I promise you I won't look. *Move it*.'

They moved it. Swiftly the soldiers ripped off their trousers and folded them inside their ground-sheets, tying the bundle together with their belts and braces, ensuring that the package remained loose and contained as much air as possible, just as the Bull had instructed them to do.

Maltitz seemed slower than usual to take off his pants and Red Rudi, busy with his own bundle, hissed at him: 'What's up with you, you long-nosed shit? We're all men here, except Ross. We've all seen a ding-dong before today, you know, Titty!'

'Of course, Red,' Maltitz said and, pulling off his dice-beakers undid his flies, ensuring all the time that his long grey shirt hid his genitals.

Next to him Sepp Deltgen said to an ashen-faced Ross. 'Don't worry, kid, I'll see you across that puddle of piss. Just stick by me.'

The Bull flung a glance to left and right. 'All right, you girls, you've had enough time. Now I want to see some action. I want you to move — and move fast! 'Cause over there on the other side of that river is some garlic-gobbling perverted Frog or buck-teethed Tommy and he's just waiting to blow your turnips off if you're too slow.' He shrilled a blast on his whistle.

On the other side of the river, other NCOs started to throw thunder flashes into the river, sending up great sheets of crazy white water, while on both flanks skilled marksmen started to fire quick control bursts of tracer, which skimmed just above the surface.

The Bull nodded his approval and bellowed above the sudden racket, 'And just so you know this is not the boy scouts, you bunch of perverted banana-suckers, that shit flying over there is the real stuff. Live ammo! All right, follow me!' Pushing his bundle in front of him, the Bull moved confidently into the water. All along the bank, the NCOs led their own sections after them. Suddenly the river was full of struggling, gasping men, pushing their bundles in front of them, trying to keep their heads and shoulders burdened by thirty kilos of rifle, pack and steel helmet above the tormented water.

Halfway across Ross panicked. 'I can't go on ... I'm gonna drown, Sepp!' he screamed.

Deltgen let go of his own bundle and splashed across to where the terrified Ross was beginning to sink, thrashing the water with his hands, being dragged down by the weight of his equipment. 'Hold on, you stupid shitbag!' he cried desperately. 'Hold on, I'm —'

'Let that man go!' the Bull's tremendous voice boomed across the river from the opposite bank. 'Let him go!'

'But, Sergeant-Major...'

'No buts. In war there would be no time for weak sisters like that. *Let him go. This is an order!*'

Sepp hesitated, treading water, listening to the screams coming from the drowning youngster only a few metres away. Should he disobey the enraged swine standing dripping with water on the other bank and take the consequences? Or…

Tracer hissed over his head. Ross gave one last scream and suddenly he thrashed the water no longer, but lay slumped face downwards on the surface, slowly beginning to sink. The decision had been made for him…

'Dead,' the Pill pronounced and awkwardly he closed Ross's eyes.

'Shitty warm-brother, if I ever saw one,' the Bull sneered and spat drily into the reeds. 'Good riddance, if you ask me.'

Sepp Deltgen clenched his fists, taking his eyes off the dead boy's face. He was disgusted with himself, disgusted with the Army, disgusted with his fellow-men for being the creepers and arse-crawlers that they were. He, the lot of them, had failed Ross; now he was dead, stretched out in the mud with his skinny legs naked and hairless and absurd, revealed to everybody. It was then that he swore a great oath, dead serious for the very first time in his life. The Bull would pay. By God, he would pay for Ross's death!

CHAPTER 4

All that last week of August, the hardening and brutalization of the 69th Infantry Regiment continued at a hectic pace, as if time was running out fast and every last minute had to be crammed full with learning the business of killing.

While the Czech peasants harvested the great golden fields, their days were full of violence and strain: hoarse bellowed commands; unrelieved activity which left them gasping like ancient asthmatics their hands and legs trembling uncontrollably. The gruelling routine was broken only by hastily snatched meals of weak beer and cold greasy tins full of 'old man', cheap pork in reality but reputedly made of the corpses of pensioners from the Reich's workhouses.

Bull was in his element. His little piglike red eyes gleaming evilly, he harassed the red-faced, sweat-lathered infantrymen by day and by night. He would chase after them, prodding at the laggards with his stick and, if the officers were not looking, levelling great vicious kicks at them, all the while lashing them with his filthy tongue. '*You shitty boy-scouts ... too much of the one-handed widow, I'll be bound ... get going, you bunch of asparagus Tarzans ... open those legs, nothing'll fall out. At the double ... did you hear, you candycracks? AT THE DOUBLE!*'

In the morning, with the red ball of the sun hanging over the peaks of the Polish mountains in the far distance, he would stand on the square, legs spread in his gleaming boots, hands set contemptuously on his big hips, and begin the day's torments: 'Soldiers you call yourselves! Oh, my aching arse, I've shat better! But by the Great God and all his triangles, I'll make soldiers ... yes, I said, *soldiers* ... of you yet!'

Then the familiar hell would commence once again. They would be chased over the bakehouse-hot Czech fields, their eyes blank and unseeing, brick-red faces streaming with perspiration, huge beads of sweat gleaming in their eyebrows, to dash at each other with their bayonets, urged on by screeching NCOs with their cries of '*KILL!... KILL!... STICK IT IN HIS GUTS!... SLICE THE EGGS OFF'N HIM... I WANT TO SEE BLOOD!*'

Nor would nights bring any rest for the exhausted young men. It was rare that the Bull and his cronies would allow them more than a couple of hours' sleep. Returning from the sergeants' mess, their bellies swollen with beer and schnapps, eyes red and evil, they would fling a thunder flash through the open window of one of the barracks and bellow as the crash of the explosion flung the alarmed young men from their bunks. '*STAND BY YOUR BEDS!... COME ON, LETS BE HAVING YOU WARM-BROTHERS OUT OF THOSE BEDS NOW... YOU HAVE HAD ENOUGH CUDDLING AND KISSING... AT THE DOUBLE!*'

In a frenzy of fumbling and frightened activity, tearing off their striped nightshirts and tumbling into their fatigues, boots and helmets, they would stand rigidly to attention, the sleep still in their eyes, while a contemptuous Bull and his cronies would swagger up and down the barracks room before they would commence the nightly torture.

There would be the 'dancing lesson'. With their rifles held out at arm's length, they would be forced to hop up and down the length of the barracks room until they thought their arms would drop off and their back muscles were ablaze with burning agony. This might well be followed by 'pumping' — press-ups — their arms and legs trembling crazily with the strain, while the Bull and his cronies, puffing easily at their cheap cigars, pressing them down to the floorboards with their heavy nailed boots.

But the worst torture of all was the 'masked ball'. It entailed furious changes from one uniform to another, just as the Bull's whim took him. '*Fatigues!*' he would bellow, standing poised, legs spread wide apart, in the centre of the room; and there would be a frantic scramble to rip off one uniform, pull the fatigues out of the metal cupboard and put them on.

The Bull had no mercy. He gave them no time to catch their breath. '*PT kit!*' he'd cry the next moment, and the same mad rush would be repeated with the Bull's cronies whacking the harassed, crimson-faced soldiers' naked rumps with their canes and making malicious remarks about their manhood — or their lack of it. PT kit might well be followed by 'parade uniform', and the Bull would have them goosestepping the length of the room in their best uniforms, chortling hugely when they collided into each other in the narrow confines of the corridor.

And so it would go on until finally the Bull and his cronies would tire of the sport and would leave for their own bunks, finally allowing the exhausted tortured young men to slump fully dressed on to their clothes-and equipment-strewn beds, their eyes hollow with despair, their chests heaving with the effort, a burning rage in their hearts.

As Sepp expressed it, after one particularly gruelling 'dancing lesson' that lasted fifteen minutes and had them swaying over the floor like drunks, 'I'll get him... Oh, I'll get the bovine bastard... Even if they slice off my turnip.' He looked round the room with burning eyes. 'As sure as my name is Deltgen, the Bull won't live to see 1940!'

Consumed by that look, Maltitz shuddered. It was no empty boast, he knew. The little Rhinelander meant it.

Thus as the great events took place behind closed doors in the capitals of Europe, which would — unbeknown to them — decide their fates, the young men of the 69th Infantry Regiment were prepared that last week of August for the slaughter to come.

In the evening Colonel von Ostermann, moody and withdrawn now, brooding on the terrible secret known only to him, caught a glimpse of Major von Dietz walking slowly across the parade ground, stark black against the lemon-yellow rays of the setting sun. His head was bent as if in thought and his skinny shoulders rounded so that from a distance the young officer looked old, very old.

On Saturday, August 26, 1939, Colonel von Ostermann was summoned hurriedly to the headquarters of Army Group South, to which the 69th Infantry Regiment belonged. He could see immediately that the headquarters was in the grip of a flap of the kind he remembered all too well from his days as a young staff officer in 1918. Dusty dispatch riders roared down the narrow white Silesian roads, trailing a white wake behind them. At the entrance to the HQ itself the sentries were edgy and nervous, and everywhere white-faced anxious staff officers hurried back and forth. From within the building typewriters clattered and telephones shrilled incessantly.

Just before the conference commenced, he spotted an old comrade, Tietz of the 172 Flak Brigade. He pushed his way through the crowd of officers standing in excited little groups, discussing the possible reasons for the abrupt call to HQ. They shook hands and then taking Tietz, a white-haired artilleryman, to one side, he asked *sotto voce*: 'What's up, Tietz? Where's the shit hit the fan?'

Tietz chuckled, revealing a mouthful of gold teeth. 'That's just the phrase for it, von Ostermann.' Cautiously he indicated with a jerk of his head a small group of soldiers in dusty uniforms and unfamiliar square caps standing in the courtyard below, looking forlorn and a little bewildered. 'Polacks,' he exclaimed.

'Polacks!' von Ostermann echoed, puzzled. 'But the offensive is not scheduled to start yet.'

Tietz chuckled again, obviously enjoying the situation. He was too old now to attain the rank of general; therefore he was without ambition and enjoyed seeing the staff officers 'wet their knickers', as he always put it. 'Tell the Greatest Captain of All Times,' he said scornfully, using the Army's contemptuous name for Hitler. 'He decided that the Jablunka Pass — you know, between Czechoslovakia and Poland — should be taken by a *coup de main* before the declaration of war so that old Rundstedt's tanks would have a clear run for Warsaw. Now there's been some sort of political mess-up with Mussolini and our dear Führer has been caught with his pants down. The war has been postponed — till further notice — and old Rundstedt is fuming.' He indicated the staff officers bustling to and fro with sheaves of documents and maps. 'I wouldn't like to be in those chaps' fancy boots this evening. The Old Man's got a damned rough tongue on him when he wants.'

General von Rundstedt, commander of Army Group South, had indeed. He stood there in front of the wall map in the huge conference room, flanked by his chief-of-staff General Manstein, looking incredibly old and wrinkled, wrapped up in a heavy greatcoat despite the intense August heat. 'An incredibly impossible gaffe has taken place,' he rasped in that cognac-thickened voice of his, 'a piece of piggery of the worst kind!

Elements of Admiral Canaris's special troops clad in civilian clothes took the Jablunka Pass this lunchtime on the Führer's specific orders. Now we've actually killed Poles and taken their men prisoner.' His faded eyes blazed suddenly. '*In peacetime!*' he raged, the veins standing out on his skinny throat.

'General, calm yourself,' Manstein urged. 'Remember your heart.'

'Damn my heart!' von Rundstedt croaked, twisting his scraggy neck to one side as if he were choking. 'At this moment I would gladly meet my Maker. If only the damn ground would open up and swallow me!' He stared around at the concerned faces of the assembled officers who filled the big panelled hall and shook his head sadly, as if he could not comprehend the foolishness of his fellow-men. 'Not only have we given away our intention to attack Poland — bad enough — we have, more importantly, revealed Army Group South's plan to attack via the Pass. Now, of course, those damn Polacks will be waiting for us when we come!'

'But, General,' Manstein objected, screwing his monocle more firmly in his right eye, 'because of Signor Mussolini's intervention, there is some doubt whether there will be any offensive actions against the Poles at all.'

'*Offensive actions against the Poles!*' von Rundstedt mimicked Manstein's prissy, fussy voice maliciously. 'Of course there will be an attack! That man…' he caught himself just in time. Even he was afraid to express his true feelings about the man he called the 'Bohemian Corporal' in front of a roomful of officers. 'Explain the original plan, Manstein,' he commanded and clicked his fingers for his orderly.

The white-jacketed orderly appeared as if by magic and presented the old general with his regular, half-hourly glass of cognac. Tietz winked knowingly at von Ostermann.

43

Von Ostermann smiled back at him and waited for Manstein to begin his exposé. 'The Poles have mobilized their forces in seven major groups all along the frontier, which I don't need to tell you, gentlemen, is indefensible. Fundamentally, our plan of attack is two main pincers heading for the heart of the country, supported by subsidiary prongs moving outwards on the sides of the prongs. Our role is that of the southern prong with our objective Warsaw, with one subsidiary thrust towards the River Bug and the major city of Lwow.'

Manstein let them absorb the information that most of them knew already, while von Rundstedt sipped his cognac moodily, sunk in thought. Outside the motorbikes roared as the dust-covered dispatch riders, heavy leather pouches slung across their chests, came and went. The bewildered Poles, prisoners in a war that had not officially begun, stared at them open-mouthed.

'Now let us assume that this operation will really get off the ground after all,' Manstein continued, flashing a glance at von Rundstedt, who ignored it. 'Then the Poles will still expect us to take the most obvious path into their country, the Jablunka Pass. Since the unfortunate incident of this afternoon, I have been giving some thought to the problem, gentlemen. When we march again let them continue in their belief that we shall take the obvious route.' Manstein looked directly at Colonel von Ostermann and the commander of the 69th Infantry Regiment knew with a sudden sinking feeling that he and his men had been picked as sacrificial lambs.

Behind him von Rundstedt frowned, as if he could already visualize what would happen to the 69th, and looked pityingly at von Ostermann.

'While this feint is going in, I suggest that von Thoma's panzers of the Second Panzer Division,' he nodded at the hard-faced, wooden-headed aristocratic general, 'should move through the thick woods up there on the ridges beyond the Pass, thus outflanking the Polish position which will be fully occupied with the feint.'

Manstein looked at von Rundstedt. 'It is a rather hasty improvisation, General, but I think it could work, if the necessity occurs.'

'It will,' von Rundstedt rasped. 'War will take place.' Suddenly, with surprising energy for such an old man, he pushed by an abruptly astonished Manstein, and clasped von Ostermann's hand in a grip that was as cold as the grave. 'Von Ostermann, promise me one thing.'

'Sir?' Von Ostermann managed to stutter.

'Hold them at the Pass. *Hold them, for God's sake…!*'

CHAPTER 5

They were so obviously Gestapo agents that, under other circumstances, von Dietz would have smiled; they were almost caricatures of the feared State Secret Police, in their ankle-length green leather coats, with old-fashioned felt hats pulled down low over their jowled faces and unlit cheap cigars clenched in their mouths. But this day, as he watched them get out of the Opel Wanderer, he did not smile. Instead he felt a cold finger of fear trace its way down the small of his back. Were they coming for him? Because of *that*? Von Dietz was rooted for a moment to the window-sill, where he had been examining the large-scale map of the Polish-Czech frontier, while the two middle-aged secret policemen enquired the way of the sentry guarding the Battalion HQ Office. Then he acted.

Hurriedly he went to the stand where his cap and pistol belt hung. Keeping his eyes on the window and noting how attentive the sentry had become now that he knew the two civilians were from the Gestapo, he swiftly drew his pistol, checked the magazine, slipped off the safety and thrust it into the pocket of his tunic. If they were coming for him, he told himself, they were going to be in for an unpleasant surprise. They wouldn't drag him into the cellar of Number Ten Prinzalbrechtstrasse to turn him into a helpless, supine, willing human wreck, with whom they could do what they wished.

There was a soft knock on the office door.

That would be Sergeant Ludwig, he told himself. The orderly room sergeant had a surprisingly light hand. '*Bitte*,' he called out in a voice that was surprisingly firm and steady, he couldn't help thinking.

Ludwig, an old soldier, had been congratulating himself for days because when the balloon finally went up, he would be staying behind on account of his age. Mentally he was already counting the pickings. 'Two gentlemen, sir, to see you.' He cupped his hand around his thick sensualist's mouth and formed the word, 'Gestapo'. Von Dietz appeared not to be impressed. 'Show the gentlemen in,' he said, and rose to his feet.

The two civilians in their green leather coats came in, clicked to attention and held forward their silver police identification discs in the palms of their hands, as if they wished to conceal them from anyone but himself.

He nodded and the bigger of the two said, 'I am addressing Major von Dietz, commander of the First Battalion?'

Von Dietz felt the fear well up within him once more and automatically his hand dug into his pocket and clenched around the pistol. They had found out at last what had really happened at W— 'Yes, that is right,' he answered in a voice he hardly recognized as his own.

'Oberkommissar Weiss,' the Gestapo agent said, and indicating his companion with a hand like a steam shovel, 'Kommissar Krause from our Prague office.'

'I see. And what can I do for you gentlemen?'

Weiss looked at the chairs in front of von Dietz's desk. The officer followed the direction of his gaze and understood. 'I prefer to speak to the gentlemen of the Gestapo standing up,' he said icily.

Krause's sallow, wrinkled face flushed, but Weiss remained calm. Obviously he knew of the Regular Army's attitude to the Gestapo. 'As you wish, Major,' he said easily. 'We cops, you know, are used to standing up for long periods. That's why we've got flat feet.' He smiled, but there was no answering light in his eyes.

'Why do you wish to speak to me?' von Dietz asked, unsmiling too.

'We are making a few enquiries, Major,' said Weiss, his hard eyes boring into von Dietz's face.

'What kind of enquiries?' von Dietz forced himself to say, ready to whip out his pistol at any instant now.

To his surprise the expected question did not come. Instead it was something completely different. 'Major, I don't think I have to waste too many words on the situation in the Reich. There are some elements, as you know, who do not support the policies of the Führer. There are also those who are perverting our racial purity with their Jewish lasciviousness...'

Von Dietz held up his hand, his nerve back now that the expected enquiry had not been made. 'Gentlemen, please spare me the lecture. I am a busy man. What exactly do you want from the First Battalion of the 69th Infantry Regiment?'

'To look at the nominal roles,' Krause said, his voice harsh. It was clear that he did not like the traditional arrogance of the Regular Army officer. Probably, von Dietz told himself, he had served in the first show as a lance corporal or something like that. 'Is that clear enough for you?' He omitted the 'sir'.

'Why?'

Oberkommissar Weiss held up his hand to stop his partner from speaking. 'Sir, it is a routine matter, but now in the light of the present situation, Obergruppenführer Heydrich has ordered Obergruppenführer Müller to ensure that those regiments who will be engaged, er, actively against the enemy do not contain any of those elements which one might classify as enemies of the state. Therefore we would like to examine your roles to ascertain whether any of these people...' — as if by magic a bunch of papers appeared in his fat paw — 'who are on our black list, have found refuge in your battalion.' He smiled winningly at the stony-faced officer.

Von Dietz said nothing, and the fat Gestapo man thought he needed further information, for he continued with: 'Commies, Jews, opponents of the regime, they've all found it easy to take a dive by joining the Wehrmacht. For example, you have in your battalion, a well-known Red by the name of Rudi —' he clicked his finger urgently.

Krause supplied the last name, 'Rudolf Ratke, Oberkommissar,' he said hurriedly.

'So you see, Major, everyone has a, er, little skeleton in his closet, what?'

Von Dietz told himself the fat cop little knew what kind of tremendous skeleton he had in his own personal closet. But his face revealed nothing of his thoughts. 'Oberkommissar, I cannot allow you to look at my roles,' he said firmly. 'I have no time to waste on police business.'

'What?' the fat cop exploded, the smile vanishing from his face.

'Do you know what you're letting yourself in for?' Krause threatened. 'We're from the Gestapo, don't you understand that? We are the official organ of the State. You can't refuse us to allow to look at your roles.'

'I can and will,' von Dietz said calmly. He crossed to the desk and pressed the button.

'Sir?' Ludwig appeared immediately, as if he had been listening behind the door, waiting for this summons.

'Show these gentlemen out of the barracks, Sergeant.'

'Sir!'

Krause's face flushed an angry red. 'I hope to hell you know what you are doing, Major?' he cried.

'I do,' von Dietz answered.

'You know that we will return with an official order from the Army commander, which I am sure will cause some personal unpleasantness for you,' said Oberkommissar Weiss. His tone was neutral, but the threat was there all right.

'Undoubtedly,' said von Dietz, allowing himself a tight little smile, 'but by that time, gentlemen, I will be either dead or a hero.' He shrugged. 'I wonder what you will do then with an official order from the Army commander? Ludwig, show them out. Good day.'

For a moment it seemed as if the two Gestapo men might well refuse to leave, but after Krause had shot him a murderous glance, they went, escorted out by Ludwig.

Von Dietz watched them drive away before returning to his desk to replace the pistol in its holster. His hand was trembling slightly, and he realized for the first time just how afraid he had been during the brief interview.

For what seemed a long time he sat there, head in his hands, thinking of the events, long buried in his subconscious, of that winter in W——, telling himself that now he had really burnt his boats behind him. Undoubtedly the two fat cops would soon be on their way to Army HQ to seek an interview with Field Marshal von Rundstedt.

Suddenly he smiled at himself in the full-length mirror at the other side of the office with its traditional legend painted in white across the top: 'ARE YOU CORRECTLY DRESSED? ARE YOU A CREDIT TO THE 69TH?'

What did it all matter, the past and the present? Soon there would be the war and he would be either a hero or a corpse. The coming battle would decide everything. He went back to his maps, the Gestapo men forgotten.

CHAPTER 6

For August 28th, Colonel von Ostermann ordered a regimental route march. There was nothing unusual about the appearance of the order on the company notice boards the previous night. Once a week ever since the regiment had been mobilized the previous spring there had been a route march, growing progressively longer as the months went by. Those who were wise greased the insides of their foot rags, poured talcum in their dice-beakers and went to bed early; those who weren't filled their water-bottles with schnapps and water.

At first light that Monday, with the sky a dull purple, flushing scarlet to indicate the hot day to come, the bugler roused the men from their beds. Breakfast passed swiftly, as did the normal morning inspection. The men were eager to cover most of the usual thirty-kilometre course before it got too hot. They moved swiftly and briskly, rolling their blankets, balancing their packs, loading their mortars and heavy machine-guns into the little handcarts. Thus by six o'clock, just as the Czechs started to throw open the wooden shutters of their half-timbered houses and hang the fat goose eiderdowns out of the upper windows to air, the long column of field-grey was crunching over the cobbled streets, heading east towards the mountains, each company led by a mounted officer.

The morning was fine and the men of the 69th Infantry were in good spirits, thinking nothing of the fifty kilos of ammunition and equipment strapped to their shoulders. Their pace was steady and brisk, exactly 108 paces per minute, giving exactly five kilometres to the hour (or fifty minutes to be exact, for there was a ten-minute break each hour, when the men would fall flat on their faces in the dusty verges and rest until the whistles shrilled again), as was the tradition in the 69th.

By ten o'clock the sun was already hot and their marching had stabilized into an automatic, almost hypnotic rhythm. One hour later Colonel von Ostermann, riding at the head of the long dusty column ordered that collars could be undone and talking allowed. A blue cloud of smoke began to rise from the marching ranks and the men, removing their helmets from sweating, red-rimmed shaven skulls, turned and chatted with their neighbours, maintaining their rhythm, robots still from the waist downwards.

At midday, with the sun at its zenith, von Ostermann ordered a song. All along the column, the wing-man of each company bellowed the time-honoured formula: 'A song — *one, two, three!*' and they burst into the old marching song of the '*Nut-brown maiden … hi-di, hi-do.*'

By one o'clock the 'nut-brown maiden' had lost her attraction and the marching men, the backs of their tunics wet and black with sweat, slogged on doggedly through the dust.

At two Colonel von Ostermann ordered a one-hour halt and now the men, cooling their feet in a little stream that chanced to run parallel with the dusty white road east, started to grow uneasy. In slow, heat-weary phrases the little groups of sweating soldiers, bathing their feet and munching dully on their hard dry sandwiches of blood-sausage and bacon, gave expression to their doubts: 'But we've already done thirty klicks… He can't expect us to do any more… How we gonna get back to the barracks — that'd be another shitting thirty klicks… *What's going on, eh?*'

When they resumed their weary march towards the mountains at three, Major von Dietz, after checking his own battalion, cantered up to where von Ostermann rode in splendid isolation at the head of the column. For a while the two of them rode side by side in silence, the only sound that of the horses' hooves and the swish of their tails as the animals tried to get rid of the flies that buzzed around their steaming flanks. In the end von Dietz said drily, 'So we're not going back, Colonel, eh? It's the real thing.'

Von Ostermann did not answer for a moment and when he did, he didn't turn — as if he could not bear to face the younger officer. 'No,' he said in the end, 'we're not going back.'

At four Colonel von Ostermann ordered the column to rest just outside a typical Czech village of the border area: a collection of low, white-painted thatched cottages surrounded by picket-fences, grouped around a slate-roofed church, with a modest country house on the hill beyond. It was about then that the Bull came up, leading the convoy of motor vehicles, dragging the goulash-cannon behind them and carrying the Regiment's heavy equipment. Weary as they were, the dusty men squatting on the verges raised a hoarse song of contempt as they saw the kitchen-bulls, the postal clerks and the rest of the Bull's pets and cronies looking out at them as if they were creatures from another world:

'If the sergeant's pinched yer rum, never mind,
If the sergeant's pinched yer rum, never mind,
He's entitled to his tot, but he's supped the shitting lot!'

The Bull's beefy face flushed with anger, but he knew better than to let go in the presence of Colonel von Ostermann. So he accepted the traditional ditty with a fake grin on his thick sensualist's lips as he strode over to report with a flourish to Colonel von Ostermann. 'Everything as ordered, sir. The Czechs think we're out on a two-day march.'

'Let us hope so,' von Ostermann said without much conviction in his voice. He knew the Poles would have their spies everywhere in the border area. He pointed to the big house on the hill. 'Get hold of that house over there and, er,' von Ostermann hesitated, well aware of the full meaning of his words, 'put it into a state of defence.'

'Sir!' The Bull flung him a tremendous salute, his face set now in an unholy grin.

During the invasion of Czechoslovakia the previous March they had put several large Czech houses on their route of march into a 'state of defence'. The procedure was simple and very rewarding. You kicked out the Czechs, knocked a couple of holes in the walls for the cannon and machine-guns, piled mattresses against the windows and turned the place into a fort. But that wasn't all. As he had told his cronies after his first experience of this kind of looting, 'If you're hungry or thirsty, what's the good of leaving good sides of bacon or fancy wines in the cellar?' Here he had winked. 'And if the fancy Czech milord happens to have a nice full stocking under his bed, why shouldn't an honest German soldier take it with him — for safe keeping, of course.' Thus he swung round in alacrity and bellowed to the waiting kitchen-bulls, 'All right, get the lead out of yer arses! Get the goulash-cannon going!' He turned to the group around Red Rudi stretched full-length in the dusty grass. 'You … you … and you … on yer feet! Follow me. We're off on a little mission for the Colonel.'

Wearily Red Rudi, Maltitz and Sepp, murder in his heart, rose, grabbed their rifles and trailed after the big NCO, scattering the noisy ducks and chickens of the awed barefoot peasants as they went through the miserable village street. Behind him, Dietz looked at the little group and then at von Ostermann. He didn't say anything, but von Ostermann knew what his look meant. He shrugged wearily and slapped thick dust from his cavalry breeches. 'In a few days, my dear von Dietz, you're going to see worse, much worse…'

The Bull did not bother with introductions. He thrust out a hand the size of a small ham, palm upturned, and slammed the ancient, white-haired servant against the wall, making the yellowed photographs of bewhiskered nineteenth-century worthies which decorated the dark hall rattle, as if they might fall down at any moment. 'Come on,' he ordered and stepped over the groaning old man from whose nose a trickle of black blood was now beginning to curl. 'Silly old shit. He should have known that no self-respecting German could understand that monkey chatter of theirs!'

'He said "welcome" in Slovak,' Maltitz said, eyes full of pity for the old man.

The Bull didn't even turn. 'What are you, Titty, a shitty Jewish professor or something?'

Maltitz turned pale and Red Rudi shook his head urgently, warning him to say no more.

But the Bull would not have heard anyway. He was too busy flinging open the doors along the corridor, making swift assessments of what might lie there in the way of loot before the rest of the Regiment got into the place. At the end of the corridor, he opened the last door to the right and exclaimed: 'The best room. This is where Milord and Lady have their tea.' He stood there, fingers curled, little finger extended, as if he were daintily sipping tea. To left and right of his broad back which blocked most of the view, the others could see a long dark room, both walls lined with cracked oil portraits of men and women in the powdered wigs and ornate clothing of the eighteenth-century. At the far end was the gleam of what looked like an expensive silver tea service grouped around a high silver samovar.

The Bull's little eyes sparkled. 'The far end of the room,' he said, 'that looks like a good spot to set up the machine-gun. You and you, break open the window.' He licked his lips in obvious greed. 'I'd better secure that tea service, though, before one of you crooks organizes.' He stepped forward.

It was then that the cool, collected voice behind them said quietly, '*Dobra dan.*'

As one they spun round.

A tall woman was standing, dressed in riding habit, her raven-black hair swept back severely and tied with a black bow to the nape of her head, her black eyes cool but commanding. 'Who are you when yer at home?' the Bull growled, taking in with some approval the woman's high full bosom and shapely hips in the tight-fitting riding breeches, and telling himself he'd give *her* a bit of a gallop every night — for free.

'My name is von Muzarki,' she replied, her gaze meeting his so that momentarily even the Bull was embarrassed and forced to lower his eyes. 'Countess von Muzarki.'

Maltitz took in the perfect German and the '*von*' and said: 'Are you German, madam?'

The woman shook her head firmly and a small smile formed on her full red lips. 'Once we thought of ourselves as being international. There are branches of our family in Poland, here, Austria, even Germany.' The smile broadened for some reason it was unknown to a red-faced Maltitz. 'But now we consider ourselves simply as Poles.'

'And what are Polacks doing at this side of the frontier?' the Bull growled, finding his voice again.

'We've been here a couple of hundred years,' she replied. 'Perhaps it would be more fitting to ask what are Germans doing here?'

Red Rudi, overcoming his aversion to the aristocracy, whatever its nationality, grinned and nudged Sepp Deltgen in the ribs. The Polack had really given the Bull what he had asked for.

'Don't risk a big lip with me, Polack,' the Bull began and then suddenly he stiffened into the position of attention, as did the others, when they saw von Dietz standing there, beating his riding crop against the side of his boot in a decidedly angry manner.

'Sergeant-Major, be on your way and get this place sorted out. The men will soon be needing their quarters for the night. Put the Countess's people in the cellar.'

'That won't be necessary,' the beautiful Pole stopped the Bull. 'We'd prefer to be under our *own* roof,' she smiled challengingly at von Dietz, and he flushed, knowing exactly what she meant. She did not want to be under the same roof as the Germans. 'We will go into the barn.'

'As you wish.' Angrily von Dietz turned and went out, followed by the soldiers. As the Countess watched them, the smile vanished from her face and was replaced by a look of brooding sad premonition.

That evening, with no sound from outside save the soft rustle of the wind in the ancient oaks, Colonel von Ostermann assembled the First Battalion in the hall.

The men were crowded everywhere, all eight hundred of them, squatting on window sills, crouched on the floor, propping up the walls, but there was none of the usual shoving and pushing, complaining and joking that normally took place on such occasions. Von Dietz could see that the men were worried and somehow subdued, as if they could already have guessed the reason for this sudden summons.

While he waited for von Ostermann to appear, he stared around at the faces of his soldiers in the flickering yellow light cast by the oil lights strung along the walls. They were youthful, unlined, the cheeks firm and bronzed, their eyes glowing with good health and determination. Suddenly he felt a warm glow of pride in them. They were young and inexperienced, but they looked like soldiers. Yet his pride was tinged by sadness at the thought of what must invariably happen to them soon.

Colonel von Ostermann came in. At the front of the room the Bull opened his mouth to bellow the order for them to stand to attention, but the Colonel gestured at him to stop, almost angrily as if this was not the time and place to play soldier.

The Bull sat down grumpily and stared at his gleaming boots.

'You may smoke, comrades,' the Colonel said noting, just as von Dietz had, the good health and determination of the battalion. But he now assessed those qualities as a commander who had to make some calculation of the ability of these men to carry out the task that would be assigned to them.

When the scratching of matches and the first hectic puffing had ceased, he began very simply and straight to the point: 'Comrades, it is very probable that our country will be at war with Poland within the next forty-eight hours.' He paused, and waited for the gasp of surprise to subside.

He gave them exactly ten seconds then continued, his voice the same as before, as if he had just announced that a routine training exercise would take place in two days' time. 'The political reasons for this new conflict do not concern us, comrades. We are soldiers, *not* politicos.'

Von Dietz felt he caught a trace of irony in the CO's voice, but he couldn't be sure.

'The 69th has never concerned itself with such things. When ordered to fight, the Regiment fought. It has always been that way and always will. We fought at Leipzig in '13, Königgrätz in '66, Saint Privat in '70 and between 1914 and 1918 in battles too innumerable to be mentioned here. But always, we have done our duty to Germany.' Colonel von Ostermann's normally gentle voice rose and there was absolute conviction in it now, which every man in that hushed room felt. 'The 69th has never let the Fatherland down, and it won't now!'

For a long moment there was a tense silence in the big room, while every man there considered the Colonel's words, trying to imagine what the real thing would mean to them. Most of their fathers had fought in the First World War and they had heard tales enough of the battles in the trenches of Flanders and the blood bath of Verdun. Were they fated to suffer the same terrible experiences and come home crippled, gassed, blinded like their fathers had?

Somehow the Colonel seemed able to read their minds, for he said, 'Comrades, rest assured your lives won't be wasted unnecessarily. This is a different kind of war. There will *not* be the tremendous slaughter of the old war.' He flashed a glance at Major von Dietz, and could tell by that bitter smile of his that the Major didn't believe him. The knowledge made him suddenly angry, for he knew that von Dietz was right: the feint could well end in the kind of slaughter that had decimated the flower of Germany's youth at Langemarck in '14. 'What is our mission, comrades?' he demanded harshly, and the men in the front row started and looked in surprise at the Colonel's suddenly red face.

'I shall tell you. You, the men of the First Battalion of the 69th Infantry Regiment, will have the great honour of leading the whole of Army Group South across the border into Poland. The details are still secret and I can only reveal them to you when the time comes. From now onwards, though, you — we — are on a war footing and you must reveal to no one what you have just heard. But remember, comrades, it has always been the right of the 69th to lead the attack, ever since the days of Old Fritz himself. Now you have that right once again, and you must honour that right, for with you when you march will march the ghosts of your fathers, your grandfathers, yes, and their fathers before them —' He broke off abruptly, knowing that he had lost them; there was no enthusiasm in their eyes, just a kind of withdrawn secrecy, as if each and every one was suddenly concerned with private worries of which he had no conception and from which he was barred forever. Suddenly he wished Liesl was at his side so he could pour out his heart to her. But Liesl was long dead. In a small, deflated voice, he said, 'That's all. You may go now.'

As they started to file out, he saw in their faces the fated looks of the kind associated with old men or those he remembered seeing on old photographs of the Franco-Prussian War which had moved him so much as a young boy. They spoke of a close approach to death — and of its acceptance.

CHAPTER 7

'The big one — the one with the heavy lungs — she'll do it for twenty crowns,' Sepp said, indicating the tallest of the three buxom maids, who were hanging out washing in front of the big barn, throwing what they probably thought were coquettish glances over their shoulders.

'How do you know?' Red Rudi asked morosely, aiming a half-hearted kick at one of the farm dogs that wheedled up to him, wagging its tail violently, yet ready to turn and bolt at the slightest sign of danger from these strange-smelling men.

'This morning when she was out in the back, getting breakfast ready for the Countess, she let me have a feel of her lungs for one crown. She speaks a bit of German and told me she'd spread them for twenty.'

Red Rudi, subdued as they had all become since the Colonel's announcement the previous evening, laughed hollowly. 'And where do you think you're gonna get that kind of Marie, you Cologne clot? Twenty crowns don't grow on trees, yer know.'

'I know,' the little Rhinelander agreed. 'But I damn well would like to dip my wick one last time before —' He broke off suddenly, but they all knew what he meant. Next to Red Rudi, Maltitz shuddered violently.

'What's up with you, arsehole with ears?' Rudi snapped and then swallowed hard as the tallest of the three girls bent slowly and deliberately to reveal a long stretch of plump white thigh.

'A louse ran over my grave,' Maltitz croaked, following Rudi's gaze and feeling his heart begin to thump excitedly. Because of his special problem, he had not dared to go to

German whores that had haunted their barracks areas for months now. He, too, would dearly love to have a woman before…

'If we don't get her, the Bull will,' Sepp Deltgen said, not taking his eyes from those ample thighs, which promised so much, trying to imagine what it would be like with them wrapped around his back, while he pumped his salami into her good and hard. 'He was around sniffing up her skirts just after breakfast. I saw him. The rotten sadistic bastard is a real old lady-grabber. Shit, if I thought he'd get it, I'd fill it with powdered glass and razor-blades first.'

'Heaven, arse and cloudburst, Sepp!' Rudi exclaimed, as the girls picked up their empty wicker baskets and, balancing them on their hips, started to walk back to the barn. 'Don't even *think* things like that. It'd put a man off his grub for ever. Powdered glass and razor-blades!' he shuddered. 'What a thought!'

'We could flog the Czechs something,' Maltitz suggested, licking suddenly dry lips as the maids swayed their hips back and forth enticingly.

'Have you got a little bird in your turnip?' Sepp said scornfully.

'What could we flog them, a pair of dice-beakers or a fancy steel helmet, model '38? Drag your arse out of the mud, Titty. What's a common-or-garden stubble-hopper like us got to flog? Besides they ain't got any Marie in the first place.' He laughed scornfully. 'Why do you think she's gonna open her pearly gates for us in the first place, because she loves Germans. *Nix*! Because she needs the Marie. Those —'

Sepp stopped his angry outburst suddenly. The Countess had appeared just beyond the barn, mounted on a fine black stallion, twin jets of grey breath streaming from its distended nostrils, its flanks shining with sweat.

As if from nowhere, Major von Dietz was there, grabbing hold of the horse's bridle and extending his hand to help the Countess from the saddle.

The Polish aristocrat ignored the hand. She swung herself easily from the saddle and said something that the watching soldiers could not hear. But they could see von Dietz's thin face flush angrily. He turned without another word, not even noticing the three privates standing rigidly to attention as he passed.

It was then that Red Rudi had his idea.

'Gentlemen,' von Ostermann announced looking around at the faces of his three battalion commanders and their senior officers. 'As of twelve hundred hours today, the Regiment is on red alert. It means, therefore, that we must finalize our plans. This is the situation…' Von Ostermann spoke hurriedly, as if he wanted to get the unpleasant details done and finished with.

'Ritter von Thoma's Second Panzer Division is going to attempt to cross the ridge line, which is heavily wooded, above the Jablunka Pass and thus work his way behind the Polish defences. It will be our task to ensure that his attempt to do so succeeds. How…? We are to bind the Polish forces up there on the heights until von Thoma is well behind them, then we can break off the action.'

'If I understand correctly, sir…' — it was von Dietz, his voice dry and cold, his eyes revealing nothing — 'we will be attacking a dominating enemy position on a mountain pass, with the enemy probably alerted to our approach?'

Von Ostermann nodded unhappily and waited.

Nothing happened. Von Dietz seemed to accept the information. Instead of the objection that the Colonel had expected, the young tall officer asked simply: 'And I presume that the First Battalion will lead that attack, sir, after your talk to them last night?'

'Yes, von Dietz,' von Ostermann answered uneasily.

Von Dietz seemed satisfied, but Major Hardt, the commander of the Second Battalion, was not. As the oldest other officer there, he obviously felt it was his duty to express what probably all of them were thinking at that particular moment. 'Colonel, what kind of assignment is this for the 69th I ask you?' he demanded hotly. 'Attacking prepared enemy positions in what is, in essence, a feint? What will the glory be in that? Von Thoma will win the flowerpot. All we'll get is *the pisspot*!'

A few of the younger officers chuckled softly at Hardt's expression, but the grey-haired Major's angry look did not change. 'It is not good enough, Colonel von Ostermann. In the name of a regiment that has served the Fatherland loyally these two hundred years, you should have refused the mission!'

Abruptly there was an icy silence in the big room. The chuckles died in the throats of the younger officers. Major von Dietz looked down at his boots, as if he were suddenly embarrassed.

For what seemed a very long time, Major Hardt and Colonel von Ostermann glared at each other, two officers who had fought side by side in the trenches during the First World War, who had served as young lieutenants in the 100,000 Man Army, and had now come to virtually the end of their military careers as if they were deadly enemies instead of lifelong friends. Then von Ostermann's expression changed, and he said softly: 'Paul, times have changed. You know it. I know it.

64

The days of the old 69th died in 1933, you know what I mean?' Out of the corner of his eye von Ostermann caught the look on Major von Dietz's face and with the finality of a revelation knew what had long been troubling the young man. 'Honour is dead, at least the kind we once knew is. We have to do what we are ordered to do.'

Hardt didn't hesitate. 'What are your orders, Colonel, for the Second Battalion?' he rapped.

Von Ostermann smiled, obviously moved. 'Thank you, Paul,' he said softly. 'Now these are my plans for the Second and Third Battalions…'

Red Rudi grinned down triumphantly at Sepp and Titty sprawled lazily in the straw fanning away the flies that were everywhere while their comrades snored all around them.

Sourly Sepp looked up at him and snarled, 'What you looking so shittingly well pleased about? You won the flowerpot or something?'

Rudi, obviously very pleased with himself, shook his head and by way of reply, opened his hand. Resting on his palm, there was a heap of silver crowns.

Maltitz gasped.

'Who did yer kill?' Sepp snapped, flashing a quick glance to the left and right at his sleeping comrades, as if he really thought that Red Rudi had murdered someone to obtain the money.

The Berliner tapped the side of his stub nose knowingly. 'No names, no pack-drill, Sepp. Just put it down to my well-known political acumen.' He grinned at his two running mates happily.

'Acumen — what's that when it's at home?' Sepp asked.

'How much?' Maltitz asked more importantly.

'Enough for all three of us,' Deltgen answered grandly, 'and I'm inviting you two to dip yer wicks at my expense. *After* Red Rudi, naturally, I don't want to stand on a wet deck.'

'Naturally,' Sepp said eagerly, licking his lips as if in anticipation. 'When?'

'After supper. As soon as Big-Tits has cleaned up, she's gonna come out behind the barn — you know where that haystack is?'

They nodded swiftly, minds already racing with delightfully lecherous thoughts.

'Then she'll let me have it. You two can decide who's going next. It don't matter to me, as long as I get mine, in *my* way.' He chuckled coarsely. 'They don't call us the men of the 69th for nothing, you know. Now come on, let's see if we can screw those mean sods of kitchen-bulls out of a bit of bread and sausage. Got to keep our strengths up for tonight, haven't we?'

Laughing happily, the three comrades staggered away to where the goulash-cannon smoked lazily in the heavy lazy afternoon air, while standing at the little window of his quarters a sleepy Sergeant-Major Bulle, his hair still tousled from his afternoon nap, stared after them, wondering what three slack-arsed stubble-hoppers, who looked to him as if they well deserved to end up as cannon fodder, had to be so happy about.

CHAPTER 8

'An arse,' the Bull pontificated as they sat on packing cases in the Countess's cellar, each with a bottle of her prize plum brandy at his feet, 'is an arse, you lot might think. But it ain't so. No, it ain't — and I'm not shitting you!' There was a rumble of agreement from his cronies. In the Regiment it wasn't wise to cross the Bull; you could find yourself shovelling shit in the latrines that way — very quickly.

'Now look at your average short-legged wench's arse, for example. I'd classify it as a sand-digger.'

'Sand-digger?' they echoed as one.

'Yes!' He took a tremendous slug at the potent schnapps and shuddered, whether with enjoyment or pain no one dared to ask. 'It hangs so low, the cheeks dig a couple of grooves in the sand. *Ha, ha!*'

'Ha, ha!' they laughed fawningly. 'That's a good one, Bull! *Sand-digger arse!* What next?'

Encouraged by their laughter and fired by the potent spirit, the Bull continued his scientific appreciation of the female arse. 'Then there's the arse on stilts. Two little, high balls of flesh,' he held his big hands up, fingers spread greedily like sausages, to illustrate what he meant. 'Or you might call that kind, an apple-arse. Really something to get your paws on!' The Bull took another tremendous pull at his bottle, while the others stared at him in admiration.

'Then there's the pear-arse, the kind you see on big-titted wenches who sit around a lot. You should design an arse-brassiere for that kind of arse, Engineer-Sergeant Metzger.'

Engineer-Sergeant Metzger laughed uproariously at the thought and gasped, 'Course I'd have to do a lot of fumbling around first to get the right idea, Bull!'

'But the best kind,' the Bull said, no longer listening, 'is what I call a full-moon arse.'

'*Full-moon arse!*' they chortled in unison.

'Yer,' the Bull said, grinning evilly. 'I once knew a widow who always wore black lace underwear and when she took her drawers off there was that beautiful arse of hers coming up like a full moon. By Christ my ears used to glow at the very sight of it, filling the bedroom!' He tugged at the front of his pants at the memory. 'You had to have a real length of salami to satisfy that full-moon arse, I can tell you bunch of warm brothers. None of your dangling ding-dongs for that wench!' He wiped his eyes, as if they might be full of tears, and staggered unsteadily to his feet. 'Gonna grab a piss outside,' he slurred, 'and don't you greedy sauce-hounds dare to put yer dirty paws on my bottle, or I'll have the nuts off'n you with, a blunt razor-blade!' And with that terrible threat, he clattered blindly up the steep stone steps into the night outside.

A happy, satisfied Rudi came round the back of the haystack, flies wide-open, uttering soft moans, as if he might be hurt.

'What's up, Rudi?' the other two whispered anxiously, keeping their voices low because of the nearness of the barn, which housed the Countess and her Czechs. 'You injured?'

'Yer,' Rudi answered, positioning himself against the haystack, supporting himself with one hand, while he prepared to urinate. 'That Czech wench has got nipples like daggers, right up underneath her chin. Took lumps out of my chest! But it was lovely, *lov-er-ly!*' He let out a tremendous stream of urine that glistened silver in the moonlight that flooded the yard.

With a groan, he stopped the flood, then let it go again, once, twice, three times. 'Case, she's got the pox,' he explained. 'Cleans out the tube. Can't get a dose that way. But even she had, it would be worth it. Now I can die happy.' He fastened his flies and adjusting his cap correctly, said, 'All right, comrades, she's all yours. But treat her gently, lads, because after what she's been through with me, well, you know?' And with that he was gone, sauntering across the cobbled farmyard like a man well satisfied with himself and the world.

Deltgen eyed Maltitz. 'Well, who's next?'

Maltitz, hardly able to control the quaver in his voice at the thought of the woman waiting for him just round the corner, said: 'We'll toss for it, Sepp.'

'All right, Titty.' Deltgen took out a ten-pfennig coin, his sole cash, and spun it in the air. 'Call,' he commanded. 'Head or eagle?'

'Eagle.'

The Rhinelander clapped his hand down hard on the coin as it landed on his palm and together they craned their heads to make out who had won. Deltgen cursed. 'Eagle! All right, Titty, she's yours. But don't shittingly well take too long. I'm ready to shoot my wad as it is.'

Maltitz forced a laugh. 'If I'm not back in sixty seconds flat, come and get me, you'll recognize me by the number of my boots sticking out of it.'

'Get on!' Sepp said sourly.

With fingers that felt like thick, clumsy sausages, his heart in his throat, Maltitz hurried around the corner already fumbling with his flies. She was waiting for him, spread out on the straw, a little lamp burning at her side, breasts hanging luxuriously on her stomach, ample thighs already open, stroking her great bush of black hair, as if it were the fur of some pet cat.

'Come, soldier,' she said in throaty, heavily accented German. 'You come now!'

Maltitz swallowed hard. He hadn't seen so much female pulchritude since the night they had burnt down Rachel's house during the Crystal Night. His knees trembling, already feeling that tremendous first urge coursing through his skinny body, he let his pants drop to his ankles and stood there before her ready, exposing himself to her as he had not dared to do so to anyone for nearly two years.

Her dark-brown eyes narrowed and she said something in Czech, which he couldn't understand. Then she said in German, 'I won't tell. Come... *Come now!*'

And then he was on top of her warm welcoming body, his every limb trembling with joy, and everything was forgotten.

How he had got there, the Bull did not know. A few moments before he was enjoying a luxurious leak outside the cellar and now he was wandering around behind the barn which housed the Polack and her band, his flies still ripped open. What had brought him over here he asked himself? Then he remembered. The whispered voices and the little squeaks and gasps and pleasurable moans which he knew only too well from brothels and lonely widow-women all over the Reich. Someone, somewhere, was ramming home the old salami!

Suddenly the Bull was overcome by a great fury and sense of outrage. Why should anyone else be getting his ashes hauled on this night when soon he, the Bull, might well die in battle for his Fatherland, his desires stilled for all time? At that moment he could have wept hot tears at the sheer injustice of it. Wasn't it his due as the Regiment's senior NCO to get the first cut of any tail that might be available?

Now the rustling in the straw had ceased and there was the sound of heavy army dice-beakers walking slowly across the cobbles. The very sound heightened his rage. He knew it well. It was that of a satisfied man, going back to his bunk where he would sink into a deep enjoyable sleep, full of pleasurable dreams of naked wenches lying legs-spread in feather beds. Blindly, his beefy face flushed with almost unbearable anger, he swayed towards the shadowy outline of the haystack.

He turned the corner and skidded to a drunken stop. The Czech woman lay there in the straw naked. Deltgen towered above her, his pants around his ankles, watching open-mouthed as the Czech woman knelt in the straw, wagging her great arse with pleasure, while that bastard of a Rhinelander thrust back and forth. Her moans of delight broke the spell.

'*Get yer dirty flippers off that woman*!' he bellowed.

The pole collapsed at once. The tent went down. The Czech woman clasped her ample thighs together with an audible snap like a safe being shut, and Deltgen spun round, his face a mixture of alarm, rage and surprise.

'What the —' the words died on his lips, as he saw who stood there, the Bull, his face a fiery-red, his pig-like eyes filled with rage and desire. 'Sergeant-Major!' he managed to gasp.

'Don't give me, Sarnt-Major,' the Bull exclaimed, showering his face with spittle, his eyes taking in all of the Czech's ample charms, feeling an all too obvious urge in his lower regions. 'Pull up those trousers at once! What are you — some kind of pervert or something!'

'But, Sarnt-Major —'

'No buts!' the Bull bellowed. 'Christ on a crutch, man, you're damn lucky that I don't bang you on a fizzer for this kind of piggery! Fu — er — attempting sexual intercourse with a racially inferior female of the opposite sex. No, hit the trail, you slack-assed barn-shitter, before I change my mind!'

Miserably, his heart afire with rage, hands trembling uncontrollably, Sepp Deltgen pulled up his trousers and fastened his flies.

'And don't forget the sign of honour!' Bull rubbed pepper in the wound, smirking now in anticipation, telling himself this would be a fine tale to tell his drinking cronies — 'and there she was in the hay, with her legs spread like ready money, and I made him salute before he went.'

Deltgen flung the big NCO a semblance of a salute. 'Permission to dismiss, Sarnt-Major?' he said in a strangled voice.

'Permission granted,' the Bull said, dismissing the soldier from his thoughts now, his mind concentrating solely on what was going to happen in the next few minutes.

The Czech whore waited till the sound of Deltgen's boots had died away on the cobbles; then she said in a sultry inviting voice. 'You come — me?'

'I come — *you*!' the Bull chortled, ripping down his trousers drunkenly, his breath coming in short, sharp, almost painful gasps.

'You like?' the whore said, spreading her legs in seductive invitation.

The Bull's eyes nearly popped out of his head at the sight. At his temples the purple veins started to tick violently, as if he might have a stroke at any moment. 'I like,' he gasped in a voice that he hardly recognized as his own.

'Come ... come, then!' she sighed, thrusting out both arms, great tufts of jet-black, sweat-laden hair revealed in the armpits.

Bull's eyes were too full of other things to see what she had clutched in her right hand. With a great sigh he fell upon her, sinking deep into the soft cushion of her flesh. An instant later the sigh changed into a shrill, almost feminine scream of sheer absolute agony, as the Czech woman played her little trick on him with the sharp length of a twig; and he was writhing back and forth in the hay, all thoughts of sex vanished immediately, clutching his injured organ, whimpering like a badly hurt child, while she ran back to the barn, giggling uproariously as she did so.

It might have been Bull's scream that woke von Dietz out of a troubled sleep. Later he didn't know or care. But as the blubbering outside finally died away and the Bull limped slowly and painfully back to his bunk, completely sober now, he became aware of the soft, muffled clip-clop of a tired horse approaching the house.

For a few minutes he lay there listening to it, then he turned angrily and closed his eyes again. But he couldn't sleep. Who was out riding at this time of the night he asked himself? It was long after lights-out for the soldiers and curfew-time for the civilians. In the end he gave up. Throwing on his long greatcoat over his pyjamas, clambering into his boots and then as an afterthought slipping a pistol into his pocket, he left his room and made his way carefully through the long lines of snoring soldiers who lay packed like sardines in a can in the big hall.

Outside all was silence. The courtyard was empty, bathed in the cold-silver light of the moon. His eyes searched the deep shadows. Nothing. Then he saw it. A gleam of yellow light coming from a crack in the wooden stable behind the barn! He hesitated and then slipping off the safety catch of his pistol and telling himself he was a fool to do so after all it was still peacetime, he crept towards the light.

'Caution is the mother of the china cabinet,' he quoted the old saying to himself, and peered into the stable. It was the Countess, dressed in her black riding habit, her back towards him, currying her still steaming mare. The animal had fresh splashes of grey mud on its fetlocks in spite of the fact that there had not been any rain in the area for three weeks.

Von Dietz hesitated. The Polish woman angered him yet attracted him, too. She was of his own kind, with the same sort of background — for all he knew they might even be related through the West Prussian line of the von Dietz's. And in the back of his mind he knew, too, that he desired her.

His mind made up, he opened the door. She spun round startled.

'Good evening, Countess,' he said formally, although he knew instinctively that this was not the occasion for formality.

The Countess said nothing, but underneath her eyes the delicate waxy skin suddenly became translucent, as if the blood was draining from her face before his very eyes.

'You've been out for a ride?' he said.

'Obviously. And I know, too, I've broken the curfew rules.' Melodramatically she threw out both arms as if she were suspended on a cross, her breasts pressing excitingly against the thin material of her blouse so that he could see the big nipples outlined against the silk. 'Arrest me — shoot me, if you will.'

He forced a smile and tried to control the thickness in his voice. 'I don't think that will be necessary, Countess. A lot of your people break the curfew all the time. I was just interested in what a beautiful young woman like yourself could be doing on a horse at this time of the night.'

'Riding,' she answered woodenly, her beautiful face revealing nothing.

'I can see that. But where?'

She said nothing.

For an instant von Dietz did not know what to do or to say; then suddenly his gaze fell on the horse's muddy hooves once more and he knew where she had been. There was only one place where a horse could get hooves like that within kilometres of the village: the border stream between Czechoslovakia and Poland. She had been there, and she had waded the stream into Poland on her mount!

She followed the direction of his gaze, read his mind and stifled the involuntarily gasp too late, her hand clasped to her pale lips a little absurdly as if she did not know whether to cry or yawn.

'You went into Poland?' von Dietz said slowly.

She nodded, hand still clasped to her mouth.

'Why?'

'Can't you guess?'

'I asked you a question,' he said after a moment, not wanting to articulate an answer to her words. It would be too terrible.

'I answered it — in my fashion.' Her voice was without emotion. 'What are you going to do *now*?'

Von Dietz said nothing. His brain was racing furiously. She had gone to her people to tell them what was going on up in the Czech mountains. That was it. It was the only explanation possible.

A heavy silence descended upon the stable, broken only by the little metallic noises made by the mare, as they froze there like characters in the third act of some fourth-rate melodrama. It seemed to go on forever. Then she ripped at the front of her silken shirt and the heavy breasts with their great dun nipples tumbled out, unrestrained by any brassiere.

'Well, German,' she said almost contemptuously, 'would you like my body as the price of your silence?'

The spell was broken. Without a word, von Dietz swung round and went back the way he had come, leaving her, breasts naked and heaving, staring at the swinging stable door,

BOOK TWO: *THE EDUCATION OF MAJOR VON DIETZ*

'One of the great fallacies of our time is that the Nazis rose to power because they imposed order on chaos. Precisely the opposite is true — they were successful because they imposed chaos on order. They tore up the commandments, they denied the superego, what you will. They said, you may persecute the minority, you may kill, you may torture, you may couple and breed without love. They offered humanity all its great temptations. Nothing is true, everything is permitted.'

John Fowles, The Magus

CHAPTER 1

In late 1937 the then Captain von Dietz was posted to the provincial town of W— in the remote border area of the Eifel. It was now over a year since German troops had marched into the demilitarized zone of the German Rhineland and everywhere in the small towns and villages along the long frontier with Belgium and Luxembourg, new Adolf Hitler barracks were being thrown up, and the undersized pudding-faced Eifel farmboys called to the colours to do their two years' military service. Thus it was that Captain von Dietz, serving as adjutant and second-in-command of one of the raw new battalions, found himself in the sleepy provincial town, where the peasants still kept pigs and oxen in the back streets and the all-pervading smell was that of horse manure.

He didn't like it. He liked neither the town, the people, nor the new battalion and its commander, Major Mueller. Mueller, a northerner like himself, felt only contempt for his men. For him they were 'animals', 'half-frogs', 'water-heads' and the best *'proteten'*.

In the morning, striding up and down in front of the battalion in the cavalry breeches he affected (although he was an infantry officer from a very unfashionable regiment), whipping his riding crop against his highly polished riding boots to punctuate his words, he would lash his miserable, pasty-faced recruits with some new edict: 'I know you are pigs! I know that at home you eat from the trough with the other swine. Well, now you are honoured by being members of the Greater German Army, thanks to *our* Führer Adolf Hitler and, by the great whore of Buxtehude, the Führer does not want any pigs in his forces! At nine hundred hours, the whole battalion will parade for eating drill.'

Thus it was that an amused Captain von Dietz came to supervise eight-hundred young farmboys, eating imaginary soup out of soup plates with imaginary spoons and cutting up imaginary meat with imaginary knives and forks, two instruments that most of them were acquainted with only from wedding feasts and wakes.

On pay day Mueller would announce to von Dietz: 'Today the animals get fed. We must ensure that the fartsuckers don't puke their greedy guts up all over some innocent civvy's new boots.' So the two of them would patrol the cobbled streets of the little town, visiting each inn and amateur brothel (the Army had wished to introduce correctly supervised official brothels, but the local Catholic bishop had objected: 'We can't have my sons being corrupted that way, General. Besides we must give our daughters locally a chance, too, to get pregnant; otherwise we'll never get them married off!'). The cynical Mueller would say loudly in the presence of every soldier he spotted with a girl, 'the price of pork being what it is, you can still buy a whole swine for five marks' or 'hope you've signed for the Parisian, because if you get a dose this night, you're for the high jump, soldier!'

That winter von Dietz spent three months of his life composing the battalion's so-called 'Hair Order'. It began '*HAIR*!… Hair on the head will cease at the forehead (the front) and at the top of the earlobes (to the rear). In both cases, the hair will cease with a clean-shaven, perfectly straight horizontal line…' It ended with '*MOUSTACHE*!' and the remarkable discovery that: 'Only officers were permitted to wear moustaches (see appendix 1/33, Section A). Moustaches do not exist for private soldiers!'

It was not surprising that Captain von Dietz ended 1937 as cynical as his commander and much more bored, for Mueller had ambitions to become a general which he finally succeeded in doing, only to end the war doing a last dance for his war crimes at the end of a Greek rope. But by that time, Colonel von Dietz had been long dead.

Von Dietz went about his duties in that remote border town in the last year of peace, teaching his rural cannon fodder how to eat with knife and fork, take a weekly bath, change their underclothes once every two weeks, talk an understandable German instead of 'that damned half-frog of theirs' (as Mueller called it) and prepare to die for 'Folk, Fatherland and Führer' in the non-too-distant future.

There were compensations, of course. There was Vera, the plump wife of *Kreisleiter* Schmier. The shaven-headed, enormously fat Nazi County-Leader, who looked as if he might burst out of his brown SA uniform at any moment, had once been a local pork butcher. But in the period prior to 1933 when Hitler came to power — the 'Battle-Time', as the Nazis liked to call it — he had fallen down the stairs of the local Communist party's piss-corner in a moment of drunken confusion when he had mistaken the Reds' local inn for that of the Nazis, and had been found covered with blood, his unconscious face resting among the cigarette butts in a pool of stale brown urine in one of the lime-encrusted stalls. The Goebbels' propaganda machine went to work immediately and proclaimed the drunken pork butcher as a victim of Red terror, who has spilled his blood heroically for the cause. Hitler personally awarded him the 'Blood Order' in Munich and it had been his making. In 1933 he gave up his pork butcher's shop for good and devoted his energies to politics. As the *Westdeutscher Beobachter* stated: 'Today National Hero Kurt

Schmier is the "man-of-the-hour". Without doubt, this old comrade of the "Battle-Time", who has repeatedly shed his blood for our Führer Adolf Hitler, will show those treacherous elements, those parasites, perverts, work-shys and *JEWS*, that a new wind blows in Germany!'

Now County-Leader Schmier dominated the political life of the little town. He organized the boycotts outside the remaining Jewish stores and shops ('He who buys at a Jew's is unworthy of being a German'). He inspected parades of the new Hitler Youth and more importantly the 'Hitler Maiden' ('Oh, what a beautiful German bum you have, Female Group-Leader!'). He quietly ensured that 'the water-heads', the mentally retarded results of centuries of rural inbreeding with their monstrous heads and slack drooling mouths, were moved to 'hospitals where they'll receive proper treatment, you understand?' And he enjoyed spending quiet evenings with his cronies in the cellar below the local police station supervising the cops 'interrogation' of some Red swine or other ('Bend 'em down, *Wachtmeister*, for Chrissake! Make 'em bite their own balls! Stick it up the Red Jewish arse!').

Due to the immense political activity of her husband, Vera Schmier, a good-looking blonde in her mid-thirties, was bored, tremendously bored. For a while she had tried to escape her boredom by parties, given with the liberal funds that came from the Party HQ in Berlin and the even more liberal 'gifts' with which the local big farmers and store owners hoped to keep County-Leader Schmier happy. But soon parties bored her, too. As she said to Captain von Dietz on the occasion of their first meeting, bending low as she poured his tea so that he could get a good look at her ample breasts in the low-cut evening dress: 'There is simply no society whatsoever in this God-forsaken place!' She fluttered her false eyelashes and accepted the cigarette he offered her. 'A German woman does not smoke, the Führer says, but just this once.' Adding 'my husband, naturally, he has his politics. But what have I got — *nothing!*'

Exactly thirty minutes later she was on her back in Kreisleiter Schmier's own big double bed, stripped naked, with her plump white legs spread high in the air, gasping for breath frantically as if she were in the last throes of an asthma attack, getting a great deal, while on the wall a heroically posed Adolf Hitler frowned down at the pair's frantic antics in his loyal follower's bed, as if the new leader of the 'One Thousand Year Empire' was wondering whether he should condemn such disloyalty or praise their worthy attempts to produce 'new heroes for a new heroic Germany'.

Thus Captain von Dietz spent the last year of peace, dividing his attention between the Adolf Hitler Kaserne and Kreisleiter Schmier's Vera; not happy, but then again not unhappy; blind to the drastic changes taking place in Germany all around him (perhaps deliberately so); a little contemptuous, a little cynical, a little bored as befitted a young man of his lineage and background who found himself in the circumstances he did. But things were soon going to change; the education of Captain von Dietz was about to commence.

CHAPTER 2

It had been a rotten day in the Adolf Hitler Kaserne. Major Mueller had been in one of his moods. He had read in the *Völkischer Beobachter* that morning, that a former comrade of his had been promoted to colonel in the Condor Legion currently fighting as 'volunteers' against the Reds in Spain. He had thrown the National Socialist paper down in a burst of rage, muttered something about 'God, I'll creak as a hundred-year-old major in this God-forsaken shit-heap!' and then bolted on to the parade ground to give the waiting battalion hell.

'*DOWN!*' was his first word.

As one, the eight hundred young men dropped to the concrete, pressing their noses down hard into the puddles, lying at attention, arms stretched rigidly down their sides.

Mueller let them lie there. There was no sound save the caws of the crows in the skeletal winter trees around the barracks square. Suddenly, startlingly, Mueller bellowed: 'Do you feel it, you frog swine?... The cold creeping into your rotten bones? Well, do you? *ANSWER!*'

'*Jawohl, Herr Major,*' the unfortunate cannon fodder yelled back.

He stood there, staring down at their inert bodies, their uniforms turning black quickly in the thin bitter rain that was now beginning to fall. His broad face was full of infinite contempt. Then he screamed: 'On your feet, you good-for-nothing swine! *UP!... UP!... UP!*' He thrashed his cane against his right boot in a paroxysm of fury. 'By God, I'm going to crack your lazy Eifel arses for you this day!'

And he did. All that long wet miserable winter's day, Mueller had chased his leathern-lunged, strained, red-faced young soldiers up and down the Eifel hills until with twenty men being sent to the dispensary for sundry gunshot, bayonet and other wounds, he had had enough and the battalion had been dismissed for the day.

Now a weary, somehow depressed von Dietz, dressed in civilian clothes — an officer never went into an inn in uniform, just in case he followed his inclination to go into some bar and get blind-drunk — wandered through the glistening-black evening streets of the little provincial town. He was hardly aware of the swastika banners flying from virtually every house, or the occasional barricaded window of a Jewish store, or the inns with the sign smeared across the door in white paint, '*Juden unerwünscht*', so engrossed was he in his own thoughts: Should he get drunk? Or should he indulge in Vera Schmeier's ample and willing body, and then get drunk?

It was in this mood that he became aware of the small group of local citizens crowded together in the Pariser Platz, staring upwards through the grey drizzle at something on the steep roof of the half-timbered medieval Gasthaus zum Ritter. He paused and followed the direction of their gaze.

A small man in a dark business suit, now soaked black with rain, sat on the edge of the roof, legs dangling, staring down with no apparent curiosity at the group of morbid onlookers.

Von Dietz frowned. What the devil was the little man doing up there? He shifted and walked to the edge of the crowd. 'What's going on?' he asked a man eating a bratwurst out of a piece of grease-proof paper, routinely dipping the sausage in the smear of mustard on the paper without taking his gaze off the little man on the roof.

'It's the Jew … Ernst Solomen… Has the fur shop at the corner of the Rathausplatz,' the man answered between bites. 'Been up there … since four o'clock, silly Jewish bastard.'

'But what's he going to do?'

The man with the bratwurst shrugged carelessly. 'Who knows what goes on in a man's 's head? Perhaps commit suicide.' He finished the sausage, neatly crumpled up the piece of paper, and still without taking his eyes off the roof, placed it in the nearest trash bin.

Von Dietz absorbed the information, staring upwards too now, and noted that the little Jew sitting there in the dripping rain wore the black, white and red ribbon of the Iron Cross, first class, around his neck, and had the Silver Wound Medal pinned on his skinny chest. He wondered why.

It was just about then that Kreisleiter Schmier swaggered up in his gleaming ankle-length leather coat, tugging at his Alsatian, which he had recently bought in imitation of the Führer, followed by a little crowd of fat, middle-aged SA, all obviously drunk.

'What's this?… What's this?' he cried, pushing his way through the crowd, the citizens jumping back as Wolf, his dog, snapped at his ankles. He acknowledged von Dietz's presence with a wave of a fat hand and looked up. 'What's the man doing up there?' he asked of no one in particular.

'Running off at the mouth that he's had enough or something,' a dozen voices informed him self-importantly.

'*So-so*' Schmier said, swaying back and forth on his heels, complete master of the situation, while his dog tried to get its snout under the long habit of an embarrassed young nun in the crowd. He cupped his fat hands around his mouth and shouted, 'What's this, Ernst — kosher canyon or something?'

'I've had enough,' the Jew quavered, staring down at the crowd. 'Had a noseful. I fought for Germany in the last lot and was wounded three times. Shed my blood for the Fatherland, I did.'

'Boo-hoo!' Schmier sneered. 'Did little Ikey get hurt by the naughty frogs in the big war?'

'Boo-hoo!' his drunken cronies took up the chant and pretended to dab their eyes, while the crowd laughed and the young nun, no longer so embarrassed now, leaned ever closer to the Alsatian's greedy snout.

'I'm gonna jump!' the Jew shouted.

'Jump,' Schmier said carelessly. 'You've got your audience now — *jump!*'

In spite of the rain and the growing darkness, von Dietz could see the fear and uncertainty on the little man's face, and he felt a mixture of pity and contempt for him. Did he think the crowd below really cared? This was a spectacle for them, something to talk about for a few days, make their dull provincial lives interesting. Hell, they *wanted* him to jump!

'I'm gonna jump,' the Jew's voice was at the edge of a scream.

'Well, shitting-well jump,' Schmier yelled back, 'and get it shitting-well over with! We've got families and homes to go to, Iky, even if you —'

The Jew let himself slip from the eave. At ten metres a second he came sailing down, his sudden scream lost in the whoosh of air. He smacked into the wet cobbles below like a bag of wet cement, his skull bursting on impact, littering the cobbles with gobs of thick red gore and white fragments of bones.

'Typical pig, typical Jewish pig,' Schmier broke the sudden awed silence. 'Just look at my boots! All covered with bits of Jew!' He tugged the Alsatian's head from underneath the nun's skirt and touched his fat hand to his peaked cap, 'Excuse him, Sister, he's young.'

'It's all right,' the young nun gasped, telling herself she would faint at any moment. 'He's a very nice animal, very nice indeed.'

Von Dietz turned, sickened. He got very drunk that night.

Two months after the incident with the Jew, von Dietz was hastily summoned in his role of adjutant to one of the barracks by an excited, pale-faced NCO, who kept muttering something about 'they pushed him too far … just too far…'

As he had climbed the four flights of stairs leading to the attic, the young awed men standing at every floor, had stared at him, as if he had just landed from the moon. When von Dietz was ushered into the slope-ceilinged room, what he saw there made him stop in his tracks. He gulped hard in order to repel the bitter bile which threatened to choke him.

A young man was hanging there, his neck stretched at least ten centimetres, his field-grey trousers soaked with faeces and urine. A three-legged issue stool was overturned at his feet.

Overcoming his repugnance, von Dietz forced himself to approach the dead youth and check whether the body exhibited any sign of life. It did not. The eyes bulged horribly from the twisted purple face, the tongue hung out like a long strip of leather, and the rope had almost vanished into the deep furrow of his neck. Hardly recognizing his own voice, he ordered, 'Cut him down, cover him with a sack, and take him downstairs. Then report to me with the details.'

'Well?' von Dietz demanded of the NCO five minutes later. 'Give. What's the story?'

'He was a Bible student, sir,' the man replied, his face a shade of green from what he had just been forced to do.

'A what?'

'Bible student.'

'What in God's name are they, man?'

The young NCO swallowed hard. 'I don't know exactly myself, sir. All I know is they ain't Catholics like us. I mean, like the lads of the battalion. They ain't even Lutherans like that lot from the North.'

At another time von Dietz would have been amused at the NCO's attitude to the religion of fifty-million-odd other Germans, but not now with the picture of that poor tortured boy before his mind's eye.

'Well, what did he do? What was the trouble?'

'Not much really, sir, just read that shitty — excuse me — read the Bible all the time. It got on the lads' nerves. I mean reading the Bible, that's the job of the priest, not the likes of us. He read it all the time. In the barracks room, in the cookhouse, even in the latrines, sitting on the damn thunderbox.'

Von Dietz controlled his temper. The NCO was a typical pasty-faced, Eifel farmboy, who probably had never been out of his one-horse village before he had been called to the colours. Carefully he asked, 'Why then do you think he committed suicide? He seems to have been a harmless type of boy, Corporal.'

'He got on the lads' tits — excuse me, sir — their nerves … and —'

'And?' von Dietz prompted.

'They started to tease him.' The NCO was suddenly hesitant, picking out his words with more care.

'How?'

'The usual things, sir!'

'What usual things?' von Dietz snapped, iron in his voice. 'I don't know the *usual* things.'

'Putting fae —' the NCO couldn't find the word he sought and in red-faced frustration, he growled, 'putting horse-crap in his bed, tearing up his letters, hiding his Bible, putting —'

Von Dietz held up his hand and the NCO stopped lamely. 'But why?' he demanded. 'Why? Just because he read the Bible?'

'Yes, I suppose so, sir, and because it didn't seem right for a soldier to be always sitting around, reading a shitting book. Excuse me, sir.'

'God in Heaven, man, stop saying "excuse me" all the time. I know what shit is. Get on with it!'

The NCO flushed unhappily. 'A soldier isn't supposed to be like that. We're supposed to be like — what do they say on the radio these days? A German soldier is as tough as leather, as hard as Krupp steel…'

'Get out!' von Dietz interrupted savagely. 'Get out, damn you, at once!'

Almost forgetting to salute, the red-faced corporal staggered out of the office, leaving von Dietz to ponder angrily over the fate of a young man hounded to death by his so-called comrades because he had read the Bible.

But if von Dietz took the suicide of the soldier hard, Major Mueller simply laughed when he told him the news and said cynically, 'I suppose he must have come to the end of his particular rope, what, Captain?'

Perhaps it would have appeased Captain von Dietz somewhat if he had known then that within exactly seven years, the general, as Mueller would be in 1945, would also come to the 'end of his particular rope' in a stinking Greek jail. But he didn't.

One week later he made a formal application to the War Ministry in Berlin's Bendlerstrasse to be returned to his parent regiment for 'personal reasons'.

The request was turned down on a standard reply form without any explanation why. On the day that he received the rejection, Mueller had laughed across the table at him in the mess and said, his voice thickened a little by the cheap *Korn* he was drinking: 'My dear von Dietz, obviously you gentlemen of the aristocracy don't have the pull you once did in the Greater German Wehrmacht'. He formed his forefinger into a circle and looked through it as if he were some aristocratic Prussian officer looking through his monocle at some particularly sloppy soldier. 'Pip-pip!'

It was then at the age of twenty-six that Captain von Dietz started to learn just how tenuous the life of the soul was and that the old Prussian concepts of honour, loyalty and truth meant little in the 'glorious New Age' in which he purportedly now lived. His soul, if he truly had one, was beginning to die.

But there was worse to come before the education of Captain von Dietz was finally completed.

CHAPTER 3

It all started harmlessly enough.

In the last week of October, 1938, Reichsführer Himmler decided that all Jews within the Reich who possessed Polish passports would be arrested and deported back to their native land. In the end, fifteen thousand of them were arrested. Unfortunately the Poles didn't want them. As their representatives explained to Reichsführer Himmler, 'We've got enough Jews' — though they didn't really say 'Jews' — 'of our own.' As a result Himmler found himself with fifteen thousand Jews on his hands. For twenty-four hours he worried about the problem. They might well be Jews, but they were *not* Germans. What power had he over them? But in the end, he reasoned, the Polacks wanted them even less than he did and would be undoubtedly pleased if they, the Germans, found a nice satisfactory solution to the problem: Sweep it under the carpet, in other words. In the first week of November he ordered that the Polish Jews should be quietly placed behind the barbed wire of those lonely establishments called concentration camps, after the 'reservations' the British Army had founded for their Boer prisoners, civilian and soldier, during the Boer War.

One of those Polish Jews thus transported to the camps was an undersized master-tailor called 'Grynszpan' by the Poles and, because that name was impossible for a German tongue to pronounce, 'Gruenspan' by the camp authorities. Somehow the news of his arrest in Hanover managed to leave the country, and thus the humble Polish master-tailor was fated to become a footnote in the bloody history of the 'Thousand-Year Reich' before he disappeared into the ovens.

Gruenspan had a seventeen-year-old son named Herschel, who somehow had escaped from the Third Reich in time and was now living in Paris illegally, managing to keep alive by selling his skinny, undersized body to rich homosexuals. One of his customers was a German — an important German in fact, namely Third Secretary Ernst vom Rath serving in the Chancellery of the German Embassy in the French capital.

On November 7, 1938, young Herschel Gruenspan, for whatever reason, met his 'friend' in one of the *bistros* frequented by their kind, pulled out a somewhat antiquated revolver and pumped five slugs into the Third Secretary. The elegant, affected diplomat fell to the floor, bleeding profusely, hands grabbing at the damp sawdust in mortal agony. Herschel allowed himself to be arrested by the gendarmes without resistance.

On November 8, Hitler's own paper *Der Völkischer Beobachter* stated ominously that the 'German Folk will draw its own conclusions from this new Jewish crime'.

The following day Hitler met his old Party comrades of the 'Battle-Time' in Munich, where together on November 9, 1923, they had attempted to *putsch* and failed. In the Munich Bürgerbräukeller, their old Party pub, he gave his usual speech, full of threats and sentimental references to the 'old days', but made no reference, surprisingly enough, to the attempted murder of a German diplomat in Paris. In the wings, those who were actively preparing the reprisal hesitated. Perhaps their *aktion* was going to be stopped at the very last moment?

They need not have worried, those hefty middle-aged gentlemen in the brown and black uniforms, the good family fathers with their generous bellies, who patted blonde children on the head and had damp eyes when they stood before the decorated fir tree on Christmas Eve. Help was on the way.

At eight-thirty precisely, just as the brown-shirted veterans were sitting down to sauerkraut and sausage and half-litre steins of good Munich beer, a telegram reached them that Third Secretary vom Rath had died of his wounds. Now there was no holding the men in the wings. They had official sanction for their *aktion*. Telephone calls and telegrams flashed from one end of the Reich to the other. *Die Reichskristall-nacht*, as it would later cynically be called, was about to commence.

'Spontaneously' the mobs went out into the streets in every German city where there were Jews. The synagogues were the first target. Everywhere the howling, torch-bearing mobs, faces lathered with sweat, eyes gleaming wildly, set fire to the houses of worship, tearing the precious Torah scrolls from the hands of the weeping Jewish custodians and throwing them back into the greedy, all-consuming flames. The cemeteries came next. In the smaller rural towns, brown-shirted farmers appeared — also 'spontaneously' — with their oxen and ploughs to rip up two and three-hundred-year-old Jewish graveyards, while the drunken stormtroopers stamped up and down on brittle bones with their heavy hobnailed boots. The Jewish stores and businesses were next. Everywhere, while their owners cowered in the bedrooms, the mobs smashed the plate-glass windows, tossing goods and garments into the gutters and dancing on them or, if they were smart, quietly thrusting them in their pockets or down the front of their beer-stained khaki shirts.

But, of course, it did not end with the synagogues, cemeteries and stores…

In W— Kreisleiter Schmier had about ended his annual stag night for the local *Prominenz* and officers of the garrison when the news of vom Rath's death reached him. Ever since 1933 he and the local stormtroopers had celebrated the 9th in the local Party inn, with plenty of schnapps and beer, and sausages traditionally served in a chamber-pot full of mustard to cries of drunken delight. This November 9th had been no different, and by now most of those present were in the last stages of intoxication, including Captain von Dietz, who got drunk easily and often these days.

A snoring SA man lay sprawled over the back of one of the armchairs. Another crouched shivering on the billiard table, legs curled up in the foetal position, completely naked save for his jackboots. A third was vomiting noisily out the upstairs window, to the annoyance of some unfortunate passer-by below.

Mueller's officers were in no better state. Their tunics ripped open, they sagged there in their leather armchairs, glasses and cigars dangling from their nerveless fingers, watching a rubber-kneed naked second lieutenant attempting to catch the goldfish in an aquarium with a pin attached to the end of his dress lanyard.

But drunk as he was, Kreisleiter Schmier knew the importance of the telegram he had just received. Leaving the drunken SA men and their officer guests to their own devices, he staggered out of the door to attempt to supervise the burning of the local synagogue as best he could. But Schmier was too late. The building was already burning merrily when he arrived there and the local citizens, drunk with schnapps and excitement, were busy looting not only the synagogue but the houses and shops of the nearby Jewish settlement

It was then that Schmier had the brilliant idea which, unfortunately for the ex-pork butcher, would ensure one day in March 1945 that his bloated body would be fed by a group of

American-Jewish soldiers who had just slit his fat throat to the self-same pigs it had once been his duty to slaughter.

What better way to celebrate the 'Glorious Ninth' and punish the Jewish people than to have a bit of fun with their virgins? 'Said — done,' he chuckled to himself and bellowing to Police Sergeant Weissgarten, who was standing discreetly in the shadows watching the destruction, to follow him, Kreisleiter Schmier, laughing drunkenly to himself, set off to find the 'Jewish girls'.

'Da ... *da*!' Schmier almost fell into the big room, pretending to blow on an imaginary trumpet.

Behind him an embarrassed Sergeant Weissgarten pushed the four frightened Jewish teenagers into the room, one of whom was hugging her bleeding swollen mouth.

'Jewish girls!' Schmier proclaimed triumphantly, as Sergeant Weissgarten, a clever man who had been a policeman under the Kaiser, the Republic and now under Hitler, made a hurried exit, telling himself he wanted no part of what would probably soon happen in that room. As he clattered down the stairs, he heard the one of the women scream.

That scream roused von Dietz from his drunken stupor. He blinked open his eyes and took in the bottle-littered, smoke-filled room without comprehension. He licked his thick, parched lips, wondered where he was and what he was doing there — then decided it wasn't worth worrying about and closed his eyes once more.

The second scream, shrill, high and hysterical, made him sit bolt upright, suddenly wide-awake and apprehensive. Cowering at the end of the room, there were four dark-haired girls between fifteen and eighteen with a swaying drunken Schmier staring at them greedily with his pig-like red eyes, the saliva of desire trickling slowly from the side of his slack mouth and down his fat chin.

Schmier reached out a soft pudgy hand and touched the nearest girl's left breast. She shrank back with a little cry of alarm. 'No!' she whispered.

'You should be glad I touch you, Jewish bitch!' Schmier drooled.

Next to her a bigger girl with a tough face said, 'Take your damn pork-butcher paws off her, Schmier! She's only fifteen.'

There was a shocked gasp from those still sober enough to understand what was happening. Jews never talked back to Germans. They were the inferior race; the Germans were the new *Herrenvolk*.

Schmier gasped hard as if someone had just punched him in his massive paunch. 'What did you say, you Jewish bitch?'

'You heard me. Leave her alone —'

She never finished the sentence. Schmier's big fist slammed directly into her face. Von Dietz could distinctively hear her nose break, as she crashed into the wall, gobs of dark-red blood spurting out everywhere.

'That's enough, Schmier!' von Dietz heard himself shouting, coming to his feet as the woman wiped the blood as best she could from her ruined nose and glared at Schmier with burning-black defiant eyes.

Schmier spun round to see who had spoken. He saw von Dietz and his face flushed even more. 'What right have you to tell me what I can do and what I can't do? *You* of all people! Don't you think I don't know about your rotten goings-on behind my back, corrupting my wife, making —'

'Kreisleiter Schmier, Herr von Dietz,' Mueller's voice cut into the trembling fat man's tirade, '*please*. Let us remember we are officers and gentlemen!'

Leaning weakly against the wall, the blood beginning to stream down into her mouth again, the woman laughed. 'Gentlemen!' she sneered thickly.

Mueller flashed her a glance and she returned it boldly, her face completely unafraid.

Von Dietz turned to Mueller. 'As an officer of the German Army, Major, you cannot tolerate being a party to this kind of behaviour, surely?' he asked, trying to keep his voice steady despite his raging anger.

Mueller laughed easily. 'Of course I can. What in three devils' name do I care about a couple of Jewish wenches? They mean nothing to me.'

'They're women!'

'Of course, they are,' Schmier sneered, 'and that's why we're all gonna fuck them. What about it, boys? Like a bit of Jewish woman before it goes out of fashion?'

Von Dietz smashed into Schmier's back propelling him forward. 'You filthy swine —' he began and swung round at the grunt, but it was too late already. The rubber club slapped down on the back of his head. He went down on his knees, still fighting the roaring blackness which threatened to engulf him at any moment. The SA club smacked against his skull once more. Without another sound, he pitched forward on his face on to the beer-wet carpet.

November 9th, 1938, was over, and nobody ever saw the four Jewish girls again.

CHAPTER 4

Major Mueller, white-faced with dark smudges under his red-veined eyes, apologized formally at midday and said he would approve von Dietz's transfer to his parent regiment if he cared to apply to the Bendlerstrasse once again. At the ranges that afternoon, officer after officer who had taken part in the horror of the previous night sidled up to von Dietz at the butts during breaks in the firing exercise and apologized, too. Kreisleiter Schmier sent a case of Moselle wine with a note attached upon which he had written in a shaky hand: 'Hope that you will do my wife and me the honour of calling in the very near future.' He had underlined the words 'wife' and 'in the very near future'. That night von Dietz, watched curiously by his fellow officers from the tall French windows, solemnly broke every bottle in the gutter behind the officers' mess and let the wine run down into the drains.

For the first time in his young life Captain von Dietz had learned to hate. All his life he had been brought up in the belief that, as a future Prussian officer, one had to be objective and that hatred distorted one's judgement and was a luxury that only civilians could afford.

But now von Dietz hated. He hated Germans and everything German. Now he realized just how hypocritical they and their whole way of life was, with the formal bowings and scrapings and their *bitte schöns* and *danke schöns*, the handshakes, the talk of *kultur*, their cloying sentimentality. All of it hid a black sadistic nature, which would always come to the surface once their petty little clerks' minds knew they could not be punished for their savage, unthinking cruelty. And he, von Dietz, had the misfortune to be a member of that cursed race at a time when all of them knew they couldn't be punished; that they were ruled by an evil perverted man who actively encouraged that cruelty. He wrote to his father, the General, a long rambling, highly emotional letter, in which he made a very poor job of explaining his feelings, but in which he expressed his desire to resign his commission and leave Germany. If the Bendlerstrasse refused (for he had signed on for life as a regular officer, as had always been the case with the von Dietz's), he would simply desert.

By return of post he received a long angry letter from the General, in which the old man pointed out that the family had served a variety of foolish, perverted and, probably in some cases, crazy masters ever since the von Dietz's had first entered the service of the Prussian princes; and that in spite of the failings of their political masters, the von Dietz's had soldiered on, remaining honourable, just men, true to their own consciences. He would have to do the same. Adolf Hitler would not rule Germany forever.

The typewritten letter stopped abruptly as if the old General, sitting on the saddle which he used as a chair in his study and dictating to the pretty young blonde who von Dietz suspected was his father's latest mistress, had suddenly pulled the unfinished letter from the machine and dismissed her before writing in his own hand at the bottom: 'Discount the above rot. You are right, my son. But do your aged father a great favour and remain in the Regiment. *Pray for an early war!*' He had underlined the last phrase with a vicious slash of the old-fashioned wooden pen he used so that the nib had actually ripped the thin paper.

On December 1, 1938, his request for a transfer back to the 69th finally came through. Mueller called him in to hand it over personally extending his hand as he did so. Von Dietz, cold, hard, and withdrawn now, as he would be for the rest of his short young life, refused, just as he refused to give one of the customary farewell parties for his fellow officers at the mess. He could not, it seemed, get out of W— quickly enough. In spite of the heavy snow that was beginning to fall, he left that very night, telling his soldier-servant to pack the best he could and forward his luggage to the regiment. At the gate, the duty sergeant, at Major Mueller's express order, turned out the full guard. Von Dietz passed the Eifel farmboys without even a glance as they stood rigidly to attention in the falling snow, heads turning woodenly as he went by, as was the drill.

'Aristocrat shit!' one of them said when they got back into the guardroom. 'Didn't even salute us.'

'Don't bother about him,' his mate replied contemptuously, slinging his helmet on his bunk. 'Everybody knows he's a warm brother like all those aristocrats. Kreisleiter Schmier says he likes young boys, and *he* should know.'

In Trier, after buying a first-class single to Berlin, von Dietz changed into civilian clothes at the Hauptbahnhof and took a room in one of the many shabby hotels around the station, where they did not ask for identity documents as long as one paid in advance. He spent a long night wide-awake, planning and listening to the hectic squeak of rusty bedsprings above him as some whore serviced half-a-dozen customers.

Next morning he went to a second-hand gunsmith off the Pferdemarkt and, showing him his civilian 'weapons' pass', bought a somewhat antiquated hunting rifle and ten rounds of ammunition. The gunsmith asked no questions and neither did he. Nor did he quibble about the price. He didn't want the man to remember him, just in case.

The rest of the day he spent in his bedroom, listening to the clatter of the whores' high heels as they brought their customers up and down the rickety stairs. He adjusted the sights and working parts of the gun and filed a cross into the nose of six of the bullets until he was satisfied that they would be as effective as any machine-made dum-dum bullet. Although the propellant was not very powerful, anybody hit by one of them would be splattered all over the furniture.

December 3, 1938, was a grey dull day, with the hint of further snow in the dry air. He paid his bill, telling the greasy, unwashed owner that he would be taking the morning train to Cologne. The man wasn't interested, but von Dietz felt it was important to plant that particular idea in his mind, just in case the police came investigating. The hotel owner would be only too happy to have something to tell the bulls and be rid of them before they started asking more awkward questions about the kind of establishment where guests registered without showing their *Ausweis*, as the law required.

He walked across the square to the station for the benefit of the greasy hotel owner, took a fourth-class ticket to Cologne, ducked across the lines and rode illegally as far as the suburb of Trier-Ehrang, where he managed to fool the ticket collector with a platform ticket he had bought the day before, then caught one of the antiquated yellow post-buses as far as Daun, to the north of W—.

Here he spent the night in an abandoned barn, freezing in the bitter night air yet warmed in a way by the burning thought of revenge, which had now become almost an obsession with him. At five, even before the first weak grey light of the winter dawn began to creep through the rotting planks of the barn, he was awake and busy, greasing the second-hand hunting rifle for the task ahead.

It was the day of the St Hubertus Hunt, the traditional hunt of the Ardennes-Eifel area, named after the saint who had once, according to the pious legend, been lured into the endless forest by the glowing, haunted stag. From far and wide, the Party officials had gathered outside Daun, at Kreisleiter Schmier's invitation, to enjoy the on-the-foot hunt. The clarions blared, the dogs howled and the would-be hunters complete with green hunting costume and slouched hat indulged in their last icy *Korn*. Now the hunt could commence. They went off in fine style, fat, clumsy, hopeless city-folk shooting and slaughtering everything that the contemptuous beaters could drive into their sights. An obliging Kreisleiter Schmier personally slit the throats of the various hares and rabbits they slaughtered with the ivory-handled hunting knife that the Führer himself had given him as a token of his esteem. He enjoyed the bloody work, executing it with a professional expertise gained over years of butchering.

By midday, with the carcasses of some two hundred animals marking their path through the forest and heath, they felt it was time for a traditional lunch of thick pea soup and sausage, washed down with ample beer and schnapps.

Kreisleiter Schmier, pleased with the success of his hunt, which would surely contribute to the realization of his secret ambition to become Gauleiter of the Moselle district once the present holder of that high office finally succumbed to his daily ration of two litres of schnapps, decided he would take a little walk. Pea soup always had that effect upon him. As he explained to his guests in his inimitable, charming manner, 'Christ, I could shit through the eye of the needle at this moment! Watch out for the green smoke, comrades!' And with that, he stalked away through the snow-heavy brush to find a suitably lonely spot, his departure marked by a series of juicy farts.

He came upon a small hill surrounded by pines and decided it would have to do, although it was open on one side to the main road from Daun to Bitburg. But, as he told himself, hurriedly undoing his breeches and squatting there, paper in one fat hand, if any peasant woman saw him now without his breeches and screamed, she'd have something worth screaming about. It wasn't every day that a common woman saw a Kreisleiter's ding-dong. He bent and took the strain, purple-faced, reciting as he did so the old, old chant: 'shit, said the King, and a thousand arseholes bent and took the strain, for in those days, the words of the King were law!'

It was thus in this somewhat undignified, though completely natural, position that it happened.

Dummmmmmmmmmmmmmmmm!

The first dum-dum bullet smashed into his guts. It exploded into a million pieces, ripping a great hole in his fat intestines, showering the snow-heavy bushes and firs all around with shit, undigested peas, shreds of sausage, and bits and pieces of Kreisleiter Schmier to a distance of at least twenty metres, as Police Sergeant Weissgarten later ascertained.

As he began to fall, the second dum dum bullet smacked into his fat pork butcher's face, destroying it as if a soft-boiled egg had been struck by a too heavy spoon, the scarlet pits of what had once been eyes filled with sudden springs of red.

The most incredible thing of all, as Sergeant Weissgarten was later to learn from the hunters who found the shattered body lying in its own shit, the monstrous white arse standing up like a tethered barrage balloon was that Kreisleiter Schmier was still able to make sounds for at least five minutes before he died, though admittedly no one could make any sense of what the tongueless horror was trying to say.

The killer was never found; and in the end Sergeant Weissgarten, who in the immediate post-war months made a great deal of his Jewish-sounding name and swarthy appearance to the American occupiers, filed the unsolved case with the note: 'Generally accepted locally to be the work of some crazy Jew — Weissgarten.'

BOOK THREE: *SEPTEMBER 1, 1939*

'He was one whose natural climate was war.'
John Hersey, The War Lover

CHAPTER 1

'Bad news, gentlemen,' Colonel von Ostermann said sourly, eyeing his assembled senior officers. 'Intelligence reports that the Poles have reinforced the Pass area with a regiment of Uhlans.'

'Good God,' Major Hardt exclaimed, 'don't tell me the Polacks still have Uhlans. I thought that sort of thing vanished twenty-odd years ago. Cavalry indeed!'

Von Ostermann smiled a little sadly. 'Antiquated, admittedly they may be, but it means two things. One, that they'll be using this new cavalry to patrol the woods on both sides of the approach road to the Pass so it will be damnably difficult to admit any kind of outflanking manoeuvre…'

'And the other, Colonel?' Major Hardt asked when von Ostermann didn't continue.

'The other?' The colonel frowned. 'Well, it looks as if the Poles know that we are here and *why* we are here.'

'A spy, sir?' Lieutenant von Sulzburger exclaimed eagerly. 'Do you think the Poles have spies up here?'

Von Ostermann looked at the eager young officer, who was currently acting as Hardt's battalion adjutant, and said a little wearily, 'Yes, I do, Lieutenant.'

'I have decided to move out of here immediately after dark,' he continued. 'As yet there are no movement orders from HQ, but I shall take the risk of independent action upon myself.' He forced a weary smile. 'They can only shoot me if they don't like it,' he quipped.

'When do we move?' Major von Dietz asked, 'and in what order?'

Von Ostermann frowned. If he had not known and grown to like three generations of von Dietz's he would have taken the young major for an impolite boor, who chose to ignore the generally accepted rules of military etiquette. 'I have worked out a plan to cover our departure. As from now, all regular duties will cease. The Regiment will celebrate its Foundation Day one day in advance. There will be extra beer for the men and champus — rather cheap champus, I'm afraid — for the officers. To the outside world at least, the 69th will be relaxed, indulging itself in good living and cheap champus. Curfew for the civilians will be at six, a little earlier than normal, but the three battalion adjutants will explain to the civilians here and down in the village that the early curfew is to insure that they are indoors and out of harm's way, once the licentious and drunken soldiery are on the streets. We want no incidents with the Czechs. We will give them two hours. The First Battalion will move off at twenty hundred hours exactly. The Second and Third will follow at sixty-minute intervals. Any questions?'

There were none.

'Good, gentlemen. Then let us enjoy Foundation Day, for God knows if we will see another.'

The house exploded with noise. The bad champus was having its effect and now the young officers, respectful and tame until their seniors left, were indulging themselves in one last drunken fling. Magazines were ripped to shreds and set alight in wastepaper bins, extinguished by swaying young lieutenants urinating upon them. They smashed empty bottles — or 'dead soldiers', as they called them — and flung glasses at the walls. They played football with a helmet, booting it back and forth across the long hall, recklessly smashing windows and glass doors as they did so. Everywhere there was the sound of splitting wood and breaking glass, the slurred cries of drunken men. Wisely the battalion commanders locked their doors and got on with their planning.

'Officers,' said Red Rudi morosely, 'I hate 'em!' Not even the two litres of special Carlsbad *pils* which had been issued to each soldier on this special day could seem to relieve his gloomy mood. 'Like stupid little kids as soon as they get a sniff of the barmaid's apron. Listen at 'em wrecking the shitting place over there!'

Maltitz and Sepp Deltgen sprawled next to him, drinking their beer in the burnt yellow grass. They followed the direction of his gaze as yet another empty bottle sailed through the shattered French window of the officers' mess and joined the rest of the 'dead soldiers' lying there in a jumbled heap.

'Oh, they're only high-spirited young fellers letting off a bit of steam,' said Maltitz.

'Besides, the place belongs to a Polack, don't it?' Sepp said. 'And who cares what happens to a Polack's property *now*? Sup up the sauce and smile. Give yer ears a treat.'

But Red Rudi was not to be appeased this hot August afternoon. His sour look did not change in spite of the hefty swig of good Czech beer he had just taken. 'That's just it,' he said. '*Now*, you said. You don't need a shitting crystal ball to know what's gonna happen *now* and why they've brought Foundation Day a couple of days forward and why we're getting this best-quality beer. Ner,' he sneered, his red face flushed with sudden anger, 'yer shitting well don't! They're fattening us up for the kill.'

His outburst was greeted by silence, and the three comrades drank their beer deep in thought, as if they had suddenly become aware for the very first time of what lay before them.

'What do you think it'll be like, Red?' It was Maltitz who broke the silence in the end.

'What?'

'Action.'

Red Rudi pulled his bottle from his lips and snapped the catch down. 'Who do you think I am — Jesus? How the hell should I know? We shoot at them. They shoot at us. We all get killed.'

'*All?*' Maltitz, his dark eyes suddenly liquid, as if he were on the verge of tears.

'That might be, Red,' Sepp Deltgen said grimly. 'I know as little about it as you do, but I do know one thing.'

Red Rudi looked at him without any particularly great interest, preoccupied with his own gloomy thoughts. 'What's that?'

'Before I go hop, I'm going to take that bastard Bull with me, even if I have to shoot the sod in the back.' He glared at his comrade. 'The Bull won't live to survive the war that's coming and draw his shitty pension, believe you me, Red!'

And Red believed him.

Major von Dietz was glad to be able to get away from the noise in the big house. His battalion was in order. The men had their gear packed and their weapons ready. The long march to the frontier would soon sober them up, though he doubted strongly whether his younger officers would be in much of a fighting shape when the time came. He shrugged. What did it matter? Although Colonel von Ostermann had not said as much, the colonel knew that they were designed simply to be cannon fodder, while the real attack took place elsewhere. He dismissed the thought and concentrated on enjoying the green calm of the firs as he walked slowly along the forest trail, inhaling the fragrance of the trees, strong, heavy and resinous in the late August heat.

Thus engrossed, Major von Dietz almost bumped into the horse that blocked the trail around the bend. It was the Countess's little cry of warning in Polish that alerted him at the very last minute. He stared up at her and instinctively blurted out 'Thank you', though after the discovery of the previous night he had sworn he would have nothing more to do with the Polish woman.

She was in the same black riding habit as the previous night. But this afternoon her face was no longer contorted with fear and rage. She stared back at him, a look almost of sadness on her beautiful oval face, as if she were registering his appearance at this moment forever.

'You knew where I had been and what I had done, but you did not report me to your superiors?' she said simply.

He nodded, looking up at her, watching the midges swarm around the black horse's sweating flanks.

'Why?'

He shrugged. 'Why should I, Countess?'

'But we are enemies now. You have your duty as ... a German.'

'*German*,' he began, his face suddenly twisted into a sneer of contempt. The look vanished as quickly as it had come, and he said baldly, 'The only duty I have is to my men, and I think it is already too late to stop what is going to happen, don't you?'

She nodded.

For a long moment they were both silent, the only noise the humming of the insects and from a long way off the muted shouts of the drunken young officers.

'Must it happen?' she asked suddenly.

He knew what she meant. 'Yes, it must,' he answered without hesitation. 'The die has been cast. It is inevitable. There is nothing you or I can do about it, Countess.'

There was sudden animation in her face. 'But I want to live! Why must you men make war? Why do you think you can abandon your families — everything — and go and fight, as if war is everything, that there's nothing else. *There is*! There is a life to be led. Why can't...' The energy drained from her abruptly, as if someone had opened a tap and let it run out, and she faltered to a stop with a last whispered, hopeless question, 'Is there no way out?'

He shook his head slowly. 'No way out, Countess.' And with that he touched his right hand to his cap in salute, turned and started to walk back the way he had come.

She watched him go, the tears streaming sadly down her face, knowing instinctively that the tall, skinny young German was fated to die, like they all were.

CHAPTER 2

The first bullet cracked out of the dark firs one hour after the First Battalion commenced its march. A newly joined officer-cadet, who thirty minutes before had been boasting he'd get the Iron Cross, second-class out of this campaign 'or be damned', clutched his throat, spat out a thick gob of blood and pitched to the ground without another word, dead.

'Shit, there's somebody in the trees, shooting at us!' the Bull yelled superfluously, as another ragged volley swept the ranks of the leading company and men began going down everywhere.

'Partisans!' von Dietz bellowed, dropping from his horse and pulling out his pistol in one and the same movement. 'Take cover everybody! Return fire! *At the double now!*'

Standing there, ignoring the white tracer-bullets which were whipping the air all around him, he watched as his men dropped into the ditches on both sides of the forest road, here and there dragging their moaning, groaning wounded comrades with them, and began to return the enemy fire.

His mind raced as he dropped on one knee next to the Bull, who cowered behind a dead man, sweating so much with absolute, overwhelming, chicken-hearted fear that he could smell it. Instinctively he loosed off a full magazine into the trees from where the fire was coming, telling himself that his bullets were doing absolutely no good, While he tried to come to some sort of quick decision.

The other three companies of the First Battalion were strung out along the forest road at half-kilometre intervals.

The Second Company would be now about seven to ten minutes' marching time behind them, and he knew exactly what the company commander would do. As soon as he heard the firing, he'd head for the sound, confusing matters even more so. No, the only chance he had of keeping the Battalion moving was to pin the partisans down with the First Company, while the Second went into the woods and winkled them out or sent them flying for their lives.

'Sergeant-Major Bulle!' he commanded, while he searched the late-evening purple gloom, stabbed here and there by scarlet flashes. 'Get a patrol together. Three or four men. I want them to —'

He spun round angrily when there was no reply, only to find the big NCO grovelling in the dust of the road, hands clasped over his helmet, as if he were trying to block out the noise of the small arms battle, like a frightened child. '*Bulle*,' he bellowed, 'are you listening to me?' He jabbed his pistol muzzle into the NCO's ribs. 'Look up at me — and listen!'

Miserably the Bull looked up and listened as von Dietz rapped out his orders, jamming in a new magazine as he did so and trying to ignore the moaning of a soldier, shot in the stomach, just to his right. 'All right, Bulle, move that yellow arse of yours and get that patrol on the way.'

A small round grenade wobbled through the air, and the Bull watched it in fascinated horror as it exploded with a thick ugly crump. Red-hot splinters of steel hissed through the gloom. A soldier screamed shrilly and then the Bull was up on his feet, running for his life, as if the Devil himself were after him.

'Holy strawsack!' Maltitz whispered in a small tense voice, as they crawled down the ditch ever further from their comrades trapped on the road behind them. 'I never thought it would be like this, Red.'

'Knock it off,' said Red Rudi. 'What did you expect the Polacks to do — welcome you with beer and hot sausages? Silly bastard.'

'Shut up, both of you,' Sepp Deltgen hissed as he cocked his head to one side, trying to hear the slightest sound to their front. 'I can't hear myself think.'

They crawled on in silence, the only sound that of their own heavy breathing and the snap-and-crack of the small arms battle behind gradually dying away. Sepp Deltgen, in the lead, forced himself to count yet another thousand, his eyes trying to pierce the gloom for the slightest sign of the enemy. He completed the count and decided that it was safe for the little patrol which was trying to warn the Second Company to start walking. 'All right! On the road, five metres' distance between each of us. You behind me, Titty. You bring up the rear, Red. Keep yer glassy orbits skinned.'

'*Jawohl, Herr Feldmarschall,*' Red Rudi said ironically, but there wasn't much conviction in his voice.

Weapons held in hands that were damp with sweat, heads swinging to and fro from one side of the road to the other like spectators at a tennis match, the three comrades moved as stealthily as possible down the forest road, their bodies tense and expectant at the thought that at any moment an enemy slug could smack into them.

It was just as they had caught the first sound of the approaching Second Company — the steady tread of marching feet — that they bumped into trouble. A dark shadow detached itself from the deeper shadows cast by the trees and hissed something in Polish.

'*Was —*'

Sepp Deltgen's startled exclamation was drowned by the crack of the Pole's pistol. He pumped five shots at the Germans at five metres' range — and missed! They didn't give him another chance. Terrified though they were, they flung themselves on the lone civilian and hurtled him to the ground, their nostrils suddenly assailed by the stench of garlic, unwashed male body and fear. They smashed the brass butts of their rifles into his ribs, slamming their boots into him and cursing in terrified obscene fury as they did so until finally a gasping Red Rudi choked, 'For shit's sake, hold up!... Don't kill the Polack shite-hawk... We need him as a prisoner!... *HOLD UP!*' Grabbing an enraged Sepp, he pulled him off the crumpled Pole and flung him to one side. 'You!' he cried, swinging round on a gasping Maltitz. 'Pull him to his feet. Let's get the hell out of here before his pals come up.'

Fingers curled around their triggers, ready to pump a burst into anything that moved among the trees, the three comrades retreated towards the sound of marching feet, with Maltitz pushing the half-conscious prisoner in front of them.

Captain Grossmann, commander of the Second Company, wasted no further time as soon as he had heard Red Rudi's excited report. He flashed a hard look at the unshaven Polish partisan. His nose was broken, one eye turning black rapidly and a thin curl of blood trickled from his badly split and swollen lips. A look of intense fear was on his face, outlined by that cold circle of light from the NCO's torch.

'Speak German, Polack?' he rasped.

'Yes,' the Pole said thickly.

The NCO gave him a vicious dig in his broken ribs. 'Hang a "sir" on that when you speak to a German officer, you Polish pig.'

'Yessir,' the Pole quavered.

'Good,' Grossmann said. 'Where are the rest of your terrorist pals?'

The Pole clamped his lips together, as if attempting to ensure physically that he would not betray his comrades in the forest.

'Did you not hear what I said?'

Still the wounded Pole did not speak. Grossmann nodded to the NCO standing next to him. The man whipped out his knife and, grabbing the Pole's long, greasy hair, pulled him forward so that the point of the knife was directly under the Pole's unshaven chin. 'Answer the officer, Polack, or I'm going to do a fandango on your ugly kisser with this.'

The Pole hawked and spat directly into the NCO's face. Next to him, Maltitz gasped and held his breath. The NCO didn't hesitate. He slashed his knife down the side of the Pole's right ear. The Pole screamed shrilly, as the scarlet blood jetted out in a solid stream and his ear flopped down on his shoulder.

The NCO gasped. 'I'll carve the nuts off'n you next if you don't answer the officer's question. *Well?*'

The words poured from the terrified Pole's mouth in the thick, heavily accented German of the border area. The partisans, who in reality were reservists of the Regular Polish Army, had come across the border the previous night. It was their job to disrupt the German concentrations the best they could. When the pressure got too great, they would slip back through the thickly wooded, hilly countryside back into Poland. Now they were in position on both sides of the forest road to a depth of half a kilometre.

'Strength?' Grossmann rapped.

The Pole hesitated, the blood streaming from his ear wound.

'Come on, Polack slimeballs, *speak*!' The NCO raised his red-stained knife.

'Two hundred … two hundred,' the Pole gasped. 'Please, please don't cut!'

Grossman forgot the Pole. Swiftly he started rapping out his orders for the Second Company's attack through the woods. Finally, while his men clicked off their safety catches and hurriedly primed their grenades for the battle to come, he swung round on the three men from the First.

'Congratulations, you've done a good job. I shall ensure that Major von Dietz hears of it.'

He looked at the bowed prisoner, who was sobbing softly to himself, and then made a gesture with his forefinger as if he were pulling the trigger of a rifle.

An instant later the Second Company was streaming into the woods on both sides of the road, leaving the three men and their prisoner standing there alone.

For what seemed a long time none of them moved. It was only when the first burst of firing startled them that they seemed to realize that they had a highly unpleasant task to execute before they could return to their company. Sepp Deltgen looked at a suddenly very pale Red Rudi and then at Maltitz. Next to him the Pole continued to sob, unaware that his fate was being decided there at this very moment.

'Who's gonna do it?' Deltgen asked in a strained, unnatural voice.

'Not me,' Maltitz gasped. 'I couldn't kill… No, not in cold blood like this.'

'Well, somebody's shitting well gonna have to do it, Titty. We can't stand around here all night like a wet fart waiting to hit the shithouse wall!'

'What about you then? You're risking a very big lip,' Red Rudi snarled.

Sepp Deltgen doubled his right fist. 'And you're risking losing a set of teeth, brother, in a minute, if you don't shut that big commie mouth of yourn!' His chest heaving with rage, he glared up at the red-haired Berliner.

'Comrades ... *comrades*!' Maltitz cried, pushing them apart, their eyes blazing with anger. 'We can't go on like this!'

The Pole stopped sobbing and, with tears still running down his unshaven skinny face, looked in bewilderment at these Germans who seemingly were ready to fight amongst themselves in the middle of the forest, while their comrades were engaged in a life-and-death struggle half a kilometre away.

'All right,' said Sepp through gritted teeth, 'I've calmed down. What we gonna do, comrades?'

Somehow the Pole realized what they were going to do to him. Abruptly he went down on his knees, wringing his raised clasped hands in the classic gesture of supplication, the tears streaming down his ruined bloody face. 'Please, don't kill... Please... Got children, two, wife ... she's got bad back... Not earn money... *Please*!'

'Hold yer water,' Sepp said gruffly, obviously affected by the sight of the kneeling Pole, 'or I'll put you out of your misery so yer missus'll get a pension.' But his heart wasn't in it. He, for one, couldn't go through with it.

Maltitz lowered his rifle and affectionately patted the shoulder of the man who only minutes before had attempted to kill them. 'Now, now,' he soothed him. 'It ain't that bad. Come on now.' He looked at Red Rudi inquiringly.

Rudi nodded and slung his rifle over his shoulder. 'Let the Polack arse-fucker go,' he said.

Maltitz raised the sobbing Pole to his feet. 'You can go,' he said. 'Go … you understand?'

'Go?' The Pole echoed the word as if it were very important. Then suddenly, as if he had just realized what its meaning was, he grabbed hold of Maltitz's hand and pressed a fervent kiss on it. He did the same with the other two, though Red Rudi pulled his away hastily, saying, 'What's with you Polack? You some kind of warm-brother or something?'

A minute later he had disappeared into the growing gloom, not before he had turned, however, and waved at them, as if he were departing from good friends.

Red Rudi shook his head. 'Shit on the shingle,' he cursed, 'this is gonna be a fucking funny war, mates.'

In silence the three comrades began to trudge back to their company.

CHAPTER 3

'*Shit, shit, shit*!' Captain Grossman groaned, his voice a strangled mixture of agony and rage as the battalion MO went to work with his scalpel, the young soldiers crowding into the barn and watching in awe. 'They've shot the bastard off'n me before the shitting war even starts! Now I'll be running around with a peg-leg for —' His outburst ended in a groan, as the white-faced doctor started to cut through the ragged tenacious length of red flesh and white muscle that held the foot to the rest of the shattered thigh.

Major von Dietz stared without pity at Grossmann, a blowhard *par excellence*, whose dreams of glory and promotion in the coming war had been rudely shattered by the burst of Polish machine gunfire which had virtually nipped off his right leg. Indeed he felt nothing, save a sense of satisfaction that he had driven off the Polish attack successfully. He had come through his first taste of military action well and he knew, without any sense of pride, that he would be a good soldier and commander. He had not lost his head when the Polish fire had hit them in the forest, as most of them around him had, as the wounded Grossmann had, when he went charging into action without taking the most elementary of tactical precautions.

Standing next to von Dietz in the Czech barn, viewing the operation carried out by the hissing, flaring, brilliant white light of the storm lanterns, Colonel von Ostermann watched how carefully the MO carried out his task, depositing what was left of Grossmann's foot and leg on the floor, and indicating with a nod of his head that the orderly should cover it up with a cloth in case the wounded Captain saw it. He applied the loop of the tourniquet to Grossmann's bloody stump, all the time making little soothing solicitous noises. Somewhat cynically the colonel wondered how long the MO would be able to give that kind of treatment once the real war started. Would it be only a matter of days, perhaps hours, before the young doctor would be operating against the clock, his rubber boots and apron splashed with blood, up to his ankle in bloody gore, sawn-off arms and legs strewn every way at his feet, while the casualties came pouring in, just as the military medics had worked every day during an offensive on the Western Front in the Old War? With an effort, he dismissed the gloomy mental picture and turned to the young battalion commander. 'Not bad, von Dietz,' he said. 'Not bad at all.'

'The Poles only intended to harass us, sir. It was a skirmish, in reality. They weren't prepared to stand and fight, *yet*.'

Von Ostermann noted the reservation, but made no comment on it. Instead he said, 'Well, you did a good job in your first action. But that is history now. What about the future?'

'Sir?' von Dietz snapped, his skinny face revealing nothing.

Behind him, a green-faced medical orderly, who looked as if he might vomit at any moment, carried away Captain Grossmann's leg, which lolled back and forth obscenely from underneath the blood-stained cloth. At that moment, Grossman started to sob great glistening tears of self-pity. 'Why?' he moaned. 'Why me?'

Von Ostermann frowned and raised his voice to drown the noise. 'Sixty minutes more rest for your battalion. Hardt's Second can take over point now. Give them breakfast and have them on the road again at...' — he consulted his wristwatch — 'at three hundred hours precisely. I want you in position at the frontier and under cover before dawn. That understood?'

Behind them Captain Grossmann's sobs had given way to sharp shallow gasps as the morphine began to have its effect.

Soon, for fleeting seconds, his eyes would be full of love and gratitude to the MO as was always the case with the severely wounded before the pupils rolled upwards, leaving the man either unconscious or dead.

'Understood, sir,' von Dietz replied smartly. 'I have one question though, sir.'

'It is?'

'Have you heard from Division?'

'Yes,' von Ostermann snapped, buckling on his helmet and adjusting his leather map case as if he were in a hurry to be on his way now.

'And sir?'

'It's on. We attack Poland on the first of September at zero four hundred.' He raised his hand to his cap. '*Guten Morgen, von Dietz.*'

'*Guten Morgen, Herr Oberst!*' Von Dietz clicked to attention, telling himself that at this moment he felt nothing, absolutely nothing.

'Nice salami sandwich and a canteen of black coffee, Sarnt-Major — real bean coffee, none of that ersatz shit.' It was the NCO, one of the kitchen bulls and a crony of Sergeant-Major Bulle, who had sliced off the Pole's ear. He stood there smiling fawningly, tendering the canteen and the sandwich.

The Bull, clad in clean underpants and undershirt, his second change since they had received the movement order, spun round angrily. 'Are you crazy, Schmitz?' he demanded angrily.

'Do you have all yer shitting cups in yer shitting cupboard, man?'

'But what is it, Sergeant-Major?' the NCO stuttered, taken aback by the vehemence of the NCO's outburst 'What have I done wrong?'

'Nothing,' the Bull cried, placing a metal shaving mirror into the breast pocket of his tunic to cover his heart, and then as an afterthought slipped another one into his trouser pocket. He tugged on the field-grey trousers, adjusting the mirror until he felt sure it would cover his vital area. 'Do you know what happens to a soldier who gets a slug in the guts when he's wearing dirty underwear and has his belly full of food?'

'No, Sarnt-Major, I don't...'

'He gets gas-gangrene — that's what he gets. My old man told me that, and he went through four years of the last lot. Gas-gangrene.' Pulling on his tunic, the Bull warmed to the subject with morbid fascination. 'Yer guts swell up with gas, yer flesh turns piss-yeller and yer stink. Christ, how yer stink! They can smell yer pong five klicks away — and you want me to eat a shitting salami sandwich. What you trying to do, Schmitz? Croak me or something, you fink. *Great buckets of crap, dump that sandwich!*'

But if the knife-wielding Schmitz had no intention of killing a frightened Sergeant-Major Bulle, Sepp Deltgen had.

Sitting with his comrades sipping his burning hot, bitter tasting coffee, he watched Schmitz back off with his coffee and sandwich, telling himself that the Bull was so shit-scared already, even before they were engaged in real combat, that soon, very soon, he would do what all his kind did: get himself posted to some base-stallion echelon where the only danger he would incur might be piles from too much sitting on his fat keester. Then it would be too late.

Deltgen frowned thoughtfully. *Where and how was he going to get the pig?*

Sepp Deltgen had no illusions about the kind of war that was soon to come. It would be no different than the one his father, an old social-democrat, had often enough told him about. Corruption, glory-hunting, cruelty, with 'the little man allus down on the floor with his hooter right in the shit, while the gentlemen officers bought themselves chestfuls of tin.'

The incident with the Polack had already shown him how cheap human life was and how it was only by sheer chance that he was still alive at this moment instead of lying in some ditch with the rest of the First Battalion's dead with a Polack slug in his heart, covered by a stinking tarpaulin, waiting for the rear echelon swine to pick him up and honour his passing with a rough wooden cross, '*Died a Hero's Death for Folk, Fatherland and Führer.*'

'I shit on a hero's death,' he said, not realizing that he was expressing his thoughts aloud.

'What?... *What* do you shit on?' Red Rudi asked, a little startled, stuffing the rest of his salami sandwich down his throat, as if he were frightened that someone might take it away from him. 'What's this with a hero's death, Sepp?'

'I was talking out of school,' Sepp growled.

'Windy?' Maltitz asked and added hastily, 'I am too.'

Sepp Deltgen looked at his two comrades and knew that he could rely upon them. 'Lads,' he said, lowering his voice, 'you can see just how shit-scared old Bull is.'

'Yer,' Red agreed, 'he's wearing a hole in the floor, going back and forth to the crapper. He must have been on that throne a dozen times since we hit this place. Our beloved Sergeant-Major has really got the wind up.'

'Yes,' Maltitz said. 'He doesn't look so brave as he was a couple of days ago. He could hardly stop shaking when he gave the order to contact the Second back there.'

'He's full of wind and piss!' Sepp snarled and then controlled himself. 'Now look, this is the problem: How do you croak a bastard like that, when he's allus got people around him? Hell, if he goes on like this much longer, he'll be holding hands with that warm brother of a kitchen-bull Schmitz, just so as he's not alone.'

Red Rudi rubbed his unshaven chin thoughtfully, watched the one-armed senior doctor of the Regiment, 'the Pill', enter and confer with the Battalion MO in a low voice, and told himself that the First Company must have taken some bad casualties in its skirmish with the Polacks. 'You wait till we go into action and let him have one in the back. In the confusion who would know? They say it was done a lot in the Old War.'

Sepp Deltgen laughed scornfully. 'Can you see that shit-shoveller leading an attack with us behind him, Red! Come off it, man! Wherever else Sergeant-Major Bulle might be, it won't be at the front of any shitting infantry attack.'

'There's only one place where a soldier goes by himself,' Maltitz said hesitantly. He hated violence, always had. He would have never dreamed of joining the infantry, where violence was the stubble-hopper's trade in wartime, if it had not been for his special problem. Yet he knew he must help his comrade, even if it meant sanctioning 'violent action' — he dare not, even mentally, use the word 'murder'.

'And where's that, Titty?' Deltgen asked.

'The thunderbox — and the Sergeant-Major looks to me, as if he's going to be using it a lot in the next twenty-four hours, Sepp…'

The Pill offered von Dietz his one hand, saying with, perhaps, false heartiness, 'Take the flipper, young von Dietz. I hear you did very well back there.'

Von Dietz forced a smile. The Pill had served with his father on the Western Front in 1916. Indeed it was his father who had carried the young officer-cadet back to their own lines after he had had his hand blown off during the attack on Fort Vaux at Verdun and had won the Blue Max doing it.

'Well, we didn't panic altogether, Pill, I must admit that. Though I imagine you must be doing quite a thriving trade in anti-diarrhoea tablets at this particular moment.'

'Possibly,' the Pill answered, smiling though his wise old grey eyes remained somehow sad, as if he felt sorry for what he saw in von Dietz's face. 'Listen, von Dietz, I'm old enough to be your father so I can talk to you like this. I'm not here to be your mother or the mother of any of the others of the Regiment for that matter. I'm here to tend your wounds and to — if I can put it in the terms of the machine age in which we live — to *maintain* you as an efficient combat officer.'

'So?'

'So, young von Dietz, I've been watching you for a long time now and there's something troubling you, something very serious. What is it — girls, promotion, the age in which we live?' he ventured, looking at the tall young man from the corner of his eyes.

'Speak up, what is it?'

Major von Dietz laughed in the old doctor's face. 'Pill, you've been reading too many books by that Jew Freud — and you know they're on the list, you naughty fellow, you. Quite frankly, Pill, I've never been happier than at this moment for a damned long time. Believe me.'

And in a way it was true.

'But —'

The Pill's protests were drowned in the NCO's shrill whistles and the cries of the young lieutenants. The Regiment was moving on again and Europe had exactly twenty-four hours more of peace left.

CHAPTER 4

The tanks of von Thoma's Second Panzer waddled up the hill like metal ducks towards a pond, throwing up a cloud of dust on this burning hot last afternoon of August 1939. Behind them slogged the sweating, bare-headed panzer grenadiers, rifles over their shoulders, laden with belts of machine-gun ammunition, bundles of stick-grenades stuck in their belts and in the sides of their dice-beakers.

Von Ostermann watched them pass sourly. 'The heroes, gentlemen,' he announced to his waiting officers. 'Undoubtedly we will be seeing them smiling at us from the illustrated papers in due course — if we live. "The victors of the Jablunka Pass", or something of that sort.'

'Sour grapes, sir?' Major Hardt, the senior battalion commander, winking at the others, ventured.

Von Ostermann forced a smile. 'I suppose so, Paul. I attended the War Academy with von Thoma, you see, and it doesn't seem fair that that somewhat wooden-headed gentleman should win every damn flowerpot that's going. After all, he is already a general.' He paused a moment, then addressed von Dietz: 'Major, report please.'

Von Dietz took the centre of the group. '*Meine Herren,*' he commenced his briefing in the correct crisp, clear Prussian manner, 'my men are already in position up there on either side of the road leading to the Pass. At ten o'clock near that pine wood and on the other side at two o'clock in the large patch of ferns. As far as I know the enemy hasn't spotted us. Probably because the Poles have not dared to send reconnaissance planes across the frontier.'

'Too much like a deliberate provocation,' von Ostermann added hastily.

'At midnight precisely my battalion will commence moving up both sides of the road and engage the Polish positions covering the road.'

'Thank you, von Dietz. Hardt, your turn.' Colonel von Ostermann snapped, raising his voice above the rumble of von Thoma's horse-drawn artillery.

'Thank you, Colonel. Well, gentlemen, as instructed the Second Battalion will cover Major von Dietz's right flank, moving through the forest at a distance of some five hundred metres from the Pass road. If the Uhlans attack, we will see what they can do against the Second Battalion's machine-guns.'

'Exactly,' von Ostermann said.

'Your battalion, Kunz?'

Kunz, an eager, ambitious soldier and the only National Socialist amongst the three battalion commanders, pulled a face. 'We are to remain in reserve — at the Colonel's disposal.' And then, no longer able to restrain his anger that the Third Battalion was not playing a more active role in the attack on the Pass. 'Though, in my considered opinion, the Third should be used —'

'Please leave the planning to me, Major Kunz,' von Ostermann interrupted coldly. 'Never fear, Kunz, you'll have glory enough before this bloody business is finished with.' He forced a smile. 'You'll make general yet.'

The others grinned at Kunz's sudden embarrassment, and the Third Battalion commander looked at his feet.

'Now then,' von Ostermann said. 'I know you are all completely new to this sort of thing save for last night's skirmish, so let me tell you *this* right from the start. It will be an awful balls-up. Yes, you heard me correctly — an awful balls-up! It always is. Nothing will go right. Some of you will probably lose your heads. Undoubtedly some of the men will attempt to run away.'

Kunz opened his mouth to protest, but von Ostermann silenced him with a glance. 'Everything that can go wrong, will go wrong. But,' he paused and then raised his voice, 'the regiment will carry its objectives, because the 69th always has, for two hundred years.' He clicked to attention, hand touching his cap, his gaze swinging from face to face, as if he might well be seeing them for the very last time. 'Gentlemen, I salute you. *Hals und Beinbruch!* Report to your duty stations.'

Sepp Deltgen crouched in the hot ferns, which were alive with stinging flies, though he felt neither the sweat which was pouring off him nor the bites of the flies. His whole attention was concentrated exclusively on the little hessian-and-wooden structure which had been erected at the edge of the stretch of ferns and served as the NCO's latrine.

For nearly an hour now he had been crouching there, hardly daring to breathe in case anyone discovered him, stick-grenade clutched in a sweaty hand, ready to pull out the china pin as soon as the Bull sat himself down on the non-coms' thunderbox.

The afternoon dragged by on leaden feet. Earlier on when the Major had announced that the First Battalion would be moving across the Polack frontier, there had been a steady stream of non-coms to the thunderbox. Probably the news of imminent action had had a disastrous effect on their guts, but now the stream had dried away to an occasional NCO strolling down to the latrine, a bundle of newspaper in his hand, his braces dangling, as if he were prepared for a long luxurious sit.

Deltgen wiped away the sweat, and concentrated on poor Ross's dying face as they had dragged him out of the water, his chest ripped open by their own fire, trying to stoke up the blaze of his hate and forget the burning heat, which made him want to fall asleep. The Bull and his kind of sadistic bastard should not be allowed to get away with their kind of piggery.

There were plenty of his kind of root-swine around in the German Army; at least he should put paid to one of them as a warning to the rest of the striped animals.

Suddenly he caught his breath. A massive figure was hurriedly coming towards the latrine, already ripping open his flies, as if he couldn't get to the throne quickly enough. It was the Bull!

Sepp Deltgen took a deep breath, his red face taut, his heart suddenly beating furiously and so loud that he told himself the big NCO must surely hear it. He lifted his arm, stick grenade in hand, and prepared to throw. Nothing happened!

He tried again.

Nothing! It seemed that his arm was deliberately refusing to obey his brain. 'Shit,' he hissed to himself angrily. 'Move, will you!'

Still nothing. Next moment the Bull was inside the latrine and Sepp could hear his deep sigh of heartfelt relief as he slammed his fat arse down on the thunderbox.

'Why?' he asked himself, his arm still sticking up in the air absurdly. '*Why?*'

But his brain could give him no answer. Slowly he got to his feet, ignoring the noises coming from the latrine now, put the grenade into his dice-beaker and trailed sadly back to the camp.

Maltitz and Red Rudi were waiting for him, sprawled in the shade, trying to beat off the flies with newspaper fans. They sat up immediately when they saw him. Red Rudi saw immediately from the look on the little Rhinelander's face that something had gone wrong and said nothing. Maltitz was not so perceptive.

'Well, Sepp?' he hissed. 'Did you?'

Sepp Deltgen sat down carefully, saying nothing.

'Well?' Maltitz persisted.

'*I couldn't … I couldn't…*' Suddenly choked with emotion, he put his hands over his face and began to shake with dry sobs, while Maltitz looked at Red Rudi in open-mouthed amazement.

Now they waited.

In front of them, in the purple gloom of the August night, lay the Polish frontier. Only metres away was the red-and-white striped barrier of the border crossing, bearing the proud eagle of Poland, manned by a handful of frontier guards. But in the woods to left and right of the road they knew there would be Poles enough. Before the morrow was over there would be German dead littering that peaceful road leading up the Pass.

They all knew it as they lay in the grass, waiting. Some took the knowledge philosophically. Many were afraid, their pulses beating too rapidly, their breath coming in sharp hectic gasps, as if they were under great physical strain. Most of them concealed their fear with whispered obscenities and crude boasts. But a few couldn't. Their field-grey trousers were already black with urine and they moaned softly to themselves as they sought frantically for some way of getting out of what was to come. A bullet shot through a loaf of bread (to hide the powder burns) and a finger gone. *They couldn't expect a man to fight with a finger gone, could they?* When the rest advanced, remain here in the bushes until it was all over. *Who would notice in the confusion?* Throw away yer rifle in the first rush and surrender to the Polacks before the shit started flying. *But would the Polacks take prisoners?*

Thus, as the minutes ticked away, they waited and wondered, as young men always do the first time they go into battle: some brave, some fearful, some terrified, only a few saying their prayers...

Major von Dietz crouched in a ditch, fifty metres from the frontier post, and watched the minutes to midnight slip by. *Fifteen ... ten ... five ... three... He rose to his feet*, slipped the catch of his pistol holster off, his eyes fixed on the green-glowing dial of his wristwatch... *Two minutes.* He flung a glance to his left and right, noting the tense faces of the young soldiers crouching there. *One minute to go...*

Midnight!

As if some unseen hand had thrown an immense power switch, a tremendous flash of light split the sky to the west. For one fleeting second there was only that great burning white-red light, but no sound. Then the fury of that huge booming noise swamped them, tearing the words of command from von Dietz's mouth, buffeting his tense face with shock, as the whole of the Corps' artillery slammed into the Polish positions in the hills to their front.

In an instant, smaller weapons joined in. Mortars belched. Machine-guns chattered. Flak cannon screamed white death. To the east a fantastic pattern of stabs and forked jabs of scarlet flame erupted in the sky in a kind of terrible, awesome beauty, while from the Polish positions signal flares hushed into the sky, summoning help, advice, God knows what.

'*LOS!*' von Dietz screamed desperately above that tremendous din. '*LOS STURMANGRIFF...!*'

Crying hoarsely, the young men of the 69th streamed forward, bayonets at the ready, impelled by some wild atavistic fury. All fears forgotten now, they crashed down the flimsy frontier pole, stabbing and slashing the handful of Polish officials to death and pelted up the road and fields beyond, as the first slow chatter of the antiquated enemy machine-guns, like the hammering of some old, irate woodpecker, indicated that the Poles were beginning to fight back.

It was September 1, 1939. World War II had commenced.

CHAPTER 5

The skeleton of the First Company came down the hillside, led by a second-lieutenant with a blood-stained bandage around his head, leaning on a stick, his eyes wide and staring with shock. His soldiers followed in small, mincing steps, zig-zagging as if they were drunk. It was hard to tell their faces from their field-grey uniforms. Mud or sand or shock had turned them into one.

As they stumbled by the men of the Second and Third Companies, waiting in the ditches on both sides of the pass road, their grey mute faces were crying out the unbelievable horror of the martyrdom that they had just undergone.

Maltitz swallowed hard as they passed and gripped his rifle tighter in sweaty hands. Red, next to him, whispered, 'Oh, my holy arse!' Sepp Deltgen crossed himself, as they did in Rhineland when a funeral procession went by.

'My God, they're not soldiers,' someone cried, 'they're walking corpses!'

Von Dietz grabbed the white-faced second-lieutenant with the staring crazy eyes. 'What happened?' he demanded harshly.

The young officer mumbled something unintelligible, the saliva dribbling down from his slack lips.

Von Dietz shook him. 'What happened up there?' he demanded once again.

The officer gave no answer.

Von Dietz did not hesitate. Von Ostermann's words had been right. This was a complete balls-up! He knew nothing, except that his First Company was finished and that the First Battalion's drive towards the Pass had come to an abrupt halt.

He reached back his hand, grunted and slapped the officer hard across the face.

The man gasped. 'What…' Suddenly the blank look had gone from his eyes to be replaced by one of pain and shock 'Major, why did you do that, please?'

Von Dietz ignored the question. 'What happened up there, man? Come on, out with it!'

'Bunker, sir… They've got this bunker to the right of the road… We walked straight into it. My God, I didn't know.' Suddenly the young officer broke down completely, falling to his knees in the dust, sobbing as if his heart would break. 'My God! I didn't know…'

'Sergeant-Major Bulle!' von Dietz snapped.

'Sir!'

'Get Lieutenant von Hass to the rear and see that his wound is taken care off!'

The Bull's face lit up. This was the chance he had been looking for ever since dawn had broken and it was clear that the First Battalion was running into ever-increasing opposition, now they were no longer covered by the corps' artillery barrage. Casualties were mounting rapidly and Sergeant-Major Bulle had no intention of becoming one himself. Bending down hastily, as if he were scared that Major von Dietz might change his mind, he raised the sobbing young officer and began to lead him to the rear.

Von Dietz dismissed him and what was left of the First Company. He had set up a cordon of regimental policemen, armed with machine-guns, at the rear of the battalion; they would pick up the broken survivors. At the moment they were no good to him; their nerve was already gone. 'All right, on your feet, everybody!' he snapped cool and businesslike, knowing that the sight of the survivors had unsettled his men. 'Forward!'

Cautiously, bodies bent double as if they expected to be hit at any moment, the remaining three companies started to move forward over the steaming, broken ground, so heavily pitted with shell-holes that it was hard to imagine that anyone who had to defend it could have survived. But von Dietz, in the lead, knew the Poles were still up there, waiting for them.

Maltitz waded through a shell-hole that somehow or other had filled up with dirty water, tinged pink with the blood of a headless German corpse that floated in it. He gulped and looked away. He clambered up the other side, his uniform stained with thick grey mud that stank of cordite and death. The ground was littered with dead Poles and Germans. To his right a Polish truck was burning furiously while its driver, head trapped through the shattered windscreen, burned with it. To his left a German machine-gun crew, caught by a sudden burst as they attempted to set up their MG34 in a ditch, crouched there, feeding a belt of ammunition into the breech.

'God in heaven!' Sepp Deltgen cried just behind him. 'Is it never gonna end?'

'*Voda!*' a voice at his side croaked.

He spun round, ready to fire.

'Hold it!' Red Rudi yelled. 'It's a wounded Polack… He wants water.' He indicated the green-uniformed soldier lying in a pool of blood, his stomach sticky with gore.

Maltitz reacted first. He pulled out his canteen and bent down to offer the water to the dying man. In that very same instant the Pole pulled out his grenade with the last of his strength. Deltgen was quicker. His rifle cracked. The Pole reeled back, dead, an ever-widening circle spreading across what had once been his face. Maltitz stared down at him in horror, canteen still in his nerveless fingers, whispering, 'But I only wanted to give him a drink…'

Von Dietz worked his way across a slope, littered with abandoned German and Polish equipment, helmets, gas masks, cooking pots, canteens, overcoats, even rifles, pistol in his hand, heart beating hard, every nerve tingling, ready to throw himself down at the first sign of trouble.

Then it happened. There was the single crack of a high-velocity rifle. Behind him a man screamed and pitched to the shattered ground. '*Hit the dirt! Quick!*'

Just in time they fell to the ground in untidy awkward groups, as the Polish machine-gun swept the earth at metre height.

Von Dietz's mind raced. He was green, very green, he knew that. But he knew, too, that once his men went to ground, they would stay there or run to the rear. They were not to be given time to think.

Ignoring the tracer cutting the air just above his head, he wriggled frantically to the top of the slope and took cover behind the body of a dead German, listening to the unpleasant thwack of the Polish slugs hitting the corpse time and time again, making it stir and twitch. Taking off his helmet and hoping the old dodge he remembered seeing in the old Wild West films of his youth would work, he raised it on the muzzle of his pistol.

In the same instant that the first volley of slugs slammed into it and made it ring like a bell, he flashed a look over the top. It was only a fleeting glimpse, but it was enough.

There was the enemy bunker, a low squat structure, made of concrete and packed earth, grass-sods piled on its roof as camouflage against air attacks, with sandbags stacked around the entrance and a heavy machine-gun spitting fire from the nearest slit, covering the tangle of rusty barbed-wire which blocked the approach to the place.

Von Dietz crouched there for a moment and considered the situation. There was little possibility of outflanking the position. The bunker had a free field of fire on all three sides. There was no other alternative except a frontal assault.

His mind made up, he slithered down the slope and faced his men. He could see they were scared — most of them had eyes that were glazed as if with tears, as if they might cry at any moment, and their lips moved constantly, twitching, trembling — but he ignored their fear. The time of indulgence was over. Now they would have to prove they were men and not boys, even if it might cost them their lives to do so.

'Second Company,' he commanded harshly, 'fix bayonets!'

The young lieutenant who had taken over from Grossmann repeated the order and for a moment there was no sound save that awesome, sinister one of steel being slid out of metal scabbards and clamped home with a note of finality on the end of rifles.

'No bunching! Keep your distances! No falling back to help the wounded!' Von Dietz rapped out his orders in short, harsh sentences, each one like a blow from a hammer on the heads of the numbed waiting soldiers. He rose to his feet and drew his pistol. 'Second Company… *AFTER ME!*'

The NCOs blew their whistles and then they were running forward awkwardly, bursting over the top of the ridge right into the fire of the Polish machine-gun. They started taking casualties at once. Here, there, everywhere, men were suddenly galvanized into action, arms and legs flailing like puppets in the hands of a puppet-master suddenly gone mad, before finally falling to the ground — some stilled forever, some still writhing in mortal agony.

The survivors ran on, men dropping all the time, their ranks growing thinner and thinner by the second, the cries of 'stretcher-bearer' and 'mother' drowned by the cruel chatter of the guns.

The wire stopped them. Abruptly they were fighting off its treacherous barbs, as it ripped and tore at their uniforms, holding them trapped there to be sacrificed like dumb animals to the merciless machine-guns.

'Come on, men,' von Dietz called, his voice utterly calm, raising it only when the chatter of the guns threatened to drown it. 'We've only fifty metres to go.' He gasped and freed himself from the last barb of the wire and stared at the squat grey outline of the bunker, calculating swiftly where he should attempt to break in. 'Come on, for the honour of the old 69th! *Mir nach, Jungs!*'

Firing his pistol quite purposelessly and watching the slugs whine off the concrete, he doubled towards the bunker. The survivors followed. There were very few of them now.

A soldier reached the concrete. For a moment he crouched there, out of sight of the machine-gun, wondering what to do next. He decided to climb on to the roof. He reached up, just as the Pole appeared from the trap and emptied his magazine into him. He slithered backwards, fingers clawing the concrete, face turned upwards as if pleading for mercy. But there was no mercy to be granted this day.

A corporal ran straight towards the spitting machine-gun. His body was riddled with bullets, blood spurted from holes everywhere. Somehow he managed to stagger forward the last few metres, carried on by the crazed energy of men in combat. He thrust his shattered chest against the gun's muzzle, effectively blocking it for a few seconds, crying as he died, 'Now get the fuckers!'

But his sacrifice was in vain. The Second Company had vanished. There was not enough men to carry the bunker. Von Dietz gave up. 'Get back,' he cried. 'Everybody back…! *Back*!'

Five minutes later the handful of bloody survivors were hobbling past the horrified men of the other companies, painfully and silently, like sleep-walkers haunted by some terrible nightmare.

Von Dietz gave himself ten minutes to recover. Someone gave him a flask of cognac. He emptied it and didn't feel a thing. His body was tired, admittedly, but his mind seemed perfectly calm and at ease. Was it because he was a born soldier? Or was he afflicted by some strange combat neurosis that left him devoid of emotion, prepared to take up the challenge of the bunker once again without the slightest fear that he might suffer the same fate as the men of the Second Company? Or was it simply that he *wanted* to die?

At that moment he neither knew nor cared. All that concerned him was the capture of the Polish bunker; it seemed the most important thing in the whole world.

He rose to his feet and put on his battered helmet. 'Third and Fourth Companies, *fix bayonets*!' he ordered.

Nothing happened.

He looked round the faces of the men crouched in the dirt. They avoided his eyes, or bent their heads to look at their boots, while their NCOs and officers looked aghast, here and there whispering urgently to the soldiers closest to them.

Von Dietz took his time. When he spoke again, his voice was dangerously soft: 'Third and Fourth Companies, *fix bayonets*!'

Again nothing happened.

To his right a red-faced older NCO swung back his foot as if he were about to kick the pale-faced trembling youth next to him. Von Dietz shook his head. The NCO poised there stupidly with one foot still in the air.

'I gave you an order and you refuse to obey?'

'It's sheer suicide up there,' someone to the rear ventured. 'We've all seen what's happened to the First and Second.'

'Ay … ay,' voices agreed with the unknown speaker everywhere.

'*The best soldiers in the world… German infantry,*' a little voice in the back of von Dietz's head sneered scornfully. '*Big mouths, but nothing behind them*!' But he did not say that to his men. Instead he said, almost conversationally. 'You realize that by disobeying an order in combat, you run the risk of being shot for cowardice in the face of the enemy?'

'We'll be plugged up there anyhow,' an anonymous voice called.

'I see.' Von Dietz pulled out his pistol. 'I shall give you one last chance. If you are not on your feet by the time I count three, I shall shoot one of you!' He clicked off the safety catch. '*One … two…*'

He picked out his victim, a pasty-faced fat youth, who wore steel-rimmed spectacles and who had been charged more than once for wetting his bed back in the barracks. It would be Piss-bed, as his comrades called him contemptuously. '*Three!…*'

Nobody moved.

Von Dietz raised his pistol and fired. Piss-bed reeled backwards, glasses tumbling absurdly over his suddenly shocked face, and collapsed in the dirt, hands clasped to his heart — dead.

The men stared in shocked silence.

'But you *killed* him!' someone said, voice full of frightened resentment 'In cold blood!'

Von Dietz slapped his pistol butt as if to reassure himself that the magazine was correctly in place, watched by his awed men. He felt absolute master of the situation. If necessary, he would shoot each and every one of them. 'Well,' he demanded, apparently satisfied with his pistol, 'will you fix bayonets now?'

Maltitz looked at von Dietz standing there, legs astride, pistol balanced easily in his hand, eyes cold, emotionless, even indifferent, and then at his two comrades. He knew he wasn't a brave man, but he did think of himself as a man with a heart, who felt for his fellow-men. He could see Rudi and Sepp being shot in cold-blood. Deliberately he rose to his feet and fumbled for his bayonet, his fingers trembling like leaves in a wind. Somehow or other he managed to get it out and trapping his rifle between his knees, fixed it to the muzzle. Then he stood there, feeling very much alone and absurd somehow.

'Aw shit!' Red Rudi cursed in disgust. 'What a shitting life!' Face flushed with anger and self-disgust, he rose to his feet and did the same.

One by one, the others followed the two comrades' example, while von Dietz watched them with a mocking smile on his skinny face, knowing he had won but feeling no sense of triumph at that knowledge — just contempt.

CHAPTER 6

Fortunately for Sergeant-Major Bulle he had experienced the well-known pains and heard the familiar rumblings five minutes before it happened and had gone to find a latrine in a hurry. It was additionally fortunate for him that the field dressing station's latrine, to which he had escorted the wounded lieutenant, was running over with the yellow-green, bloody waste of dysentery cases forcing him to flee backwards, holding his nose, to find a better place in the middle of a grove of firs, some fifty to sixty metres away from the tented encampment. Thus it was that Sergeant-Major Bulle survived the Polish Campaign and indirectly won his Iron Cross, First Class.

The Polish insurgents, a rough bunch of local farmers hastily armed with World War I vintage weapons, burst into the first tent and found it full of unconscious men lying on the floor. They all snored heavily with the heavy grating rasp of men under sedation and on each one's forehead there was his dosage pencilled in with yellow crayon. Here and there blood leaked from wounds on to the dirt floor. But the Poles saw neither marks nor blood. They saw simply hated German soldiers. One of them pulled out the pin of an incendiary grenade with his teeth and flung it into the tent. They backed out hastily as it exploded in a searing flash of brilliant white light. In an instant the tent was aflame, the wounded still within, unaware that they were being incinerated.

The Poles rushed into the next tent. It was crowded with more lightly wounded men, arms and legs attached to complicated pulleys and counterweights so that most of them couldn't move. The Poles bayoneted them to death easily, going from man to man and stabbing him with systematic cruelty. One big man tried to rip off his pulleys and escape, but a massive Pole in a ragged overall thrust his bayonet so deep into the man's stomach that his spine arched taut and high with absolute agony. 'Just like sticking a swine in winter, eh, Piotr?' another farmer called over to him as he finished off his own German.

'*Ja*,' Piotr called back, wiping his bayonet clean on a straw mattress. 'Only these Fritz swine are easier to catch than our Polish pigs.'

They all laughed at that and their amusement continued as they ran to the next tent and slaughtered the terrified wounded, who were trying to slash their way out of the canvas with their knives. A concentrated burst from an old French machine pistol soon put an end to that.

Now the Polish insurgents were seized by an all-consuming blood lust that could only be satiated by slaughter and more slaughter as they raced from tent to tent, bayoneting, slashing, pulling the drainage tubes out of the shattered lungs of those with chest wounds, forcing water by the litre into the stomachs of those shot in the guts, flinging bottles of ether into the orderlies' quarters and throwing in lighted matches after them, setting the tents alight in an instant and watching the screaming orderlies burned alive.

It seemed to take the Pill a long time to become aware of what was happening all around him; perhaps it was because he was quite deaf or perhaps it was because he was engaged in a complicated leg amputation. No one ever knew, for the Pill did not live to tell anyone what really happened. But he was to play an important role in the Goebbels' account of the 'Blood-Bath of the Border'.

The Poles apparently watched for some time as he unwittingly carried on with his operation, making menacing gestures with their weapons whenever the scared orderlies, who had seen them immediately, threatened to drop their instruments. But one of them had started to retch thickly, as the one-armed surgeon began to saw through the thigh bone and that was the end of the performance. A machine pistol opened fire, and suddenly the hissing white lantern shattered in a thousand pieces, splattering the wounded man's naked chest with burning oil.

The Pill spun round, blood-stained saw still held in his gloved hand, eyes blazing with anger above his mask, 'What in three devils' name…?'

The cry of rage died on his lips as he saw the bearded civilians crowded there, blood-stained bayonets clutched in their raw-boned peasant hands. But there was no fear in his eyes as he snapped, 'You speak German?' And then, 'What are you doing in my hospital? Don't you know I — we — are protected by the Red Cross, eh?'

The one called Piotr threw back his head and guffawed loudly. 'Fritz — he protected by Red Cross!' he stuttered as if very amused. 'Poland — he protected Red Cross as well?'

The Pill was afraid, but he dare not show his fear. Without turning round, he snapped, 'Apply the clamps — quick! The poor shit'll bleed to death, otherwise.'

The orderlies, apparently more afraid of the Pill than the Poles, hurried to carry out the MO's orders.

The Polish machine pistol chattered, making a tremendous racket in that confined space, filling the tent with the acrid stench of cordite.

Two of the orderlies screamed and slammed against the wall of the tent. A third, with what appeared to be bloody buttonholes suddenly opening up across the front of his white overall, fell with his head into the bloody ragged stump of the unconscious man stretched out on the table.

'You murdering pigs!' the Pill shouted, ripping off his mask with his one hand.

'Look at that, Piotr, the Fritz sawbones has only got one paw!' someone cried in amazement.

'Now he's got none!' Piotr roared, picking up the gleaming steel hatchet that lay among the instruments at the foot of the table and bringing it down with one swift stroke. The Pill screamed as the tremendously sharp surgical instrument ripped right through his wrist, and he stood there swaying, staring stupidly at the dripping stump.

The Poles roared with laughter. 'Fritz sawbones, he got no hands!' they cried in delight. 'Hey, *Herr Doktor*, you operate now!' They pushed the instruments in front of the dying Pill and gestured, as if they wished him to pick them up. 'Come, come, your patient, he die. Hurry, *Herr Doktor* ... hurry!'

But the Pill's knees were beginning to sag beneath him and his eyes, clouding over rapidly, were rolling wildly like those of a very drunken man.

Their cries and taunts obviously were no longer registering, and the Poles grew tired of the little game. One of them stepped forward and pressed the trigger of his machine pistol, which burst into high-pitched life. The Pill's head shattered like that of a wax dummy, his features seeming to slide off the surface of the face like melting wax. Blood and cracked white fragments of brilliant white bone flew everywhere, dyeing the whole side of the tent a bright scarlet.

Then they were gone, running past the blazing tents, with the murdered, wounded, naked bodies swathed in bandages, scattered everywhere, and along the trees which covered a trembling Sergeant-Major Bulle's hiding place into the woods from which they had come.

Then, and only then, did the Bull pull up his trousers and venture forth to see what all the noise had been about. Five minutes later he was fleeing through the woods in the direction of the frontier, screaming incoherently, unbuckling and throwing away his pistol belt as he ran, and an instant later his helmet and equipment straps, for now there was only one thought uppermost in Sergeant-Major Bulle's mind: flight.

They took him to Major Kunz, the commander of the Third Battalion, two men supporting him as if he were a very old man, looking at each other aghast as the dishevelled NCO continued to blubber, the tears streaming unheeded down his big face.

Kunz gasped, his rage at his own inactivity abruptly forgotten. 'What the devil … what the devil happened to you, Bulle?' he managed to stutter.

Sergeant-Major Bulle gave a caricature of his once immaculate salutes, aware only of two things: he was safe with the Third Battalion; and he'd better produce a good story, quick. They shot deserters from the front. 'With permission, sir, may I sit? Up there it was — well — hell.'

'Of course, of course, my dear Bulle, I can see you must have been through something terrible.' Major Kunz thrust his own treasured collapsible chair under the Bull's big arse. Once during the winter manoeuvre of 1938, the Führer himself had rested for a few moments on it. He had not dared to down his own loyal buttocks on it for weeks afterwards. As an afterthought he pulled out his silver brandy flask and offered it to the NCO. 'Rest yourself for a moment, my dear chap, and take a drink. We've got all the time in the world.'

The Bull drained the flask in one go, his eyes flooding with tears as the fiery liquid burned down his throat and slammed into his stomach with a red-hot punch. Belching pleasurably and wiping the back of his pig paw across his red-gleaming lips, he handed the flask back to Kunz, who frowned at the fact that it was empty, but said nothing.

'No time for my problems, sir,' he said bravely. 'It was hell, but *I* survived, although, by God, there were moments when I thought I simply wouldn't make it — there were so many of the Polack swine.'

'What happened, Bulle?'

'Polacks, sir. They attacked the Second Clearing Station, bayoneted every one there, wounded and doctors alike. A few of us tried to fight back,' he shrugged modestly and hung his head, as if to say that his own desperate battle was not worthy of mention. 'I did for six or seven of them until my magazine was empty and one of the murderers knocked the pistol out of my hand. Then I'm afraid I took to my heels.'

'Don't reproach yourself, *mein Lieber*,' Kunz said hastily, and laid his hand on the Bull's shoulder. 'You did more than your duty. By God, you did!' Then Major Kunz's face darkened. He pulled out his map case and studied the map of the border area for a few minutes, before announcing, 'Sergeant-Major, just across the border there is a little hamlet — here.' He stabbed the map with his forefinger. 'Do you see it?'

The Bull nodded, wondering what was coming.

'The Polack Army fled the place this morning, according to Intelligence, but there are, perhaps, some one hundred civilians left there.'

'Yessir.'

'Now, Bulle, those damned Polacks who murdered our helpless comrades at the Clearing Station might well have come from that hamlet.'

'Could be sir,' the Bull said dutifully, not caring where they had come from, as long as he, personally, never met them again.

'Sergeant-Major Bulle, it is time that these infernal sub-humans realize with just whom they are dealing. I want you *personally* to lead a little expedition from the Third — a couple of platoons armed with flame-throwers will suffice.'

'To do what, sir?'

Major Kunz smiled darkly. 'To teach the Polacks a lesson that they will never forget. Now I want you...'

CHAPTER 7

Major von Dietz was seized suddenly by an all-consuming rage. His men were bogging down once again, just when the bunker was within grabbing distance. Instinctively, not thinking of the danger, remembering suddenly his father telling him — more than once — how he had dealt with his 'reluctant heroes' back at Verdun in '16, he pulled the china pin out of the stick-grenade. Hastily he counted, *one*, *two*, *three*, and flung it to the rear of the crouching panting infantrymen. 'Enemy attacking from the rear!' he cried, as the grenade exploded in a vicious flash of scarlet. '*Advance!*'

The trick worked. The infantry sprang up from their hiding places and hurtled forward. Men went down everywhere as the Polish machine-guns opened up on them once more. But this time a good score of the 69th made the outer wall of the bunker, gasping frantically as they slammed against the concrete and collapsed there in the safety of the dead ground where the deadly Polack machine-guns couldn't reach them, while to their rear their comrades who had survived that crazy rush went to ground once more. Von Dietz flung them a quick glance. There were enough of them for his purposes.

'You,' he commanded the Jewish-looking private who had been first to stand up after he had shot Piss-bed, 'get your grenade.' He turned to his companion, the one they called Red Rudi for some reason or other: 'You, too.' Not waiting to see if they followed his instructions, he snapped, 'follow me — at the double now!'

They doubled around the back of the bunker, ears deafened by the hammering Polish machine-guns close by, the air full of the stench of explosive, until they came to the rear entrance to the Polish fortifications. Von Dietz skidded to a halt. The two soldiers were still with him. 'You, over there!' he gasped. 'Be prepared to throw.'

Maltitz rushed to the other side of the entrance.

'You stay here.'

Red Rudi nodded his understanding.

Von Dietz replaced his magazine with a full one. 'All right, throw your grenades. *Now!*'

The two stick-grenades sailed into the dark shaft of the bunker. There was a thick throaty crump, followed by a scream. Dense smoke streamed out of the entrance in the same instance that von Dietz sprang forward, pumping a stream of slugs into the gloom. Almost without thinking, the two comrades followed, although the Major had not ordered them to do so.

Von Dietz sprang over the armless Pole still writhing on the floor. Further up the narrow passage, another Pole tried to flee. Von Dietz fired. The man jack-knifed. He went down, his hands frantically fanning the air as if he were climbing the rungs of an invisible ladder.

Red Rudi booted open a wooden door to his right. He caught a quick glimpse of three men crouched over a machine-gun and, tossing in a grenade, slammed the door shut again hastily. For a long moment nothing happened. Abruptly the door bulged outwards. In an instant the room was filled with the screams of fear and agony of the dying men within.

They ran on. A man swung round the corner in the green uniform of the Polish Army. Instinctively he screamed when he saw Maltitz's field-grey. Maltitz recognized the language; it wasn't Polish, but the tongue *his* parents had once spoken. But it was already too late. His forefinger pressed the trigger of his rifle. The man in the green uniform smashed against the wall and slowly began to slide down it, his dark eyes looking directly at a horrified Maltitz in silent dying accusation. Maltitz could not stand the look any longer. He turned and ran after the others.

They swung into a large room. Perhaps it was some kind of dormitory. Everywhere there were Poles, some of them lying on the rough bunks, wrapped in blood-stained bandages; most of them, however, armed. But the German attackers reacted first. Standing at the door, they fired as one. The Poles came tumbling from their bunks, slamming to the floor in a bloody welter of flailing shattered limbs, like beetles fleeing from a suddenly upturned stone. And then it was all over. As the rest of the battalion started to enter the bunker, what was left of the defenders began to raise their hands everywhere.

Suddenly von Dietz felt all the energy drain from him. He leaned against the wall and let his men get on with it, pistol hanging from his nerveless fingers, watching the Poles being herded outside with their hands on their strange three-pointed caps. Some of their eyes were fearful. Others flashed looks of pure hatred at the officer slumped against the wall, and as exhausted as he was von Dietz was forced to look away. He could not stand those looks.

Thus Major von Dietz was sole witness to a strange ritual carried out by one of his soldiers. Kneeling by the body of one of the dead Poles, the soldier was swaying back and forth almost ecstatically and muttering what might well have been prayers, though they were spoken in language that the major could not understand.

First Bible student and now this strange kneeling soldier, he said to himself. Turning wearily from the scene, von Dietz began to thrust his way through the Polish prisoners, down the corridor until he emerged into a strangely transformed evening. For a moment he stood there bewildered, watching the blood-red ball of the setting sun sinking rapidly below the peaks to the rear, and then he realized what was strange about the evening.

Silence reigned over the battlefield. It looked as if the Poles had given up everywhere; yet down below, in the direction from which they had come, there was the leaping flickering pink of what could only be a large fire.

What could it signify?

The villagers stared at the Germans, as the angry infantry drove them from their little tumbledown, straw-roofed cottages and forced them into the dusty square around the onion-towered church. Their faces were those of men who had always worked outdoors, gnarled and russet brown: the faces of men who were humble, honest, slow-thinking, harmless.

But the Bull and his men did not see that. Indeed they saw only the fear in the Poles' eyes and took a sadistic delight in it; the Polacks were shit-scared of them. Thus their chests swelled out with pride and they stood tall, as they herded the last of the white-shawled women and sobbing, barefoot children into the square to join their menfolk, telling themselves that old 'Poison-Dwarf' with his clubfoot had been right all the time: they *were* the superior race and these Polacks were nothing but animals. They could crush them under their boots like insects; they could play God!

But that was not to be just yet.

Standing, legs apart, hands set on his hips, his face set in a contemptuous sneer, telling himself that he must look every millimetre a select member of the new 'master race', the Bull was surprised to see a small black-robed figure emerging from the onion-towered church, bearing what appeared to be a banner or flag with him. Christ, he told himself, of course, those shits of cardboard soldiers from the Third had forgotten to search the church! The sneer fled from his suddenly anxious face and he shot a quick glance up at the tower. He breathed a sigh of relief. No sign of some Polack sniper busily engaged in drawing a bead on the very precious person of Sergeant-Major Bulle. He swallowed hard and watched in silence as the black-robed figure came closer, the crowd of peasants parting to let him through, crossing themselves reverently as they did so.

The block-robed figure stopped in front of the Bull, who saw now that the man was a priest and that he was scared, deadly scared. Coward that he was himself, he could recognize another immediately, and there was no mistaking the fear in the priest's dark-jowled, fat face and constantly flickering eyes.

'What do you want, Polack?' the Bull asked, running his gaze up and down the priest's plump little figure, as if he were something that had just come out of the woodwork.

'The Holy Black Madonna of Cracow,' the priest quavered in good German. 'She protects us.'

The Bull was momentarily puzzled. 'What the hell's that supposed to mean?'

'No harm can come to us while she protects us. We are honest, good people. We have done no wrong. For that reason she protects us.' The priest said the words as if reciting some sort of litany, as if he desperately wanted to believe in them, but knowing in his heart of hearts that the words had absolutely no power whatsoever. Swallowing hard, he looked up almost pleadingly at the stylized figure of the Madonna worked into the banner in cheap, bright colours.

'Honest, good people, who have done no wrong!' the Bull exploded, the complete master of the situation now. 'Why you crappy-arsed warm-brother of a roman candle, three hours ago your honest good people slaughtered my comrades in their beds while they were wounded and could not protect themselves!' His beefy face flushed beet-red. 'Treacherous, slimy murderers, that's what you Polacks are, I tell you!'

The priest cowered, the banner shaking in his trembling hands. 'We ... we had nothing to do with that!' he quavered. 'They ... were not from here. We are peaceful people —'

'*So you knew*, you Polack puker!' the Bull roared, splattering the other man's face with spittle. 'And now you come to me, waving that shitting old woman on a flag, crying stinking fish, and thinking you can get away with it. I know we Germans have got soft hearts, too soft, in my opinion, but this time you've gone too far.' Seized by a tremendous rage, he reached up and, grabbing the banner from the priest's unresisting grip, he bent his right knee and snapped the pole in two. Contemptuously he tossed the pieces into the dust of the square.

There was a shocked gasp from the assembled Poles. Here and there a man clenched his fists and took an angry step forward. Women crossed themselves hastily. Children sobbed.

The Bull flung an abruptly frightened look around the edges of the square and relaxed again. The stubble-hoppers had their rifles at the ready and the flame-thrower operators were holding their matches prepared to light their weapons at a second's notice. There would be no danger from the Poles; his men could slaughter them in minutes. He decided he would enjoy these moments of absolute power, with no officers to check him or rebellious cardboard soldiers to answer him back.

'Well, priest,' he announced slowly, 'your days of enjoying the old five-fingered widow are over,' he made an obscene gesture with his right hand, while the priest lowered his eyes like a shocked virgin. 'Just like the rest of those slime-shitting Polacks of yours!' He grabbed forward and pulled the priest to him, lifting his feet right off the ground, and pressing his own red face into the terrified priest's. 'Let me give you one last piece of advice. *Last*!' he repeated the word, savouring the horror in the priest's dark rolling eyes. 'I'm gonna do you and the rest of these Polacks a favour. You're gonna to take a little trip up there earlier than you thought. Why in a couple of hours you could be drinking china tea with the Big Guy himself! Now isn't that good of me? So I suggest you go through some of those roman-candle games of yours. Give the Polack currant-crappers a last whirl of the old prayer beads or something.' He dropped the priest suddenly so that the man sprawled on his back in the dust. '*You've got exactly five minutes, Polack*!'

Thus as the kneeling Poles chanted fervently, crossing themselves at regular intervals at the priest's command, ignoring the growing wet stain at his feet, the German soldiers watched and smoked in silence, letting the blue smoke of their cigarettes rise into the still purple gloom of the evening, relaxed and at ease like labourers who felt they well deserved a rest before the hard work of killing commenced.

BOOK FOUR: *THE PASS*

'Oh, what with the wounded and what with the dead
And what with the boys who are swinging the lead
If the war ain't over and that bloody soon,
There'll be nobody left in this bloody platoon.
Tra la la…'
Infantry marching song, World War I

CHAPTER 1

'*My God!*' Colonel von Ostermann breathed in awed shock and reined in his horse, holding the bridle tight as the animal kept shying at the flames of the burning village further up the dusty road.

An old woman lay dead in the road, abandoned there like a bundle of ancient rags, her toothless face withered like a mummy's shrunken skull by hard work and the cruel summer sun. Beside her were two half-naked children, both with gaping raw bayonet wounds in their skinny backs.

Behind von Ostermann one of the younger officers of his regimental staff gagged and vomited over the side of his horse. But there was worse to come as they cantered into the burning village, the straw roofs of the little cottages already gone, the flaming roof timbers crackling merrily and shooting up showers of fiery-red sparks as they came crashing down to the ground. The dead were everywhere — men, women and children sprawled out in the extravagant attitudes of those who have been violently put to death.

'The Poles?' an officer ventured.

Colonel von Ostermann shot him a withering look and he shut his mouth swiftly, his face colouring with embarrassment. He reined his horse, its ears pricked up with fear at the slaughter everywhere, shaking its head nervously as horses do when they encounter something they cannot understand.

Near the village pump someone had played a macabre joke. A Polish man, once a big husky fellow by the look of him, lay there, his flies ripped open and a bloody mess, on which great blue-bottles fed greedily now, where once his genitals had been. They were neatly stuffed into the mouth of the dead barefooted peasant woman next to him, her hands holding the organ as if she were sucking some monstrous lollipop.

'God in heaven, who could have done this!' Colonel von Ostermann moaned and tried not to see the little priest who had been nailed to the door of the burning church *upside down* with his crucifix propped up between his black worn boots.

'Who could have committed such piggery?'

'One-eye' Hartung, who had lost his right eye while serving with the Regiment on the Western Front in '17, swung himself off his white mare and looked around, while the rest of the staff officers sat immobile on their mounts.

In the fierce, ruddy light cast by the burning village, which stank of some oily substance that Hartung could not quite identify, it was easy to see and the middle-aged major soon found what he sought. Taking out his steel-rimmed glasses which made him look like a grammar-school teacher, he examined the casings. His face hardened. Slowly he trailed back to the others, as if he were reluctant to impart his discovery to them.

'Colonel,' he said softly.

Von Ostermann did not seem to hear.

'Colonel von Ostermann,' he raised his voice.

'What is it, Kurt?'

'Can I speak to you privately, sir.' Hartung moved off away from the others and after a moment the colonel directed his horse after him.

'Well, Kurt?'

By way of an answer, Major Hartung opened his hand. On his palm there lay two empty brass cartridge cases. 'Take a look at these, sir.'

'You know, Kurt, that I can't see without glasses,' von Ostermann said a little helplessly. 'What's written on them?' As an afterthought he added, 'please'.

'Berlin Arsenal. Issued March 1939,' the other officer answered, his voice controlled and without emotion.

Von Ostermann clasped his hand to his cheek in an oddly female gesture. 'No!' he gasped.

'Yes,' Hartung said quietly. 'They were our own people who did this?'

'But are you sure?' von Ostermann asked, his voice barely under control, his eyes filmed as if with tears. 'Quite sure, Hartung? Perhaps someone else could have used our ammunition? Perhaps —' the babble of words died on his suddenly white lips, as Hartung shook his head firmly.

'There can be no possible doubt, sir. The Poles can't use our nine-millimetre ammunition in their weapons. We had a very thorough briefing on the matter from the divisional ordnance officer last month. No, sir, they came from German rifles.' He hesitated for just a fraction of a second. 'To be more specific, from the rifles of the 69th Regiment!'

'Kunz's Third Battalion?'

'Exactly, sir. Von Dietz's is up front, Hardt's is in the woods, and there are no other German units down here at the frontier save Kunz's Third Battalion.'

For a long time the two men were silent, eyes following the progress of a lone skinny-ribbed dog, tail tucked between its legs, as it sniffed from corpse to corpse, obviously looking for its dead master.

'But why, Kurt?' von Ostermann burst out at last. 'Why?'

'A reprisal for that business of the dressing station possibly,' Hartung said and shrugged. 'Who knows why men do things like this in wartime? War is crazy and men go crazy in it.'

161

'But these were civilians,' von Ostermann objected desperately. 'There is not a weapon in sight. They are — *were* — not partisans, but just poor peasants!'

'*Pour encourager les autres*, as the French say,' Hartung said, as if to himself.

'But the men who did this,' von Ostermann seemed to have the greatest difficulty getting the words out, 'belonged … belonged to the Regiment!'

Hartung bit his bottom lip. 'Sir, can I talk clear text to you?'

Von Ostermann shook his head, as if he were trying to wake up from a deep sleep. 'What … what did you say?'

Hartung repeated his request.

'All right, but don't you understand that the honour of the Regiment is —'

'Sir,' Hartung cut in brutally. 'Times have changed. Who but us who have served it so long and have shed our blood for it understand what is meant by the honour of the Regiment?' He shook his head. 'Those days are long past. Major Kunz is, as you well know, a member of the Party — a man who has influential friends at court.'

'What has that got to do with it?' von Ostermann demanded haughtily, as the lone dog found its dead master and started to howl pitifully, licking the pale immobile face of its owner.

'This,' Hartung answered harshly. 'Kunz and his kind answer violence with violence, cruelty with cruelty, atrocity with atrocity, as the philosophy of the Party demands. An eye for an eye and all that. Condemn his action here this day and you condemn the Party. You pass a judgement on the Führer himself.'

Colonel von Ostermann drew himself up to his full height, looking down at the one-eyed major coldly. 'Major Hartung,' he said severely, 'actions of this kind *must* be punished. The honour of the Regiment demands it, whatever it may cost.'

As one of the waiting officers took pity on the howling dog, drawing his pistol and despatching it with one swift shot, Colonel von Ostermann reined his horse about and without waiting to see if his officers were following, set off at the gallop for Kunz's HQ.

'But they were only Polacks!' Kunz said, staring up at a red-faced Colonel von Ostermann, as if he could not believe his ears. 'Only Poles, sir.'

'They were human beings,' von Ostermann snapped and slapped his riding crop against the sweat-lathered flank of his stallion, as if he wished he could whip it across Kunz's face. 'And one does not slaughter civilians in cold blood. *Not* in the 69th Regiment of Infantry at least,' he added bitterly.

Kunz flushed. He recognized the insult. 'Fire can only be fought with fire, sir,' he barked.

'Cheap politico's claptrap.'

'Colonel, the Führer himself has used the phrase!'

Von Ostermann laughed cynically. 'So?' he countered, 'And how long has Adolf Hitler been concerned with the honour of the Regiment?'

Hartung flashed von Ostermann a warning look, but the colonel was beyond attending to looks from his Intelligence Officer. 'When I came back from the Old War, Kunz, I felt myself superfluous to the society in which I found myself, unable to adapt, somehow disgraced. It was the Regiment which saved me. The Regiment became my mother, my bride, my child.' His voice rose, his cheeks flushed an angry red, and for a moment Hartung was really afraid he would lash out at

Kunz. 'I will not allow my mother, my bride, my child to be disgraced *by anyone!*. Do you understand that, Kunz?'

The National Socialist staggered back, as if he had been physically struck by the Colonel's passionate outburst. 'I ... I ...,' he stuttered, while von Ostermann glared at him, eyes like gimlets. 'I did what I thought was ... best.'

'You did wrong, Major Kunz,' Colonel von Ostermann said, in full control of himself again. 'Consider yourself under open arrest. Hand over your battalion to your second-in-command.'

'But, sir —'

'There are no buts, Kunz! Do as I say or take the consequences.' He wheeled his horse round and looked down at an unhappy Sergeant-Major Bulle. 'I understand that you led this miserable expedition against the Polish village?'

'Yes, sir,' the Bull answered unhappily.

'You, too, are under open arrest,' von Ostermann said. 'I know that you were obeying the order of a superior officer who must take the responsibility for the atrocities committed there. Yet you are a senior non-commissioned officer who should have known better. You will report to Major von Dietz commanding the First Battalion and place yourself at his disposal. He has suffered serious casualties. He will need all the NCOs he can get.' Von Ostermann paused a moment and stared at the crestfallen NCO. 'My advice to you, Sergeant-Major, is to ensure that you die on the field of honour with a Polish bullet in your head, for if you don't, your punishment will be terrible.'

'But, Colonel...'

Colonel von Ostermann was no longer listening. He was staring at the lone figure zig-zagging across the meadow towards them, crying in a weak little voice, 'The Second

Battalion … the Second Battalion…' The running man stumbled and sprawled full-length.

But even before the men who rushed to his aid had picked him up and saw the deep lance wound in his side that could only have been made by a charging Uhlan, Colonel von Ostermann knew that tragedy had struck the Regiment. Major Hardt's Second Battalion had been ambushed by the Polish cavalry.

CHAPTER 2

'Hardt's battalion surprised by enemy cavalry … virtually wiped out… your fight is very much up in the air now…'

Von Dietz read the colonel's pencilled message and could tell from the very handwriting that von Ostermann was highly agitated *'Taking personal command of the Third Battalion and coming up with all possible speed to your support… Watch that right flank … Ostermann.'*

Major von Dietz frowned at the yellow piece of paper torn from an official message form and wondered what was happening. How had Hardt managed to get himself surprised like that? Why was the Old Man taking over personal command of the Third? What had happened to Major Kunz? And why was von Ostermann clearly so upset?

He shrugged and dismissed the many questions for which at present, at least, there were no answers, then turned to the soldier who had brought the message. It was no less a person than Sergeant-Major Bulle, who, on this hot September afternoon with the brazen ball of the sun beating down on them, seemed oddly shrunken, all his military bombast gone for some reason.

For a moment he was tempted to ask the NCO what the devil was going on back at regimental headquarters, then he decided against it; he had never really trusted Bulle. Instead he said: 'We march on the hour, Sergeant-Major. I have taken bad casualties, especially my officers. I want you, therefore, to take over what is left of the First and Second Companies.' He waited, as if he expected some sort of comment.

But there was none, for now Sergeant-Major Bulle's self-confidence had vanished totally and inwardly he was trembling, his knees feeling as if they were made of jelly. These damned officers — they were going to get him killed after all!

'When we move off, you'll take your men into the woods,' he said, indicating the spiked rows of firs beyond the mountain meadow of cropped burnt yellow grass. 'You will guard the flank, while I lead the other two companies up the road towards the pass. And remember what happened to Major Hardt's Second Battalion. Keep a good lookout for those Polish Uhlans. If they hit you, don't try to counter attack. Just go to ground and hold your position, do you understand?'

The Bull nodded numbly. Counterattack would be the last thing in the world he would do, if he bumped into the damned Polack lancers.

'Good, that's all, Bulle. You can go to your men.'

Sergeant-Major Bulle collected his wits enough to remember to salute the major. Then he turned and walked slowly, dejectedly, to where what was left of the two companies lay in the shade.

That morning they had discovered they were lousy. Perhaps they had got them from sleeping in the Polish bunker the previous night, no one knew. But suddenly they were lousy. At first when one of them had shouted out during the march up the road, 'Well, kiss me goodnight, sarnt-Major, I've got a bee!' using the slang word of the Old War, they had been interested and a few of them had decided to grow straggly beards like the old heads of World War I; now they were real front-swine, complete with their own private zoo of lice. But the feeling hadn't lasted long as the lice multiplied in that great heat, tormenting them as they rooted around maddeningly in the hair of their armpits, their crotches and on their chests, making them scratch and scratch all the while until their skin was sore and red.

Now they were stripped to their underpants, hard at work running their fingers down the seams of their clothing cracking the 'bees'. Sepp Deltgen had even invented his own 'bee-killing incinerator', a tin lid from a ration can, under which burned a stump of issue candle on to which he threw the louse as soon as he found it instead of cracking it with his fingers. As he explained, 'I'm gonna patent it as soon as this campaign is over. In the campaigns to come, I'll make a fortune.'

Maltitz had joined in the fun, stating, 'Yer, and with the grease that the bees leave behind, Sepp, you can make yer own boot-polish! You'll be rolling in Marie!'

Even Red Rudi managed to joke, 'Thanks for these Polack bees — they've got plenty of good fat on them. What would you have done, Sepp, if we'd been fighting those buck-teethed, skinny-arsed Tommies, eh? Where would yer fortune have been then?'

So they laughed as they enjoyed their time out of war and Maltitz, the only one of them to keep his pants on, squatted there, legs crossed in the fashion of tailors in the old days, feeling happy; a warm sense of comradeship and loyalty to men like himself condemned to death making him forget who and what he was. For a little while at least.

Inspired perhaps by the easy mood of the others, Red Rudi, who usually limited himself to sneers and bitter laconic comments on the world in general, opened up a little, expounding his own simple personal political philosophy which had little to do with the teachings of Marx and Engels and the clever writings of his former leaders who had fled Germany in 1933 for Russia, leaving him and several million other members of the German Communist Party to have their 'turds cut off at the arse', as he usually expressed it bitterly.

Someone had just said that the State had to defend itself, that's why they were fighting the Polacks, wasn't it? 'True,' Red Rudi replied, with exceptional courtesy for him, 'but what is the State, I ask you? Not the bulls and well-born gents in striped pants and fat-bellied golden peasants with their guts full of suds. No, my friends, the State is us and what are we doing fighting labourers, working men, clerks, who are just like us, even if they are Polacks?'

'Then what are we fighting for?' Sepp asked.

Red Rudi shrugged. 'I suppose your average capitalist considers that war is useful.' He made the gesture of counting coins with his thumb and forefinger. 'That's what it's about, Sepp. Besides the Führer needs one successful campaign. Every general and leader does. You see, that ensures that they end up in the history books.'

'Don't you realize that this is libellous, even treasonous?' A familiar voice said.

They looked up, shirts held across their laps like housewives interrupted in their sewing.

It was the Bull, a little shrunken somehow and much paler than usual, but still the same old Bull, hands on his big hips in that domineering pose of his, legs spread apart.

'Sergeant-Major Bulle!' someone said.

'Who did you expect — Greta Garbo with no clothes on?'

Red Rudi raised one cheek and farted slowly, insolently, and said, 'Ner, I knew it would be the usual plush-arse with ears!'

The Bull flushed angrily. 'On yer feet, bring yer shitty heels together and suck in yer gut when you speak to a superior officer, you commie bastard!' he bellowed, knowing that he must assert his authority over the survivors of the two companies if he was to survive himself during the next few days.

Rudi farted again. The men lying all around laughed.

The Bull was ready to explode, his little eyes popping out of his head with rage. 'Did you not hear my order?' He shouted, splattering Red's mocking face with spittle. 'I ordered you to stand to attention. Not only am I a senior non-commissioned officer, but also your new company commander!'

Red Rudi looked up at the Bull contemptuously. 'You're gonna bust a gut if you go on like that, Bull.'

'BULL!' the big NCO exploded. *BULL, HE CALLED ME!*'

Sepp Deltgen, who up to now had been silent, looked around his comrades and could tell by their winks, the slight nods, the silent '*jas*', that they were one hundred per cent behind him. Thus encouraged, he rose to his feet and faced the NCO, who towered above him. 'Bull,' he said emphasizing the nickname, 'you'd better get one thing clear right from the start.'

The Bull opened his mouth, but nothing came out except hectic gasps, as if he were being strangled in his attempt to speak.

'You're tolerated here, only barely tolerated, but that will have to do. You keep yer trap shut and don't pull rank on us and we'll leave you in peace.' He hesitated for a fleeting second, while all around him the sitting men nodded their approval. 'But one word too many, one wrong move and, brother, you're a dead man. Got it, *Sergeant-Major Bulle*?'

The Bull flashed a look around the faces of the men in the grass and saw that the fearful apprehension which had once been reflected there as soon as he had made his appearance was no longer there. Instead their eyes were hard and dangerous. The rage vanished as soon as it had come. Suddenly he was deflated, weak, even a little comical. He turned without another word and trailed back to the company headquarters, ignoring the mocking laughter that followed him.

Thirty minutes later the climb up the long winding mountain road to the pass had commenced once more. Sixty minutes after that the battalion separated, with von Dietz taking his men straight up the gleaming white road, while a reluctant Sergeant-Major Bulle directed the survivors of the First and Second Companies into the thick fir wood.

Exactly ten minutes later with the men strung out in the trees, heady with the odour of resin, there was the first faint whinny of a horse a long way off, followed a few minutes afterwards by the urgent whisper that flew from man to man: '*Cavalry … Polack cavalry up ahead!*'

CHAPTER 3

Major von Dietz did not like the position he found himself in one bit. For all he knew Bulle, guarding his flank, might have been a million kilometres away, vanished into the thick woods to his right, and there was absolutely no sign of Colonel von Ostermann with the reserve battalion. Twice in the last hour he had ordered the column to a halt while his radio operator had attempted to raise the Third; and twice the attempt had ended in failure. There was static enough everywhere and plenty of garbled messages in German and Polish, but nothing from Colonel von Ostermann. At that moment he felt as if he and the survivors of the Third and Fourth Companies were alone in the world, destined by fate to keep toiling through these lonely Polish mountains till the end of time.

At five, with the heat still rippling off the heights in wavy blue lines, he ordered a halt. While the weary stubble-hoppers flung themselves down in the burnt grass at the side of the road, von Dietz ordered his radio operator to attempt to raise Colonel von Ostermann once more. Then he set off to make a personal reconnaissance of the terrain to his front.

Everything was calm, heavy and peaceful under the summer heat. The birds sang lazily, the insects buzzed around without energy, and at the edge of the dusty road the tar had begun to melt, dribbling down into the verges. It was the kind of heavy summer calm that von Dietz remembered from his youth when he had spent his school holidays on his grandfather's great estate in East Prussia, where the peasants removed their caps and bowed whenever the ten-year-old boy appeared. He remembered how his grandfather had been able to claim that everything the boy could see — *to the very horizon* — belonged to the von Dietz's.

Perhaps it was the oppressive heat and the strange calm that made von Dietz grow careless, helmet slung over his arm, supporting himself with the aid of a stick as he toiled upwards towards the pass. Abandoning himself to the allurements of the summer's day, he finally sat down by a small stream that now ran parallel with the road, savouring its pure fragrance like some silly love-sick youth, listening to its sweet rippling music without any thought to where he was.

The dry crack of a rifle close by and the howl of a slug off the rock a metre from where he sat shattered the summer afternoon peace rudely. Von Dietz flung himself to the ground, his heart beating frantically, pistol in an abruptly sweaty hand, his eyes trying to penetrate the green gloom of the firs. But to no avail. He could not see the sniper.

For a long moment he lay there, calming the frantic race of his heart, forcing himself to think clearly. He knew he was trapped. The instant he moved out of his present position, either backwards or forwards, he would be exposed to the sniper's next bullet. The flies hummed over his head. In the woods the tops of the trees swayed slightly as they caught whatever faint breeze was blowing. There was absolutely no sound. He might well have been the last man alive on earth.

In the end he just gave in. He raised himself, angry with himself, angry with the sniper who had placed him in this position, and waited for the slug which *must* come. Nothing happened! It was the same when he turned and began to plod back the way he had come, a perfect target outlined as he was against the blinding white of the road. There was no sudden crack of a rifle and no frightening howl of a bullet winging his way. The sniper had vanished, he told himself.

But half an hour later the sniper's rifle barked again and the heavy late afternoon silence was broken by the agonized yelp of one of his men, who sat down suddenly, hand clasped to his shoulder, staring stupidly at the blood trickling through his tightly pressed fingers.

Instinctively the men threw themselves into the ditches on both sides of the road, rifles at the ready, hearts beating at a furious pace, eyes searching the heights for any sign of the unknown sniper, waiting expectantly for the next slug. But again nothing happened, and after fifteen minutes or so, von Dietz, angry and fuming now, ordered the column to start moving again. At this rate they would never reach the top of the damned pass!

At seven, with the dark shadows already beginning to race across the face of the mountains, von Dietz ordered his men to make camp. He would allow them to rest till zero two hundred hours the following morning, when they would be on their way again and complete the rest of the ascent before the dawn. He passed on the order that no campfires were to be lit; that would be a too tempting target for the damned sniper, who had been harassing them all afternoon. Then as an afterthought, although he wanted to give as many men as possible a good rest, he commanded that the camp should be patrolled by double sentries. Satisfied that he had done the best he could and preoccupied with the uncertainties of his situation, he slumped against a tree and chewed listlessly on the lump of hard, greasy sausage, washed down with lukewarm water, that was his supper.

If the Poles at the pass knew he was coming, which obviously they did, why bother to harass him with a single sniper? What damage could one lone Polish rifleman do against a column of some three hundred men? Puzzled and angry von Dietz chewed at the sausage, hoping that von Ostermann would soon make his appearance with the reinforcements from the Third Battalion.

Finally he gave up. Exhaustion overcame him. The sausage slipped from his fingers, his head tilted to one side against the tree trunk, and he was asleep. Far, far away to his right the growing darkness was split by the faint pink of explosion and when the wind blew in the right direction, it brought with it the subdued snap and crackle of small arms fire. But von Dietz saw neither the flashes nor heard the rattle of rifle fire. He snored on in an exhausted sleep.

They had known they were being trailed ever since the man next to Red Rudi had heard the whinny of the horse and someone else had spotted the dark silhouette of the lone rider poised on the horizon. At first they had stopped, expecting an enemy attack at any moment. By now most of them had heard the rumour that the Second Battalion had been completely wiped out by the Polish cavalry and they lay there in the burning forest, frightened and tense, waiting for the Uhlans to come charging across the fields to their left, lances tilted downwards ready to plunge them deep into their own soft flesh. But nothing of the kind had happened and an apprehensive, yellow-faced Bulle had been forced to order the march to continue.

All that afternoon they had plodded steadily upwards, eyes searching their front fearfully, rifles unslung with their fingers on the trigger, ready for trouble. Still nothing happened, although twice they had spotted the tiny black figures on the horizon, wary mounted men keeping pace with the German column.

'Great buckets of shit!' Bull had cursed when the Poles were spotted for the second time, 'What kind of shitting game do they think they're playing!'

Maltitz, trailing behind the frightened NCO, thinking the outburst was a question and not an expression of the Bull's overwhelming fear, said, 'Perhaps they're just reporting on our position, Sarnt-Major.'

The Bull seized on the statement like a dying man clutching a straw. 'Do you think so, Maltitz, *really* think so?' He looked at the undersized dark-faced soldier, expectantly, his eyes covered with a sheen, as if he might break down and cry at any moment.

Maltitz was oddly embarrassed. In the old days back at the barracks, Sergeant-Major Bulle had been a lordly figure who had strode proudly over the square like Jesus walking over the water, never deigning to notice such a lowly creature as himself, save to bellow: '*Swing those arms, that nasty man over there...*' or '*open yer shitting legs, will ya, nothing'll fall out!*' Now the Bull seemed to be hanging on his very words, as if they were highly important. 'Well, sir, if they had wanted to attack us, they could have done it long ago. They've had opportunities enough. My guess is that they're just scouts. The main force must be somewhere else.'

'Main force somewhere else,' the Bull mumbled to himself several times, as if he were repeating some comforting prayer. 'Main force somewhere else...'

But Maltitz was wrong. The Uhlans were still with them — in strength.

The heat of that long weary day was followed by the cool of a mountain night, and with the cold came mist. As the Bull pushed on, refusing to stop in spite of the protests of the weary infantry, not because he was not exhausted too, but

176

because he was too scared to set up camp and be caught by the cavalry off his feet — all that his fear-crazed mind could reason now was that movement bought safety.

Now a thin grey mist writhed between the trees as the exhausted soldiers plodded ever upwards through the hushed forest, their gaze fixed on the open spaces to their left, for all of them reasoned that if the Polack cavalry attacked, it would need a large open space. As an ashen-faced Sepp Deltgen explained to Red Rudi who trailed along at his side, limping badly with his right foot: 'I saw a cavalry attack in the pictures once. They form up at the end of this field and then they canter forward — canter's what they call it — and then they come at the infantry like a bat outa hell. They need a lot of space. I don't think they could do much in those trees.'

Red Rudi nodded and said moodily, 'Let's hope you're right, Sepp.'

But, as with Maltitz, Sepp Deltgen was wrong, too.

Half an hour passed. The thick mist thickened. They seemed to be legless as they toiled on, no sound coming from their exhausted ranks save the harsh gasp of their escaping breath. Now there seemed something eerie, uncanny about the forest. The firs dripped mournfully, with the mist curling in and out of them grotesquely, and occasionally strange unidentifiable, frightening sounds could be heard. Time and time again, the Bull flung an anxious glance over his shoulder, as if he thought he might see some mysterious rider trailing them on a ghostly silent horse, but each time there was nothing there.

Behind him, Maltitz, now as nervous as his commander, twice thought he heard the muffled cough of an impatient horse and the soft clink of metal against metal; but he dismissed the sounds as figments of his overexcited imagination. Then, when the change of wind brought with it the soft shuffle of many horses' hooves, the marching men's exhaustion suddenly vanished. There was no denying it this time. The Polish cavalry were out there, somewhere, in full strength! Here and there a man stopped, as if he had suddenly run into an invisible wall, bringing up his rifle instinctively and fumbling with it as if he were going to aim at some kind of assailant. But still there were no attackers in sight.

'*What we gonna do?*' The hushed whisper ran along the length of the frightened column, as men flashed scared glances to both sides. '*What we gonna do?*'

Maltitz repeated the question to the Bull, who stood there at the head of the now completely stalled column, wringing his big hands like a scared old woman, staring apprehensively at the mist-covered meadow to his left, his lips moving all the while.

Maltitz repeated his query.

'Do?... What *can* we do?' the Bull quavered abjectly. 'Surrender...' He spun round on the little man crouching there, rifle at the ready. 'We could surrender, Maltitz, couldn't we?' He grabbed hold of the other man's shoulder with that powerful paw of his, his fingers digging painfully into Maltitz's flesh. 'The Poles ... they don't kill prisoners, do they, Maltitz?'

Maltitz noted the 'Poles' instead of the usual contemptuous 'Polacks', and said: 'I don't think so, Sarnt-Major. But in the excitement of the attack, I don't know whether they'd be able to stop —'

'I don't want to die!' the Bull interrupted him, wringing his hands piteously, the tears streaming down his fear-contorted face. 'I haven't done anything to them. Honest, Maltitz, that was a mistake at the village... It was that maniac Kunz... And the Führer, he's to blame, too... What did he want to attack Poland for?... What did the Poles do to him?'

His own fear forgotten for a moment, Maltitz stood open-mouthed with amazement at the sight of Sergeant-Major Bulle breaking down completely like this, jabbering about things Maltitz could not hope to comprehend, save for one: the Bull had publicly condemned the Führer!

Hesitantly, Maltitz reached up a skinny hand and patted the big NCO's heaving shoulder as he leaned against a dripping fir. 'Don't worry, Sarnt-Major, everything will be all right,' he said soothingly. 'We'll get through. Weeds don't die, they say, don't they?'

'Do you really think that, Maltitz,' the Bull began and then suddenly there was a tremendous 'Hurrah' and the frantic clatter of racing hooves and bits and harnesses as the Uhlans burst from the firs.

'*Attack*!' someone screamed. '*ATT* —' The warning died on the man's lips as a Polish lance pierced his throat, the impact of the charge lifting him clean off his feet and bright scarlet blood jetting from his wide-open dead mouth.

In an instant the trail was transformed into a scene of murder and mayhem. Horses reared and plunged. Rifles cracked. Running men, their rifles long discarded, screamed shrilly as the great lances thrust deep between their skinny shoulders. Riders came crashing down heavily as they were hit by a chance bullet. Men went down beneath flashing hooves, victims of the bloody sweating riders, swirling round and round, cursing, screaming, bellowing as they sliced and hacked in the mêlée of rearing, whinnying frightened beasts and terrified running infantry.

Maltitz swung his rifle like a club. The butt caught the Uhlan racing towards him, bent low over the flying mane of his horse, lance tucked tightly to his side, across his right knee. There was the audible snap of breaking bone. The Uhlan howled and shot from his horse, flying backwards over its rump as the crazed mount galloped on, riderless. He crashed to the ground. Next instant Red Rudi's heavy dice-beaker smashed into his upturned face, transforming it into a bloody gore.

Another Polish lancer broke away from the main body of the slaughter in the centre of the glade and charged towards Maltitz, hooves thundering across the turf. Maltitz aimed, rifle clasped to his hip, and fired. Nothing happened! Maltitz stood there petrified. His breech had jammed. A German sprang from the trees and tried to grab the Pole's stirrup, but the rider jabbed his horned spur backwards, without taking his gaze off Maltitz. The German fell back screaming, his right eye hanging down the side of his cheek. Maltitz closed his eyes, the thunder of the horse's hooves filling the whole world, knowing that this was the end.

A shot rang out. Scarlet flame stabbed the darkness. The Pole's horse reared up on its hind legs whinnying piteously, its forelegs flailing the air in pain. Desperately the lancer tried to keep his seat, but in vain. As the horse rolled over and crashed to the ground, he flung himself off, straight on to Sepp Deltgen's bayonet, skewered himself right through the guts. Deltgen flung away his bayonet, leaving the Pole writhing back and forth on the bloodied turf, hands on the bayonet sunk deep into his belly as if he were attempting to pluck it out, and grabbed Maltitz's arm. 'Come on, Titty,' he cried, as more lancers started to break away from the slaughter of the First and Second Companies, 'let's get the hell out of here! Rudi?'

'I'm here!' Red Rudi wiped the blood clean from a deep gouge in his right temple. '*Where?*'

'The trees and beyond — into those thickets! They can't follow us into them on horseback!'

The three comrades turned and ran, as behind them the Uhlans finished the slaughter of the infantrymen, pressing them down in a welter of blood and gore in which they wallowed like animals, slashing, hacking, gouging, overcome by a frenzy of blood-lust and killing, ignoring the cries of their officers and the blows of their NCOs who were trying to get them moving again.

They smashed through the first line of firs, the branches ripping and tearing at their uniforms, slashing at their faces, tripping them as they ran on blindly, fear giving speed to their heels as the sound of hooves filled their ears. They clawed their way through the second row towards the dark outline of the thicket. The roar of the hooves was becoming even louder. They ran as if the devil himself were after them. The thickets were still fifty metres away. *Could they make it?*

Maltitz flung a terrified glance over his shoulder. The leading rider was only a few metres away, steed going all out, the rider leaning parallel to the flying mane, his great four-metre lance held straight to his front. Behind him there were three others, but further away. Suddenly he knew they wouldn't make it. One of them would have to be sacrificed to the lancer in order that the other two could escape.

Almost as if he were at the cinema watching someone else do it, Maltitz turned and stood there, a lone David facing Goliath, the murderous weapon growing ever larger, the thunder of the charging hooves rising to a crescendo, the rider high in the saddle seeming to increase in size until he had become a giant. And then Maltitz swung into action. Just when it seemed he hadn't a chance — that the Uhlan would skewer him with his lance — Maltitz grabbed the end of the weapon as it swung back behind the racing horse, and heaved with all his strength. The Pole yelled in alarm. Next moment he was falling from his saddle, the horse charging on without him. He hit the grass with a tremendous thump and sprawled there, arms outspread, either unconscious or dead.

Maltitz did not wait to find out. Dropping the lance which he found in his hands and trembling suddenly at the thought of what he had just done, he raced after the others.

CHAPTER 4

Just after midnight on September 3, Colonel von Ostermann arrived with two companies of the Third Battalion at von Dietz's camp, some three kilometres below the pass, at roughly the same time the young major woke up with the solution to the problem that has been occupying him when he had fallen asleep leaning against the tree trunk.

At first he hardly dared to trust his own intuition, so he listened to the colonel's account of the events of the previous day as they sipped cold coffee from the colonel's canteen. Finally he could not contain himself any longer. Interrupting von Ostermann's hesitant, shame-faced story of what had happened at the Polish village, he said, 'Colonel, all yesterday afternoon we were harassed by a Polish sniper, who surely must have informed his people on the pass itself that we are coming.'

Von Ostermann forgave the young Major's impoliteness and nodded,

'So?'

'So, why are they harassing us in this manner if they know we are supposed to be excellent. Why not let us come on and bleed to death up there in our hundreds rather than potting us off one by one. Any commander worth his salt wants the big victory, not this sort of petty thing.'

Von Ostermann noted that the cynicism had gone from the younger man's voice and told himself that von Dietz was just like his father, a born soldier who lived for action, regardless of the political background or consequences of that action.

Von Dietz was impatient for battle.

'I agree, von Dietz,' he said slowly, as all around them the camp was reluctantly coming to life. 'Why waste the time, eh?'

'Exactly, sir,' von Dietz answered eagerly.

'Well, what do you make of it?'

'This, sir, though I know I have absolutely no evidence to base my opinion on. Let us assume that the Poles have tumbled to the fact that General von Thoma is moving above the pass on the crestline with his Second Panzer. Let us also assume that originally they were not prepared for that kind of move and have been caught with their knickers down.'

'It has been known even in the Greater German Wehrmacht,' von Ostermann commented ironically.

Von Dietz, in his eagerness, ignored the irony. 'So now they realize they are going to be outflanked if they don't do something about it. But where are they going to get the necessary troops from at the eleventh hour to put an end to von Thoma's drive?'

'From the pass?' von Ostermann exclaimed, the irony and tiredness suddenly gone from his voice.

'Exactly, sir. They know we're coming. God knows we let them know that well enough in advance. So they harass us, knowing that *we* know the pass is supposed to be well defended and that we will not take any great risks. Meanwhile they slip the defenders higher up the mountain to tackle von Thoma.'

Von Ostermann was silent for what seemed a long time, while all around them men rose from the ground, yawning wearily, urinating against the trees in great hissing clouds of steam, grumbling that there was only water for breakfast. Then without a word he rose and strode over to where his radio operator squatted, earphones already slipped over his head, picking up the messages which were already beginning to fill the air waves this new day. 'Operator, attempt to raise General von Thoma's HQ,' he ordered. 'Give him my compliments and request an immediate situation report … and tell him von Ostermann from "Blue Force" is breathing down his neck once more.'

He came back to where von Dietz sat and said. 'Back at War Academy, when I was in charge of Blue Force, I captured him and the whole staff of Red Force while they were, er, at their ablutions.' He chuckled at the memory. 'The whole bunch of them with their breeches around their ankles, squatting on their thunderboxes to be exact. Von Thoma didn't speak to me for a week afterwards.'

For nearly an hour the two of them waited, passing the time with desultory chatter, while all around them the men readied themselves for another day of war. Finally the radio operator hurried over with the familiar yellow slip of paper. 'I wrote it down for you, sir,' he explained. 'The bloke at the other end seemed pretty jittery. I had to ask him to repeat at least three times.'

Von Ostermann handed the message to von Dietz. 'You read it, young fellow. My eyes are not too good at this time of the day, you know.'

Von Dietz smiled to himself. Even in the midst of total war, the colonel was as vain as ever about his physical ability. Holding it up to the torch which von Ostermann flicked on, he read it out aloud: '*Steady increasing pressure from the enemy … progress becoming very difficult… Still have not reached objective … damn your eyes, Blue Force … Von Thoma.*'

Von Ostermann slapped his hand down on his thigh hard with delight. 'My God, von Dietz, what a chance we've got! What a chance!'

'What do you mean, sir?'

'Well, you know what our role was *supposed* to be? A feint, pure and simple, with von Thoma doing the running. But now this changes everything.'

'In what way?'

But for the moment von Ostermann was not prepared to answer that question. Instead he rambled on, as if to himself, about how the honour of the Regiment could still well be saved after the unpleasant business of the village and the decimation of the Second Battalion. Finally von Dietz interrupted him firmly. 'Sir how has this business changed matters?'

Von Ostermann chuckled. 'Simple, my dear von Dietz. Instead of playing games along this road, letting the snipers hold us up while the Poles hold the pass with a handful of men, we hit them with all we've got. *Now, this very day!*' He slapped a surprised von Dietz on the shoulder. 'Young man I'll make a general of you yet.'

'Comrades ... comrades...,'/ the voice called piteously. *'Comrades, don't leave me behind ... comrades, where are you?'*

'The Bull,' Red Rudi hissed, as they dropped panting to the damp ground, hoping that the mist hid them from the Uhlans who seemed to be everywhere, trotting up and down, cutting down the survivors of the shattered companies.

'You sure?' Sepp asked.

'I'd never mistake that barn-shitter's voice,' Red Rudi answered sourly. 'Hell, that bastard haunted me in my dreams in the old days with that organ of his.'

'Comrades, please don't leave me,' the voice called again. *'Please!'*

Maltitz raised his head above the milky white level of the mist and searched the terrain to their front, hoping the Uhlans, who were now some two hundred metres away hadn't heard

Bull call. Someone was staggering carelessly across the glade to their right, arms outstretched like some crazed child looking for its mother, in full view of anyone who cared to see him. There was no mistaking that bulk. It was the Bull all right. He swallowed and told himself that they would have to make a decision fast because the Poles would soon spot him, he was making such a racket.

'What we gonna do with him?' he asked.

'Leave the shit to croak!' Sepp answered bitterly. 'There's plenty of meat on him. Let the Uhlans sharpen their penknives on his fat hide.'

'Yer, why should we chance our arms for that rotten shit,' Red Rudi added his voice to Sepp's. 'Do you think he'd help us if we were in his place?'

It was almost as if the Bull had abruptly become aware that they were there, somewhere or other. He stopped his drunken staggering and croaked, 'Comrades, don't abandon me, poor old Bulle! ... You know me ... I've always been good to you ... *Please*, comrades, don't... '

Up at the top of the glade the Polish lancers reined in their mounts, obviously trying to penetrate the grey gloom and ascertain where the shouts were coming from.

Maltitz hesitated no longer. He sprang from their hiding place and pelted across the open space, hissing, 'Sergeant-Major, it's me, — Maltitz.'

'*Maltitz!*' the Bull's voice broke with emotion. '*Thank God, you've come!*'

An angry voice called something in Polish, perhaps a challenge or warning. Maltitz didn't know. All he knew was that he had to get the great blubbering fool, standing there stupidly, under cover before the Uhlans spotted him. He grabbed hold of the Bull's hand and fought off the other man's tearful attempts to hang on to him. 'Come on, Sarnt-Major, for God's sake! *Run!* The others are hiding over there!' he gave Bulle a shove, and the big man began to run clumsily towards the hiding place, still sobbing as he ran.

The cry in Polish rang out again, sharp, angry and imperative. Waking up to his own danger, Maltitz pelted after the big NCO.

A wild volley of fire split the gloom. Maltitz ducked his head between his shoulders fearfully, hearing the bullets cut the air all around him. Now their hiding place was only ten metres away. He saw Bulle dive under cover and heard the others crying at him to get his big arse down, quick, and summoned up the last of his strength. Five more metres and he would do it. Three … two…

The bullet struck him a great blow, low in the abdomen. The impact knocked all the breath from his body in a huge gasp, but it also impelled him forward in a crazy dive into the bushes and as he blacked out, sinking into that awful pain, the last thing he felt was the bushes falling into place over his body and hiding him from the lancers who were trotting along the edge of the trees, thrusting their lances into the undergrowth.

The Uhlans had gone. They had looted the bodies and trotted away, the mist deadening the beat of their horse hooves on the blood-stained turf. Now there was that strange heavy silence that occurs just before dawn, when the night creatures are finally still and the first faint croak of the birds indicates that a new day is about to commence.

Cautiously, very cautiously, Red Rudi raised himself from their hiding place and searched the area. They really had gone. The glade was empty, save for the dead. He stared at them, mesmerized, the mist whirling around his legs as if it was trying to grab at him and drag him down with the rest of those nameless horrors sprawled on the grass: a whole bloody butcher's shop of war, burst guts, severed limbs, gaping-holed chests. He had seen the dead of the first day, but they had been nothing like this; they had died cleanly with a bullet through their hearts or heads. Impersonal, clinical even, killed at a great distance by men they had never seen. But the men now sprawled before him in the wet grass had seen their murderers, had fought with them eye-to-eye, had experienced the full range of horror, anger, outrage at the violence being done to their soft flesh, and the final, great, unreasoning, overwhelming realization that they were being killed!

Red Rudi was not an educated man but he had thought a lot which is why he had become a communist. In the chaotic last years of the Weimer Republic, when he had been one of six million German unemployed, he had believed that communism like Catholicism offered a plan, gave a man the belief that everything would work out well in the end. Now, at this moment, viewing those slaughtered young men in that mist-filled glade, he knew there was no plan to anything. Everything was chance, and that the only thing which would preserve him would be himself.

Maltitz's soft and quickly stifled moan, followed by Sepp's angry hiss, woke Red Rudi up to the job on hand. Over the last two hours they had been trying to stop the unconscious Maltitz's bleeding with bits of cloth and bandages. They had used up everything they possessed, even their undershirts; now they needed new bandages — from the dead.

Five minutes later he was back with a heap of bandages clutched to his chest, trying to ignore the stench on his hands. It reminded him of the nauseating odour that had once come from the womb of a whore he had lived with whom he had aborted with a knitting needle so that she could go back to walking the line and earn some money for them.

Together he and Sepp eased off the sticky rags and bandages that they had pressed inside Maltitz's blood-filled trousers, stifling the wounded man's moans whenever one of the searching lancers trotted by. They lifted up the flap of his shirt, revealing a great gaping wound in the soft white belly flesh just above the genitals. But it was not the bloody wound that made Sepp whistle softly and look significantly at his comrade; it was what lay below it that did.

Red Rudi breathed: 'So that was why? Poor, poor old Titty!'

But their discovery was quickly forgotten. Swiftly the two of them went to work, padding the gaping hole with bandages, wrapping others on top of the wad to keep it in place. The Bull watched, seeing nothing, hearing nothing, feeling nothing, totally concerned with his own overwhelming fear until finally Red Rudi rose and made his announcement.

With that, Bulle suddenly came to life with a trace of his old arrogant peacetime self. 'But we can't let ourselves be lumbered with him!' he declared. 'Can't you see he's had it anyway? Leave him here, and let him croak in peace.'

Red Rudi did not even attempt to argue. Instead he pulled out his bayonet — his sole weapon, for he had long thrown away his rifle — and placing the point just beneath Bull's trembling chin, hissed: 'You carry him, you shit, or I'll carve yer shitting turnip off, *now*!'

Five minutes later, as the sky started to flush the first dirty white of the false dawn, they set off, an unconscious Maltitz tied to the Bull's back. Slowly and painfully they began to make their way back to the road, leaving behind them the silent dead, watched only by the waiting, greedy crows.

CHAPTER 5

The mist had vanished, and already the morning was oppressively hot. The crickets had commenced chattering again in the burnt grass on either side of the winding steep pass road, and they racketed on in a ragged chorus which got on the men's nerves.

Von Dietz was at the head of the column, together with von Ostermann, who was doing well for a man of his age, the silence was like an explosion, and the young major could feel it almost tangibly; just as he could feel the tense nervousness of his men, who were worried about the rush for the pass and the knowledge that somewhere the unseen sniper might well be waiting for them, now that it was light again.

They marched quickly round a bend, their boots throwing up clouds of white dust. To their right the mountains were ash-blue in the windless heat. Five hundred metres to their left von Dietz could make out the shimmering heat waves rippling above the tin roofs of a small collection of huts. He flung von Ostermann a curious look. The huts were not marked on his map.

Von Ostermann licked his parched lips and said, 'Customs' post, von Dietz.'

'Do you think it's occupied, sir?' von Dietz asked, indicating that the men behind him should take cover on both sides of the road. They dropped gratefully into the ditches, while the two officers came to a halt in the middle of the road and stared at the tin-roofed huts, from which there came no sign of life.

'One way to find out, isn't there von Dietz?'

'Yes, sir. But if you don't object —'

'You are in charge, von Dietz. Do it your way. But remember, time is of the essence.'

'I will, sir.'

Swiftly the major rapped out his orders. The mortar men doubled forward, carrying the heavy parts of their weapons and the bombs. Working swiftly and expertly, they set up the tripods, securing the legs with rocks, screwed on the tubes and dropped into the firing positions behind the little weapons. Their commander looked expectantly at von Dietz.

'Six rounds — rapid fire, high explosive.'

'Six rounds rapid — high explosive!' the mortar commander echoed.

Swiftly he stepped back a pace as the first mortar belched fire, its crew turning their faces sideways against the blast, mouths opened to stop their eardrums from bursting, the commander with both fingers in his ears. With an obscene howl the fat-bellied bomb waddled into the sky, then gathered speed at a tremendous rate as it hurtled down towards the huts. Its explosion was followed almost immediately by another and then another.

In an instant the huts were obscured by grey smoke that changed to black and started to ascend slowly in a thick mushroom on the still air. Von Ostermann peered at the hamlet in that short-sighted manner of his and asked, 'What do you see, von Dietz? What do you see?'

The major had no time to answer his question. Instead he bellowed, 'One and Two Platoons! On your feet!' Drawing his pistol, he flung his arm to the right and to the left to indicate that they should form up on both sides of the road. He gave them a minute before pumping his clenched fist down and up three times in the infantry signal for advance.

'At the double!' he yelled as the hollow boom-boom of the bombs began to die away. 'At the double!'

'*Hurrah*!' the infantry cried hoarsely as they ran forward awkwardly over the rough grass, bayonets and machine pistols clasped tight to their right hips. '*HURRAH*!'

But there was no need for their feigned bravery this morning. No sooner did they reach the outskirts of the hamlet, when the first Poles started to come out of the smoke, hands raised above their head, shouting in a language they could not understand.

'Stand fast!' von Dietz cried urgently. '*Stand fast — everyone*!'

A Pole in a strange uniform was walking straight towards him, lurching, with his head tilted like someone seen in a dream, blood pumping upwards from an upraised wrist where there had been a hand. He fell in a ditch and lay still. But behind him came the others, some weeping, others vomiting blood. There would be no fight for the customs' post.

'Border guards,' von Ostermann said, as they walked through the smoking desolation of the huts, crunching over the fragments of rubble and broken beams, carefully not looking at the Pole dying in the ruins, his legs and arms gone.

'It looks as if you're right, sir,' von Dietz commented, as one of the NCOs paused at the horror, placed his pistol at the base of the Pole's skull and blew him to eternity, as if it were an everyday thing for a nineteen-year-old boy to blast the head off a dying foreigner. 'These fellows are not real soldiers.'

'Just civilians in uniform, hurriedly given weapons, and told to hang on here the best they could. Cannon fodder, in other words, von Dietz.'

Von Dietz nodded.

Von Ostermann paused at the edge of the smoking ruins and peered upwards at the heights. 'I'd give my pension, if I live to get it, to know at this moment what is going on up there, von Dietz.'

The young major stared at the silent peaks into which the gleaming white road disappeared, wondering what did lie ahead of them on the last leg of their march. In three days the Regiment had suffered nearly two thousand casualties: two thousand men, killed, wounded and missing just so that the von Rundstedt and the rest of the ancient ones could cackle, rub their hands and tell each other just how clever their strategy had been. Now there was a chance still to justify the loss of so many young men. If the survivors could seize the pass, it might help to assuage the grief of those back home. Then, at least, they could boast to their neighbours that the sacrifice had not been in vain; that the 69th had captured the Jablunka Pass!

Almost as if he could read the younger officer's mind, von Ostermann swung round, exposing his back to the enemy, if there were any of them still left up there. He gripped von Dietz's right hand in both of his and said fervently, 'Von Dietz, you've got to pull it off! It's our last chance to rescue the honour of the Regiment, the honour of all of us who have served in it, just as our fathers and *their* fathers before them did.' He looked at von Dietz's cold face, his old eyes blazing like they had once done as a young subaltern, undergoing his baptism of blood with this same Regiment. 'Von Dietz, men have always fought wars. Not for social or political reasons, not even for economic reasons as the fashionable theorists will have it these days. It is not countries which go to war, *it's men*! We go forth to fight because we want to prove ourselves. Once a man has been to war, he has some inner core for the rest of his life which tells him he is different from those who didn't go. He is not tougher, braver, bolder, but he has —' von Ostermann screwed up his face as if he were finding it damnably difficult to express himself, 'that certain something. He has laid his life on the line deliberately, even joyfully, and he has survived too. Can you just understand that, von Dietz?'

'Yes, sir, but —'

The rest of von Dietz's words were drowned by that familiar dry crack of a high-velocity rifle. The colonel's exposed back had been too tempting a target for the unseen sniper.

Von Ostermann's head shot back, mouth suddenly gaping, eyes narrowed like they always were when he was trying to see something in the far distance with his short-sighted gaze.

'*Colonel!*'

Von Dietz attempted to grab him before he crumpled to the ground, but von Ostermann waved him away with a weak gesture of his right hand. 'Take over the Reg —' he began, but then the hot salty blood filled his mouth and he could speak no more.

Hand held out to ward off von Dietz, eyes squinted trying to see what lay ahead, but surprisingly enough with a smile on his tortured bloody lips, Colonel von Ostermann pitched face-down on to the ground, dead.

Slowly von Dietz walked away from the corpse sprawled on the ground, a Polish border guard's coat thrown across the sightless face. For the first time for over a year he felt some kind of emotion, though he could not identify it. Was it a sense of sadness at the loss of this old man, who as a young captain on his grandfather's estate had bounced him up and down on his knee? Was it anger at the unknown Pole who had murdered the officer in such a cold-blooded manner? Was it a feeling of the transitoriness of life itself, the knowledge that all things were born to bloom and die? He did not know. All he knew was that he felt, *felt* something, when he had told himself these many months that he could no longer feel, that he had become an emotional cripple, fated for all time to know and perceive but never to feel again.

'Sir,' the timid young voice broke into his reverie.

He spun round. A grey-stained bespectacled soldier whom he vaguely recalled belonged to the Third Battalion stood there looking at him enquiringly.

'Yes?'

'Sorry to bother you at this time, sir, with the Colonel and everything,' he indicated the body that von Dietz had just left with an embarrassed wave of his hand.

'Go on.'

'Well, sir, it's just me and the boys ... we were wondering sort of if...' The boy squirmed with red-faced embarrassment.

'Wondering what?'

'Well, sir, whether we'd have the chance to see any action before the war ends?'

Von Dietz could have laughed out loud. '*We go forth to fight because we want to prove ourselves,*' the Colonel had said, and now this humble, skinny-shouldered specimen worrying whether the fighting would be over before he had a chance to get his stupid innocent turnip blown off. 'Of course,' he cried, a note of hysteria in his voice, though the soldier did not know that, 'of course, you'll see some action!'

'Thank you, sir.' The youth swung him a tremendous salute as if he had been greatly honoured by the CO's confidence and ran back to where his comrades of the Third Battalion eagerly awaited his news, crying, 'It's all right, comrades... It's all right, we're gonna see a bit of a scrap!'

Von Dietz's elation was soon replaced by his old contempt for his race and for himself, for humanity. They were all fools; they deserved what they got. He pulled out his whistle and blew a shrill blast on it.

Five minutes later they were on their way again. As they marched past the colonel's body von Dietz looked the other way, as if he could not bear to be reminded that for a moment or two the old man's death had caused him to feel some sort of emotion.

CHAPTER 6

'I can't go on … I can't,' the Bull gasped weakly and slumped to his knees. Tied on his back, Maltitz groaned low, but he didn't open his eyes.

Sepp Deltgen kicked the Bull. 'Get up, you big bastard, get up and march, or I'll cut you!'

But even that threat didn't seem to work. The Bull just knelt there, his great chest heaving in and out, his eyes dull with overstrain.

Red Rudi frowned at Sepp and pressed the back of his dirty hand against the unconscious man's forehead. Maltitz's skin felt hot and damp, as if he had a fever, and Rudi could tell from the way he breathed in short shallow gasps that he was in a bad way.

For a moment Red Rudi slumped against the nearest tree saying nothing, while Sepp waited. All they could hear was the buzzing of the flies, making greedy little darts from their blue circles towards the blood that stained the Bull's back. There was no other sound. Even the faint crackle of rifle fire they had noted earlier on, when the wind was in the right direction, had ceased. They might well have been alone on the mountainside; it was almost as if the war had been called off and they had been forgotten up here,

'Sepp?'

'Yes?'

Red Rudi raised himself wearily from the tree. 'The Bull can't go on much longer, he's knackered.' He kicked the kneeling NCO. The Bull grunted, but did not complain; it was as if he were some dumb beast of burden, which had known nothing but blows all its life. 'Don't you agree?'

Sepp nodded morosely.

'I think it's no use trying to catch up with the battalion. Besides the going's all uphill. The Bull would never make it'

'So?'

'We go downhill, back across the border. We'll find some Czech village or something. They're sure to have a doctor to attend to poor old Titty. He won't last much longer, if we don't get him to a bone-mender.'

'There'll be the chain dogs,' Bull gasped. 'They'll think we're deserters... No weapons, nothing... We'll be for the high jump.'

Sepp and Red Rudi ignored his quavering protest

'Those civvies, too. We ain't got no weapons ... who knows what they'll do —' His words ended in a gasp, as Red Rudi kicked him in the ribs once more.

'What do you say, Sepp?'

'All right, Red, let them fight the big war without us.' He grinned wearily. 'Eh?'

Red Rudi returned his grin. 'Who wants their medals anyway?' He kicked the Bull again. 'All right, donkey, on yer feet.' Slowly, infinitely slowly, the Bull raised himself and stood there swaying like a drunk. Sepp looked at Rudi and then he stepped forward. Putting the Bull's heavy arm over his own skinny shoulders, he grunted as he took the strain. 'All right, Bull,' he said through gritted teeth, 'let's move it.'

Together they began to stagger down the mountainside towards the frontier, bright red spots of blood dropping behind them on the parched grass. For a moment Red Rudi stood there watching their slow progress, amazed anew at the changes that these four short days of war had wrought. Two days before Sepp had been on the verge of killing the brutal, arrogant Bull. Now the would-be murderer and his victim were locked in an embrace as if they were lovers.

Red Rudi shook his head in wonder and then he, too, started to trail downhill.

Major von Dietz surveyed the pass, carefully shading his binoculars so no glint from the bright glass in the sunshine would reveal his position. Behind him his weary men lay slumped in the grass, each man silent and preoccupied with his own thoughts.

In that pure, absolutely dustless light everything stood out in clear relief against the brilliantly azure sky. The Polish positions were laid out in front of him as if he were viewing them on some peacetime sand-table.

Some hundred metres from the spot where the road disappeared over the top of the pass, there were a group of large boulders, perhaps left over when the Polish engineers had first blasted the road through the pass. It would be a convenient site to cover the approach. He searched the ground around the boulders with his glasses. There was no sign of any kind of defence among the boulders themselves, but the ground was scuffed and raked as if with branches. It was obvious why. Someone was trying to hide the fact that there were soldiers behind the boulders. He noted the point and ran his glasses up the road. Not much to see there save a tin hut that might have been used by roadmen and a blue-and-white striped pole with a sign on top of it. The height marker, perhaps?

His glasses searched the rock face to the left of the hut. In between the cracks and chasms of its almost perpendicular surface there were flowers, unseasonable flowers in this summer heat, magenta-red alpine geraniums, gentians, saxifrage. Suddenly he forgot the mystery of why spring flowers still blossomed there in late summer and fumbled with the wheel of his binoculars, focusing them on the long vague brown shape. Of course! It was a rope all right!

Excitedly he followed its progress up the steep rock face, catching glimpses of it as it wound in and about the flowers, disappearing into little crevices and bunches of the tall yellow asters until it vanished altogether just below a curved ledge of some three metres' breadth, most of the area of which was concealed from his view on the other side of the mountain.

He lowered his glasses, slowly nodding his head. That would be their main position. For a moment he remained there, working out the Polish positions. At one o'clock there was Position A, the boulders. Position B was at twelve o'clock, somewhere around the tin hut. At ten o'clock, the ledge completed the defences at Position C. He pursed his lips. All were mutually supporting, but it was clear from the lack of evidence on the road — tracks, litter, ruts, etc — that they were all lightly defended. Pull the plug out at the right spot and the water would drain out of the sink quickly. But what was the right spot?

Position C was out of the question. Too tough. They'd be slaughtered before they got to the base of the cliff and tried to climb up. Position A was a kind of buffer. The Poles would let them bang away at the boulders and when the steam had gone out of their attack, they would slaughter them from B and C. The answer, of course, was B. It was the plug which would drain the sink, once it was pulled out. *But how was it to be done?*

Five minutes later von Dietz thought he had his answer and with an air of almost malicious pleasure strolled over to where the bespectacled youth from the Third Battalion, who had approached him that dawn, lay with his comrades. 'You,' he commanded, curling his finger at the youth.

The bespectacled boy sprang to his feet, as if he were a jack-in-the-box. 'Sir!'

'I have a mission for you.'

The youth's eyes' glowed behind the thick-lensed glasses. 'A mission sir,' he breathed, as if he had just been offered the Holy Grail itself.

'Yes,' von Dietz answered, a sneer welling up within him at the young fool's naïve eagerness. 'You and your comrades will have your chance at last.'

'Action, sir?'

'Action.'

'Thank you, sir,' he breathed fervently.

'Don't thank me, soldier,' von Dietz said with mock seriousness. 'It's going to be highly dangerous. That's why I'm asking for volunteers, from your comrades.'

'You don't need to ask, sir. The boys would consider it an honour — to die for the Führer.'

Inwardly von Dietz groaned. The boy talked like one of those nauseating super-patriots in Goebbels' second-rate war movies. Suddenly he was sickened with his little game. 'Get your group together,' he commanded briskly. 'Leave your packs behind. Just rifles and grenades. Report to me in five minutes.'

'Sir!' The boy pelted back to his comrades, crying, 'we've got a mission — a mission, comrades!'

But when the volunteers, eager and grinning, as if they were going on some sort of schoolboy outing, reported to von Dietz's HQ behind a heap of rocks, they were not alone. With them was Major Kunz, devoid of badges of rank, carrying a simple soldier's rifle, stick-grenades thrust into his belt and the sides of his boots so that he looked like the rest of the stubble-hoppers around.

'Von Dietz, could I speak to you alone, *please*?' His eyes were dark, depressed and somehow sad; the old heroic National Socialist gleam that von Dietz had once told himself he had modelled after heroic soldier-posters of peacetime, had vanished.

'Of course.'

They walked out of earshot of the expectant young volunteers.

'Well?' von Dietz demanded.

'You know my situation, von Dietz. I am in disgrace. Undoubtedly I will have to face a general court-martial if I survive, and that will be the end of my career in the Army. I acted as I thought best —' Kunz broke off his self-justification abruptly, as if it didn't matter anymore. 'I must confess to you, von Dietz that I am — *was* — a very ambitious man. My wife, after all, is related to *Reichmarschall* Göring. But now that's all over.' He reached out and gripped von Dietz's arm fervently. 'As a fellow officer and, I hope, comrade, grant me this one last favour!'

'Yes?'

'Let me lead the volunteers' attack. They are my men. I know them. They know me. Von Dietz, I beg you, let me save my name and have the honour of dying on the field of battle!' he sobbed. 'I simply couldn't stand the shame of a court-martial. I'd rather blow ... blow my brains out.'

Kunz stared at von Dietz, tears in his eyes, his face contorted with unbearable emotion. The tall skinny major could have laughed out loud at his pathetic schoolboyish foolishness at that moment, but he didn't. Instead he said, 'Why, of course, Kunz, *of course!*'

The chain dog appeared suddenly out of the bushes, submachine-gun hanging across his broad chest beneath the silver crescent of his calling, face at ease, but with his right forefinger curled around the trigger — just in case. 'Now then, what have we here?' he asked in that fake good-humoured manner of cops the world over.

'What do you think, you fat slob, a group of fairies who are now going to do a little dance in their dell?' Red Rudi thought of replying. In fact, however, he replied: 'Survivors, Corporal. Ambushed in the woods up there. Bringing in a badly wounded comrade who urgently needs attention.'

'So, so,' the big chain dog said, tipping back and forth on the toes of his highly polished jackboots. 'Bringing in a wounded comrade?' He looked at the unconscious Maltitz slumped over the Bull's shoulders without the slightest interest, noting the blood dripping to the ground from his stomach, as if he were taking in the fact that some recruit was running around with his flies undone. 'How noble of you!'

'Corporal, this man will die if we don't get him to a bonemender quick!' Sepp said angrily.

The chain dog didn't seem to hear. He was enjoying this moment, as he always enjoyed them. 'Three fighting men bringing in one comrade, and one of them, if I'm not mistaken, a full sergeant-major.'

The Bull opened his mouth to protest, but he could not find the words. He was too exhausted and terrified to think.

The corporal's feigned bonhomie vanished and his broad cop's face hardened. 'Now, I'll tell you wet-tails something! You're taking off from the front. You've thrown away yer weapons and you've picked up that poor shit there and you're using him as an excuse to bug out, leaving the rest of yer pals to face the flying shit. That's what you bunch of fart-cannons are up to.' He winked one eye at them deliberately, fully conscious that he was in complete charge of the situation and that he had called their bluff. 'Don't try to shit Corporal Klemens! Experts have tried it and fallen flat on their hooters trying to.'

'But it's true, Corporal —'

Red Rudi cut the little Rhinelander's passionate outburst short with an icy-cold, 'And what do you intend to do about it, *Corporal?*'

The chain dog caught the emphasis. 'Don't use that kind of tone with me, soldier, or you'll be lacking a set of teeth, right quick. What am I going to do with you? I'm going to sit you down here until my relief comes up and then I'm gonna take you down to the captain and let him make the decision of what to do with you. That's what they pay officers for, you see.'

'Where is the captain?' Red Rudi asked, wanting the information before he did anything.

The chain dog mustered him with his piglike little eyes and decided he was harmless after all. 'Well, seeing I'm in a good mood today. I've got a nice little piece of Polack tail lined up for tonight. Only cost me five *zloty*. I'll tell yer. Down in the village, half a kilometre from here.'

'And when does your relief come, Corporal?'

'For a feller who might well be losing his turnip in a couple of days, you do ask a lot of shitting questions. But all the same, I'll tell you, soldier. In thirty minutes' time.'

'Thirty minutes!' Sepp exploded. 'He could die by then, if we don't get him to a medic!'

'Tough titty,' the Corporal answered easily. 'Yer can tell the chaplain when he comes to hold yer pinkie when yer go for yer last little stroll.' He laughed gruffly at his own humour. 'Tough —'

His words ended in a thick gasp of surprise, followed by a shrill high-pitched scream of absolute agony, as Red Rudi's knee jammed hard into his crotch. He doubled up, his false teeth hanging obscenely out of his mouth, spewing vomit, just as Red Rudi brought his clubbed fists down on the back of his neck. He hit the ground like a sack of wet cement.

'Come on,' Rudi cried, tugging off the chain dog's machine pistol from the unconscious man's chest, 'Bull, move yer fat arse!'

'But you hit him, a *chain dog*!' Bull gasped.

'Yer, and I'm gonna hit you in a minute as well, if you don't make steam. *Move it*!'

Rudi flashed a hard determined look at Sepp, and clicked off the safety-catch of the pistol. 'It's them or us now, Sepp. You with me?'

'Of course, you silly shit!' the little Rhinelander snapped back. 'You want me to draw you a shitting picture or something? Come on, you stupid Berlin bugger, let's go. Time's running out!'

CHAPTER 7

Crack! The first mortar bomb hushed into the afternoon sky and smacked down right in front of the boulders.

Plop! The bomb exploded. Immediately thick white smoke started to stream upwards. Another bomb followed it. And another. Already a dense mist was beginning to form in front of the boulders.

Von Dietz hesitated no longer. He clapped a waiting Kunz on his back. 'Off you go, Kunz — and the best of luck!'

'We die for Germany!' Kunz declared.

Von Dietz caught his laugh in time. 'For Germany!' he cried. 'To the attack soldiers!' Kunz yelled, springing up and into the open. '*FORWARD*!'

The volunteers didn't hesitate. '*FORWARD*!' their hoarse young throats echoed the cry, and they, too, jumped to their feet and began to rush forward behind the major.

Von Dietz shook his head at the hollowness of their enthusiasm and then concentrated on the attack as more and more smoke shells sailed over his head to blanket the boulder position. As yet there was no sign of any defence. Had he been mistaken?

Were the boulders undefended?

Suddenly Kunz, in the lead, stumbled. The men behind him came to a ragged halt. Then the major got to his feet again. He had tripped over something. The men cheered. They ran on heavily over the rough broken ground. Still there was no reaction from behind the boulders, now rapidly disappearing into the white smokescreen.

Kunz turned. Von Dietz could see his fanatical face quite clearly, the eyes sparkling now, carried away by some great patriotic enthusiasm that von Dietz could no longer share, that he knew, indeed, to be a lie. 'For Germany, comrades!' Kunz cried.

They were the last words he ever spoke. In that same moment the slow Polish machine-gun sited in the centre of the boulders fired with ponderous majesty, the gunner swinging the tracer from left to right, scything down the first row of the running men like grass.

But still the volunteers went on, stumbling and toppling forward, young unformed faces upturned in agony, frantic hands clawing the air as they were struck, while others sprang over the bodies of their dying writhing comrades without a glance downwards, to be hit themselves a second later.

Von Dietz watched as the rear rank halted, standing there, chests heaving just in front of the billowing clouds of smoke cut by the red and white stitched patterns of the tracer, considering whether they should turn and run or go on, taking casualties all the time. Suddenly a figure in the lead turned. He was minus his glasses now and there was a great scarlet gouge in his right cheek, but von Dietz recognized him all right. It was the boy who had wanted action. But he was no longer the eager innocent volunteer. He was primeval man now, cornered, uncomprehending, motivated solely by an angry rage; and for a moment, von Dietz could not help thinking that there was something a little magnificent about him as he stood there, shoulders bent, chest heaving, too enraged to do the sane thing, which was to turn and flee.

He cried something. Von Dietz could not hear the words because of the obscene throaty grunts made by the mortars which were still pumping smoke shells at the boulders. But they worked. The volunteers went forward once more. But this time they did not run. They plodded on, shoulders bent, rifles held across their bodies, going to their fate reluctantly like some dour farmer setting off for a day's work in a winter-soaked field. When the last of them had disappeared into the smoke, von Dietz told himself it was time to get on with the real work of capturing the pass. He shrilled a blast on his whistle and the two assault platoons, heavily laden with grenades and all the machine pistols that the survivors of the 69th could muster from their decimated ranks, slipped across the road and into the green calm of the firs lining the opposite side of the road. They were on their way.

Red Rudi smelled the Czech village before they actually saw it. It gave off that peculiar odour that he always associated with the occupied country: a mixture of wood smoke, pig stink and the sweet aroma of drying apples, which the Czechs horded in their lofts for the winter. He held up his hand and stopped them.

Gratefully the Bull sank to the ground, while Sepp helped to lower Maltitz, who was muttering to himself now, though the others could make no sense of it, save for the one short phrase he mumbled over and over again, '*Don't hit me, Sturmbannführer, please … don't hit …*'

'What is it?' Sepp asked, wiping the dried blood off his hands and smoothing the hair out of Maltitz's ghastly white face.

'The village … there's a village down there.'

'We're alone,' the Bull quavered, 'they'll kill us, the civvies.'

Red Rudi looked down at him scornfully. 'Of course, they won't. After all, we are the master-race.' He slapped the folding metal butt of the machine pistol. 'And I've got this to prove it, haven't I?' He ignored the big NCO who was mumbling to himself and said to Sepp, 'I'll go in first. You follow at a hundred metres with Titty and the Bull. If there's any trouble, leave it to me and my friend.' He slapped the machine pistol again. 'I'll sort the shits out. Clear?'

'Clear, Rudi.'

'All right, off we go.'

Two or three minutes later they emerged from the trees and saw the village before them, a collection of shabby cottages which had once been painted white, surrounded by tumbledown picket fences with chickens picking lazily in the dust and a couple of barefoot, thatch-haired children playing with a ball made of wool shreds, in the shade. But at that particular moment Rudi's eyes were neither for the cottages nor for the Czech children; they were for the long grey-painted halftrack, which bore the crooked runes of the SS on its numberplate and a large red cross on both sides of its armoured chassis. 'Shit on a shingle, Sepp!' he cried happily. 'We've really won the flower vase! Do you see what I see?'

'Medics!' Sepp echoed his enthusiasm, all weariness gone now.

'Perhaps they've got a bone-mender with them.'

'Come on then, let's see.' Red Rudi dug his Schmeisser into the Bull's bruised ribs. 'All right, donkey, open those legs — nothing'll fall out!'

But the Bull had no memory of his former saying. Wearily he staggered forward towards where the SS half-track was parked, his brain numb.

They laid Maltitz down in the corridor that smelt of chalk and unwashed children and walked a little hesitantly down the dark hall, the boards creaking under their feet as they passed the yellowing photographs of school groups of long ago, shaven-headed boys and long-haired girls in aprons with greasy faces grouped around fat-bellied teachers with Kaiser Wilhelm moustaches.

'To the right,' Sepp whispered. 'Voices coming from the right.'

The two of them moved on cautiously, past pre-1918 wall tablets bearing the lists of the dead 'Fallen for the King and Emperor of Austria', and peered in at the slightly open door.

At the far end of the big school hall two Czech policemen sat uneasily on school chairs that were too small for them, supervising the lines of naked children who were filing towards the tall, bespectacled man wearing the long white overall of a doctor. His gleaming riding boots, complete with spurs, showing from beneath the overall, the doctor was examining each child in turn, muttering his findings to a stern-faced woman in the black uniform of the SS's Female Auxiliary.

For a few moments the two unseen observers listened uncomprehendingly to the scientific terms — 'celphallic index three to four... Nordic type ... branchi-type, hair slightly curled, I'd classify as Alpine ... relationship of femur to tibia ... pelvis of the non-nordic type' — while the tall emaciated man in the overall, swiftly whipped his callipers up and down the skinny little bodies, measuring heads, shoulders, thighs and legs, making the children put up their feet, nipping their ribs to check the amount of flesh upon them, holding up their little organs with the end of his instrument, as if they were terribly, disgustingly dirty, and the SS woman wrote swiftly on the pad balanced on her ugly bony knee.

Red Rudi nodded to Sepp. He nodded back. He drew a deep breath and keeping the two Czech policemen in his sight, opened the door and snapped smartly to attention. 'Rifleman Reisser, humbly begging to report, sir!' he snapped.

'Red hair, light pigment, obviously Celtic blood. Ah, ah, and freckles too. That makes it quite certain.' The tall SS officer peered at Red Rudi through his gold-rimmed pince-nez, as if he were a particularly interesting lab rat. 'Yes, yes, definitely Celtic!'

Red Rudi felt his anger rising. 'May I ask a question, sir?' he said quickly before he exploded.

'You may, but I don't guarantee that I'll answer it, soldier. Ha, ha!'

At his side the woman echoed his laughter like a parrot.

Red Rudi bit his bottom lip. 'Sir, are you a doctor?'

'In a way — yes.' Obviously the SS man enjoyed this new game.

'A doctor — *of medicine*?' Red Rudi persisted, while the naked children stared at the two Germans in complete innocent bewilderment, wondering what this strange conversation was all about.

'Yes, one might say that.'

'Then can you help a comrade of mine, sir? He is severely wounded and needs attention badly.'

The SS doctor laughed in Rudi's face. 'My dear chap, I am a professor of medical anthropology. You can't expect me to be patching up wounded soldiers, you know.'

'You're a doctor?' Red Rudi repeated, and the SS professor did not notice the threat in the mud-stained unshaven soldier's voice.

'Yes, I am, but —'

The pince-nez nearly popped off the SS man's nose with fright as Red Rudi jammed his machine pistol into his skinny guts. 'Right, then you'd better start doing a bit of doctoring if you want to live much longer, Herr Professor!' Without taking his eyes off the ashen-faced SS man, he called over his

212

shoulder to the fat policeman. 'Hey, you Czechos, clear these nippers out of here and then bring in my comrade. He's outside.'

'*Jawohl, jawohl*,' they said in unison and started to shoo out the naked children like two old housewives. Red Rudi kept his muzzle jammed in the SS man's lean stomach, not even listening to the man's frightened babbling about his 'scientific experiments at the order of Reichsführer SS Himmler himself.'

And then the fat policemen returned, bearing in a still unconscious Maltitz, dripping spots of blood on the wooden floor, followed by Sepp Deltgen, carrying a Red Cross case he had lifted from the half-track.

Red Rudi nodded his approval and handed it to the SS man.

'All right, bone-mender,' he ordered, 'mend bones!'

Moodily Red Rudi chain-smoked outside the little schoolhouse, together with Sepp, while from a safe distance the Czech children watched them in open-mouthed silence. Inside a scared, yet tame Bull, who knew his fate was now in their hands, watched the SS man as he did his best to repair Maltitz's wound, assisted by the woman.

In silence he listened to what Sepp had found out from the policemen, who had fought in the Imperial Austrian Army in World War I and spoke good German. 'They measure up the kids, you see, and if they're blond and can be classed as — what's the word they used? — Aryan, they're sent to the Reich and put into special homes where they're brought up as Germans.'

'But whose kids are they?' Red Rudi broke his moody silence.

'The people in this village. According to that big Bull, the bone-mender has been examining kids all over this part of the

213

country for weeks now and sending the ones he selected back to the Reich.'

'And what do the kids' parents say?'

'They're not asked, Rudi. Besides they're scared. You see, if the kids don't match up to that bone-mender's scientific mumbo-jumbo, they go up the chimney.' Sepp made a spiralling gesture with his raised forefinger like smoke ascending.

Red Rudi knew exactly what he meant. Half his old pals from his Berlin Party days had disappeared the same way. 'You mean they put little turds like that in the ovens, too?'

Sepp nodded.

'Holy strawsack!' Red Rudi looked at his comrade aghast. 'What kind of people are we!' It wasn't a question, but more a cry of despair. 'Putting little kids into the camps and burning them! Sepp, Sepp! We deserve whatever is going to come to us one of these days. All of us. You and me, the whole shitting German nation! Oh, we Germans, we've got courage all right.' Red Rudi's face twisted into a bitter sneer. 'That we have. Courage to do evil, but all the eighty million of us haven't got that much courage,' he snapped his fingers angrily, '*to be good!*'

Sepp patted his comrade soothingly on the arm, 'Red, Red, don't take on like that. What can we do about it, a couple of shitty-arsed common stubble-hoppers like us? Nobody asked us nothing. What do they say?' he tried to cheer Rudi up. 'A human being begins with the rank of lieutenant! We're nobodies.'

Red Rudi slapped the butt of his machine pistol, his mind made up now. 'Listen Sepp, as long as we've got one of these in our flippers, we're somebody! These things give us muscle, courage, makes *Germans!*' He spat out the word like others said the word 'Jew'. 'Listen! *Shit, how they do listen!*'

Sepp nodded his head slowly. 'I suppose you're right.'

'I know I'm damned right!' Now Red Rudi was in control of himself, though the glint in his eyes was no longer quite sane. 'All right, Sepp, listen to this. You know what that SS bone-mender in there is going to find out soon, if he ain't found out already?'

'Yes,' Sepp answered sombrely.

'So what are we gonna do about it?'

'What can we?'

'*Don't talk like a crappy German!*' Red Rudi snarled scornfully.

'He's got to go, you know, Sepp,' he continued lowering his voice significantly. 'For *all* our sakes. He's a typical big blabbermouth of a teacher. He'd talk.'

'You mean — look at the turnips from below?'

'I do. We'll get rid of the cops. They'll be only too glad to make dust. We'll fake it to look as if their half-track has been hit by the Poles.'

'And the Bull?' Sepp asked slowly, considering the idea and knowing that Red Rudi was right; none of them would be safe from the Gestapo as long as the SS professor remained alive.

'Bull! He craps his pants as soon as I look at him, Sepp. He's no problem anymore.'

'The woman?'

Red Rudi looked at his comrade hard and then crooked back his forefinger, as if pulling the trigger of a pistol; it was the gesture Captain Grossmann had made a million years before. 'Clear?'

'Clear.'

CHAPTER 8

The sound of firing across the road was beginning to die out now, though the mortars continued their barrage, as von Dietz had ordered, maintaining the thick smoke-screen around the boulders and beyond.

Cautiously he and his men worked their way through the thick firs, each man's nerves jingling, his heart beating like a crazy metronome; for each and every one of them knew that if the smoke-screen cleared for an instant and they were spotted, it would mean the end. They would be sitting ducks.

It was an eerie feeling which von Dietz experienced too, but somehow he felt that everything would work out, that he was not fated to die — just yet.

They came level with the spot in the swirling clouds of smoke, where von Dietz judged the boulders would lie. He whispered an order. The men crouched and started to crawl gingerly through the undergrowth, trying to offer the smallest possible target. Von Dietz cursed as his hand dislodged some small rocks which rattled down the slope with alarming volume. He could feel the hot sweat spring up all over his body.

But the Poles defending the boulder position had not heard, for the half-expected burst of machine-gun fire did not come. They crawled on.

Now they were in the dead ground directly below the ledge which marked the Poles' Position C. From above they would be unable to see the intruders. From across the road in and around the hut they could, but he had to chance it. Slowly, very slowly, von Dietz raised his head, while behind him his men crouched in the burningly hot undergrowth, hardly daring to breathe. The smoke-screen blanketing the boulders lay behind him now. They had passed it all right. Directly to his right at an angle lay the hut and now he could see what he had been unable to detect with his glasses: it was defended.

To left and right of the tin hut and to its rear, there were two sand-bagged machine-gun posts, and out of the back window protruded the silver whip of an aerial. Obviously this was the little force's HQ. So he had been right all along! The pass was only lightly defended. The mass of the Polish troops were in the mountains above them trying to stop General von Thoma's panzers.

He sat back on his heels and considered the situation, calmly, objectively, aware of the young faces all around him, staring at him, wondering what he was thinking, and aware too, yet in no way disturbed by the knowledge, that in a few moments he must order most of them to their deaths.

He gave his orders. 'Two waves. At five-minute intervals,' he whispered urgently. 'Each wave in two halves, to tackle those machine-guns. Questions?' He flashed a quick look around the faces of the young men.

They shook their heads. What was going through their minds at this moment, he asked himself. Did they really understand that perhaps they only had minutes to live; that in a few moments, all their dreams, hopes, plans would come to a violent, abrupt stop? Perhaps not, for their young unlined faces revealed only tension and excitement, like athletes prior to a big race, wound-up and waiting to go.

'All right, first wave ready?'

'Ready, sir,' the NCOs answered dutifully.

He looked around the second wave, which he intended leading himself, for it would be the second wave that would capture the position. They, too, were ready.

'All right, good luck. *GO!*'

They burst from the firs screaming exultantly, firing from the hip as they ran, knowing that they had to cover the twenty metres of ground that separated them from the hut at speed or they'd be finished.

The Poles swung their machine-guns round, startled. The leading stubble-hoppers reacted exactly as the watching von Dietz hoped they would. Without pausing in their crazy rush forward, ignoring the men falling all around them, they threw their stick-grenades. Suddenly the air seemed black with them, as they slammed into the side of the hut, exploding there in great hollow booms that set the corrugated iron shaking wildly, as if caught by a great wind. But they were taking casualties, bad casualties, all the time, leaving the road behind them littered with men writhing in agony or stilled for good.

Then they were in among the Poles manning the first machine-gun. Von Dietz could hear the screams as they slaughtered the Poles. Seized by a terrible blood-lust, they would give no mercy to the enemy. It was now a matter of kill or be killed. Von Dietz cursed. They were getting themselves bogged down at the first machine-gun post. If they didn't move soon, they'd be in for serious trouble. Already the Poles had thrown back part of the tin roof of the hut and were trying to clamber out that way, handing up to those already on top, what looked like a machine-gun tripod.

'Come on, come on!' he cried, seized by tension and excitement, like a spectator of some particularly exciting action film. 'Move it, for God's sake!'

But it was too late. Engrossed in the slaughter below, the attackers only became aware of the gunners on the roof when it was too late. Frantically they dived for cover behind the sandbags next to the bodies of the Poles they had just slaughtered, but to no avail. From the roof the two Poles crouching over the ancient Vickers could dominate the whole area. They swung the gun back and forth, its barrel already beginning to glow a dull-red with the rapidity of its fire, pouring bullets into the attackers at almost point-blank range, until there were no more of them left alive and the ground to their front was covered with field-grey corpses. Then and only then did they stop.

Now von Dietz knew it was time to launch the second wave. Of course, the Poles would guess they'd attack again, but not so speedily. For the moment they'd be busy congratulating each other on their success, feeding new belts of ammunition into their weapons, pouring more water into the cooling systems of the machine-guns, taking a leak to relieve the pressure that tension had built up in their bladders. It was now or never.

'You, you … and you!' He detailed off three of his men who he knew were good shots. 'As soon as we go in, get those bastards on the roof, right?'

They nodded, tucked their rifle butts into their shoulders and snuggled their cheeks against the wood almost lovingly. Waiting until each man had taken aim, von Dietz said very clearly and very calmly, noting almost clinically that his nervous system was perfectly under control, 'This time we will do it.' He rose to his feet, pushed aside the firs and ran on to the body-littered road crying, '*ATTACK!*'

A loose track-pin rattled at each turn of the tracks, as the SS vehicle left the village, watched from behind the little windows by the Czechs. It was the only sound, save for the professor's pedantic voice as he went on and on about his 'remarkable discovery'. Red Rudi looked at Maltitz stretched out in the back of the half-track, bedded in all the blankets they could find. He was still unconscious, but he seemed to be breathing normally and there was a hint of colour in his pale cheeks. Somehow Red thought he was going to survive. Now Bull at the wheel crashed home second gear as the halftrack started to take the steep ascent that led out of the village and into the woods beyond. Red Rudi flashed a look at Sepp, who carried the two pistols he had taken off the Czech cops. The skinny Rhinelander was pale and very nervous, he could see that. He hadn't even eyes for the secretary who was squatting awkwardly in the back of the half-track and showing a great deal of inner thigh. Sepp saw the red-headed Berliner looking at him and his face hardened, as if he were trying to convey to the other man that he was prepared to go through with what they had to do soon.

Now the half-track was rumbling along the narrow road through the firs, the broken track-pin slapping against the side at every turn, the professor still chattering on, as if he were the only one present who could not sense the tension in the air. The secretary looked at her clasped hands sadly, as if she had already subconsciously resigned herself to her fate.

Clack ... *clack* ... the broken track-pin slapped the metal. The half-track rumbled on through the firs, heavy and oppressive with resin. Above them, the dead sun hung over a dead earth. The sweat dripped from all their faces unheeded. The professor talked on and on.

Ahead of them lay a dead-straight stretch of road, some two kilometres in length. Red Rudi knew this would have to be the place. It was completely empty and they could quickly see if anyone else appeared from both directions. He leaned forward and whispered in Bull's ear, 'Stop here and keep the engine running. Don't ask any questions or you'll join them. And remember, once it's done, you are an accessory and just as guilty as we are. Clear?'

Bull nodded his head, but said nothing, Rudi noted the nervous tic at the side of his jaw, which he had not had before.

The half-track began to slow down and then stopped in a clatter of rusty tracks. The woman looked, but said nothing. The professor stopped in the middle of a word, adjusted his pince-nez and enquired, like the unimaginative pedant that he was, 'Anything wrong with our vehicle?'

'No,' Red Rudi said drily and jerked his machine pistol at the professor. Out of the corner of his eye he could see Sepp release the safety-catch on one of the cops' pistols. 'Out!'

'Out?'

'Yes, out — *and quick*!'

'But why?' the professor blustered, as the woman rose to her feet, her plain face deadly pale, but composed. She knew all right what was going to happen, Red Rudi told himself, and then thought bitterly, confirming his hatred of her and the professor, perhaps she's been in on one of these little parties before? How did the Nazi papers phrase it so often before the war, '...*shot while trying to escape*'?

'Because I say so,' Rudi answered.

Still blustering, the professor rose, stumbling over a crate in the back of the half-track. Sepp opened the steel door and the professor dropped out on to the gravel road. Suddenly, as if remembering that he was an academic gentleman and an officer, he reached up his hand to help the secretary. She ignored the offer and dropped to the road, falling unluckily so that her skirt swept up, revealing that she wore no drawers. Perhaps the heat, Red Rudi told himself.

Without looking round, he said to Bull: 'Turn the half-track in the other direction.'

Gears slammed, Bull pressed his big foot on the accelerator and swung the heavy vehicle round, while the two of them on the road jumped back hurriedly. But they made no attempt to escape. For a fleeting second Red Rudi wished they would; then it could all happen spontaneously, perhaps even in anger. But they didn't. They remained standing there under that dead sun, the sweat running down their faces, staring up at the men in the back of the half-track like dumb animals who had accepted their fate.

Next to him, Red Rudi could hear Sepp swallow noisily, as if his throat were suddenly very dry. Deliberately, almost provocatively, he pulled back the bolt of his machine pistol, making the movement as noisy as he could. Sepp gasped. On the road the two of them continued to stare upwards, but now Red Rudi could see the fear beginning to sweep that stupid academic certainty from the professor's eyes and the trembling of his bottom lip.

Slowly, very slowly, Red Rudi began to raise his machine pistol.

'What are you going ... to do?' the professor quavered. 'You can't do this!'

Beside him the woman started to sob, but her eyes were wide open, as if she knew her tears would not blind her to the complete hopelessness of their situation.

Out of the side of his mouth, Rudi said in a cold voice, 'You take the woman, Deltgen.'

'But, Rudi, I can't —'

'You can,' Red cut him short brutally. 'This is the first time, but it won't be the last, German!' He tightened his grasp on the machine pistol.

The professor went down on his knees, hands raised in supplication. 'I won't say anything… Honestly, I won't tell! But let me live! Let —'

Rudi pressed the trigger. The machine pistol chattered at his hip. The professor's face disappeared in a welter of blood and gore as the impact of the burst at such close range flung him at least three metres, sending him sprawling face downwards in the gravel.

The woman stared numbly at his pince-nez which lay intact on the road, as if it were of some importance, her shoulders still heaving with dry sobs.

Sepp swallowed hard once again and raised his pistol. Red Rudi lowered his smoking machine pistol and regarded him coolly. 'Well?' Sepp did not move.

'Are you?' Rudi demanded, his voice suddenly iron.

Sepp pressed the trigger. The sudden shot startled Rudi himself. The woman was still standing there, although Sepp could not have missed at that distance. Then finally she began to sway. On the breast pocket of her white blouse a small patch of red had appeared, which grew larger and larger by the second. Still she stayed on her feet, swaying more wildly now. *Would she never die?*

Then at last her knees started to give beneath her and she sank to the ground, almost gracefully, her knees tucked tightly together, as if she wished to preserve her ladylike modesty in death as she had in life. She was dead.

For one long moment the two killers were frozen there immobile, staring at their victims. The only sound was the steady tick-tick of the diesel motor, and then there was a low moan. It was Maltitz; he was coming round. Red Rudi swung round, flashed a look at Maltitz, whose eyelids were flickering rapidly now as he tried to formulate a weak question, and commanded, '*Bull, let's get the hell out of here!*'

In the very same instant that they burst from the firs screaming at the top of their voices to keep up their courage, the three riflemen opened up. On the roof, the surprised Polish gunners flung up their arms and sagged to the metal, dead or badly wounded.

It gave them the start they needed. Almost instantaneously the machine-gun to the rear of the hut opened up, but it did not have the accuracy of the one sited on the roof.

Zig-zagging crazily, aware of the white spurts of tracer stitching a lethal pattern at his flying feet, von Dietz pelted across the road, firing from the hip as he ran. A Pole rose from the ground, dripping blood from a leg wound, and tried to grab von Dietz's feet. In mid-stride von Dietz kicked him in the face and the man went reeling back, spitting out broken teeth. A grenade sailed out of the window of the hut. Von Dietz ducked. It exploded just behind him. Men screamed, and he had the impression that one of his soldiers flew into the air and smacked into the upper branches of one of the firs from which they had come to remain there, every limb shattered like some monstrous wounded bird. He fired a burst. A man fell from the window leaking blood from a dozen holes in his chest.

A skinny Pole barred his way, thrusting at him with his long bayonet. Von Dietz twisted to the right. The Pole tumbled forward. He smashed the butt of his Schmeisser down on the

Pole's hands. The man howled and dropped the rifle to the floor. Next instant Dietz's elbow connected with his jaw and the Pole reeled back, head swinging from side to side, his eyes suddenly glazed, the very image of the comic drunk.

Now they were out of the dead ground, which had so far covered them from attack from the Poles on the ledge above. Grenades started to rain down upon them, exploding everywhere in thick angry scarlet bursts of flame, sending razor sharp slivers of steel cutting through the air frighteningly. Von Dietz did not hesitate. Summoning up the last of his energy, he dived forward, taking what was left of the brittle hut window-frame with him. He smashed down on to the floor in the corner, while the survivors of that crazy, rush came pelting down from the trap above, crashing in through the door as the bullets from the ledge began to smack into the hut.

But already his men had taken over. In the corner a blond boyish radio operator was pinned to the table on which his transmitter rested, a bayonet thrust through his hand, while the middle-aged, moustached man who was obviously the commander of the pass stood pressed against the wall, a young panting soldier holding the muzzle of his machine pistol against his breast.

Groggily von Dietz got to his feet, his head ringing, only half aware of the fire from the ledge striking the hut but knowing that the Poles up there had to be made to stop.

The young soldier did the job for him. 'Tell them to stop firing,' he commanded in short hectic bursts of speech, his chest heaving. 'Stop, or you die!'

The Polish officer made a brave show of it, although his position was hardly dignified, his tunic ripped up by the muzzle of the machine pistol to reveal his fat hairy belly. 'No,' he croaked in German and then as if he feared the young infantryman wouldn't understand, he shook his head the best he could.

Still dazed and unable to act, von Dietz watched the scene in a kind of amused detachment, as if he were watching a play: the noble Polish officer, the brutal German, the cowardly radio operator. Instinctively he knew what would happen next. The officer's refusal would be followed by the operator's cry of 'Stop, stop, I'll do it!' But von Dietz was wrong.

Suddenly the operator wrenched his hand free from the bayonet with a great cry of both pain and rage and rushed the soldier threatening the commander, his blood-dripping mutilated hand upraised. He didn't get far. A machine pistol opened fire, deafening them and drowning the operator's death cry. The room was filled with the stench of burnt explosive and smoke now, but von Dietz was able to glimpse the commander being escorted to the door by the young soldier. Stepping cautiously over the dead body of the operator, he took a towel that hung on a nail on the jamb and waved it cautiously out of the door before venturing forth into the open to shout something in Polish.

A few more shots and then the firing died away altogether. Overtaken by a strange sense of anti-climax, Major von Dietz realized that they had done it. The pass was theirs.

The men were deadened by the strain. Their legs refused to move. Their hands trembled. Their bodies were a thin skin stretched over a suppressed red-hot madness which threatened to burst out at any moment into one great roar at the monstrous crime of war. But instead of roaring, they slumped there among the dead, Polish and German, watching the blood-red ball of the sun beginning to slide over the mountains and the first black shadows slip in like silent ravens from the east.

After a while their Polish prisoners simply edged further and further away from them, until finally they slipped into the shadows with a swift hesitant look over their shoulders and disappeared for good. Nobody cared.

The shadows intensified. Still they did not move. Each man was engrossed in his own thoughts. They had killed and been killed. They had become wild beasts. And they knew, although they were alive and the victors, that they were condemned, as condemned as if some whey-faced judge in a black cap had ordered them sentenced to death. Sooner or later they would die. And the thought filled them with anger.

Von Dietz began to become aware of his surroundings at last — the shattered, bullet-pocked hut, the grotesque tangle of metal, the corpses piled everywhere. 'German order,' he whispered to himself. So this was what it meant. 'German order!'

He laughed suddenly, a strange hollow sound in that place of the dead. Slowly, painfully slowly, as if their heads were worked by stiff rusty springs, the survivors turned to look at the bare-headed officer who sat there in the dirt, his face hollowed out to a grinning death's head by the harsh evening light.

Some bit their bottom lips at the look they saw in Major von Dietz's eyes, a few shivered, one man crossed himself. There was the look of madness in those severe grey eyes now.

And then, as the mist started to rise from the craters and crannies, far away to their left the signal flares began to soar into the evening sky, indicating victory and the fact that General von Thoma had broken through. As they started to trail down the mountain, dragging their rifle-butts through the dust after them, the soldiers were wrapped in silence, grey ghosts returning to where so many of them had started and only a handful would return.

Now the dreams with which they had begun, those youthful yearnings that had made their blood uneasy, had vanished into the despair and rage of battle. They were boys no longer. They had experienced their first blood and now they were soldiers. Doomed men, all.

EPILOGUE

'Love drove me to rebel. Love drives me back to grope with
them through Hell.'
Siegfried Sassoon

The news had spread fast.

Of course, there had been nothing about it in the Party press
or in the Goebbels' radio. Naturally that would have helped to
reveal the great secret.

The news had reached W— in a different and circuitous
manner. By word of mouth; by the flushed excited looks on
the faces of the golden pheasants; by the sudden rash of new
swastika flags everywhere; by the renewed attention company
sergeant-majors were paying to ceremonial drill, as if the field-
greys crowding the border area from Saarbrücken to Cologne
were raw recruits instead of the seasoned veterans of the recent
victorious campaign in Poland; by the abundance of security
precautions, with the leather-clad middle-aged gentlemen of
the Gestapo making their appearance in every God-forsaken
Eifel village along the route He would take.

The Führer was coming!

The information was spread furtively among the civilians. It
brought a ripple of excitement to their dull winter lives, for
there had been no tremendous victories reported on the radio
to the sound of fanfares of brass trumpets making their blood
race as it had done day after day the previous September. They
whispered it to each other in the queues outside the bread
shops; passed it *sotto voce* amongst the regulars of inns;
telephoned it to one another in clumsily constructed codes,

229

hoping that the operator was not listening. Adolf Hitler, the Victor of Poland, was coming to the Eifel.

Now at last the strange peaceful inactivity that had followed the victory in Poland would cease. Soon the degenerate French and their perfidious English allies would learn what German might really was. Now it would be *their* turn.

The Führer was coming!

In Trier it snowed, as it did in Gerolstein, Bitburg and Echtenach. All along the route taken by the 'Greatest Captain of All Times', as the papers were now proclaiming him, it was snowing that day. Save in W—, which would be the last station of the Führer's visit to his soldiers before he returned to his Berlin HQ to plan for the great spring offensive in the West, which would undoubtedly make Germany the master of Continental Europe.

On the square at W—, where Major Mueller had once trained his raw Eifel recruits, who had vanished to God know's where, the men of the reformed 69th Infantry Regiment waited, eyeing the leaden sky, stamping their gleaming boots on the frozen concrete, blowing hard on their icy bemittened fingertips, casting half-shy glances at the *Prominenz* lined up behind the saluting rostrum at the far end where the ceremony would soon take place.

They were all there under the straining crooked-cross, black, red and white banners: the old ones, Rundstedt, Keitel, Guderian, the victors of Poland; and the new ones who would make the running in the offensive to come, Model, Manteuffel, Rommel, talking animatedly to one another in their elegant, fur-collared general's great coats, while the bandsmen puffed and sawed, blaring out one heroic Prussian march after another. *The Führer was coming!*

Von Dietz reined in his horse, which was made nervous by the constant banging of the big drum. He stared round the square, framed by the black skeletal trees, telling himself just how much he had changed since he had left W——.

Then he had regarded himself as a nihilistic cynic. Now he knew just what an innocent he had been. Poland had taught him that. It had taken von Ostermann's belief in the Regiment, Kunz's foolish heroism, the Countess's hatred, the cowardice of his own men under fire, the death of some three thousand Poles and Germans to teach him just how blind he had really been.

At first, after the victory in Poland was completed, he had not been able to get over the violence, the pointless deaths, the lost gambles. He hated himself for having created nothing but death; and after a while he had come to the conclusion that the only thing he could create that might atone for his misdeeds was his own death.

He had ridden out into the Eifel woods beyond W——, where they were now stationed before being sent to the Siegfried Line prior to the great spring offensive, and had sat down with his pistol with his back to a fir. He had been very cool as he had considered how best to do it, calculating the angle so that the pistol did not slip and only injure him, deciding that he would place the muzzle inside his mouth so that the single bullet would mash through his soft brain and shatter-blast the back of his skull in one final electric burst of light. He had placed the muzzle between his lips, wrinkling his nose a little at the taste of gun oil and clicked the trigger. It would work. Then, very deliberately, he had fitted a loaded magazine, cocked the pistol, clicked off the safety catch and with only the slightest of hesitations raised the weapon. It had been then that he had heard the sweet silver tone of the evening bugle as it floated up from the barracks far below, welling up out of the solitude, somehow joyful and sad at the same time. It reminded him of all those who had died and would die in the Regiment, making his own misery somehow trivial and absurd.

Thus he had sat there, unable to move, transfixed by those silver mysterious notes, while the evening sky darkened until finally its very echo had died away and he knew he was saved.

Very quickly he had uncocked his pistol, placed it carefully back in the holster, mounted his horse and ridden slowly back down to the Regiment.

The 69th had him again.

Now he sat there on his uneasy horse as the band played and the first careless wisps of snow started to drift down. In his mind's eye he saw what lay ahead as a misty vagueness, a grey uncertainty beyond which death lay waiting once more with its greedy blood-dripping maws open, while with his real eyes he saw the Regiment, the bright new faces, ruddy with good health and the freezing cold, the Class of 1919, with here and there among them the Old Heads (as they called themselves), the veterans of Poland. In some cases they were only a couple of years older than the new recruits; yet an eternity of time and experience seemed to separate their withdrawn, knowing eyes and looks from those of the others.

What were they thinking he asked himself, as he sat there on the uneasy horse, only half-hearing the band and the growing noise of cheering and *Sieg Heils* from the streets beyond the barracks walls? What was going on in the Bull's mind? What had happened to him that September, the 'Hero of the Border Blood Bath' (as the Goebbels press had called him), to deflate that beefy figure of his so to turn that once ruddy face yellow and make those piglike eyes of his cautious, wary, always on guard? Or little Private Maltitz, who seemed to have been transformed since he had returned to the Regiment from the lazaret? Why had he become so vocal, so outgoing, so happy? Or the soldier they called Red Rudi, who had become a notorious drunkard, always being brought up before him for insulting NCOs, involving himself in fights with the local golden pheasants, contemptuous of punishment, seeming almost as if he wished, wanted, *desired* to be punished? What had happened to him? And his running mate, the little Rhinelander, Deltgen, who seemed to have grown even smaller, the humour for which he had once been famous throughout the Regiment vanished, to be replaced by a hectic nervousness, which expressed itself in constant frightened glances over his skinny shoulder, as if he half expected the Grim Reaper himself to be standing there, grinning at him from cowled skull, one skeletal hand reaching out to claim him as his own.

Why? What had happened to them all in those four short days on the road to the Pass? How could... Colonel von Dietz's questions were cut short by the sudden blare of the '*Badenweiler*', Hitler's favourite march, and the shuffling for position amongst the *Prominenz* on the rostrum, as the long convoy of sleek Mercedes started to swing through the gates past the rigid guard-of-honour. He jerked his sword over his right shoulder and bellowed, his breath fogging the icy winter air, '*69th Infantry Regiment* — *ATTEN ... SHUN!*'

The Führer had arrived!

'*German soldiers ... comrades...*' that harsh guttural Upper Austrian voice echoed and re-echoed from the barracks wall, sending the crows rising from the skeletal trees in hoarse cawing protest. 'I have doubted a long time whether I should strike first in the East and then in the West. After all I did not organize the Wehrmacht not to strike. The decision to strike was always in me, for in all modesty the fate of the Reich depends upon me, Adolf Hitler. I have to choose between victory or destruction. I choose victory…'

Von Dietz no longer listened to the words, as the snow continued to drift down a little faster now. He concentrated on the man standing above him on the rostrum, the words beginning to tumble out in the usual torrent, accompanied by excited theatrical gestures. They said Hitler drank twenty bottles of mineral water during a major speech and that his shirt would be wringing wet afterwards; indeed, so it was rumoured, he insisted on a having a large piece of ice on the rostrum in hot weather so that he could cool his sweat-damp hands upon it.

It was an ordinary face save for those eyes, big, bulging, mad; the eyes of a man — perhaps monster would be better — who deliberately and knowingly could be evil. There was no denying that as Hitler threw back his head with an impatient jerk that sent his long black quiff flying from his forehead and thrust out his jaw pugnaciously, his dark gaze focused on the grey, snowy sky, as if he were challenging the Gods themselves, declaring, 'I shall stand or fall in this struggle. I shall never survive the defeat of my people! *We will march west and win — or die!*'

On the rostrum one of the golden peasants cried, '*Sieg Heil! Sieg Heil!*' the hoarse cry rose from a hundred throats as the civilians shot up their hands and the generals stiffened to attention, hands raised to their caps in salute, while the military band crashed into the '*Deutschlandlied*', the German national anthem, with a great thump of the big drum and a smash of blaring brass.

Now with that jerky walk of his, shoulders thrust back, dark eyes gleaming fanatically from that pudgy face, the Führer started to walk the length of the rigid ranks, followed by his immensely tall SS adjutants bearing the boxes containing the decorations, stopped every now and again at the whispered request of SS Major Günsche, his chief adjutant, to award a Wound Medal here, an Iron Cross, Second Class, there.

The Bull received a handshake, a few whispered words, and the Iron Cross, First Class, for his part in avenging that 'dastardly massacre of our wounded on the border'. The now Captain von Sulzberger was awarded the same decoration for rallying what had been left of Hardt's battalion, his young face, now marred a little by a lance-scar, indescribably happy. An apprehensive Maltitz was awarded the Wound Medal in Black, plus the Iron Cross, First Class, while Red Rudi, already half-drunk (though not showing it) nudged Sepp and whispered out of the side of his mouth, 'If he only knew he was shaking hands with a Jew at this minute, eh?' and then it was Colonel von Dietz's turn.

Towering high above the Führer, von Dietz raised his sword in salute and for one long instant the two of them stared at each other, the madness gone momentarily from Hitler's eyes, as if he could read what was going on in the tall, haggard young officer's mind at that moment and felt an uneasy trace of fear. And then von Dietz was bending low — too low — as if in submission to this monster, and Hitler was placing the black and white ribbon of the Knight's Cross of the Iron Cross around his neck, murmuring something about 'for outstanding courage and leadership in combat'.

Next moment he had straightened up stiffly, his horse tossing its head to and fro nervously, raising his sword to his helmet in salute, barking, 'Permission to march off, *mein Führer?*'

'Permission granted, Colonel!' Hitler said and moved back a few paces out of the way of the fidgety horse.

'*69th Infantry Regiment will advance!*' von Dietz bellowed, his command echoing back and forth across the square, muffled a little by the snow which was beginning to fall in ever-increasing strength now.

To the right of the rostrum the band struck up the '*Bayrischer Defiliermarsch*'.

'*Parade march!*'

As one, the three thousand men of the 69th moved forward behind their commander, tugging at the bit of his frisky mount, which swung its head from side to side, as if it might bolt at any moment. With their arms pressed rigidly to their sides, their eyes fixed unswervingly on some distant goal, their boots slamming home on the concrete in the goose step, the Regiment marched past the Führer with his right arm raised, the fingers of his left hand hooked in his belt, vanishing into the swirling snowflakes that wreathed them now in a white fog, on their way to a new appointment with death. And then they were gone, leaving behind them the echo and re-echo of their marching feet, and the nailed imprints of their boots, being rapidly filled in by the snow, as if Nature itself was in a hurry to hide the fact of their passing.

A NOTE TO THE READER

Dear Reader,

If you have enjoyed this novel enough to leave a review on **Amazon** and **Goodreads**, then we would be truly grateful.

Sapere Books

Sapere Books is an exciting new publisher of brilliant fiction and popular history.

To find out more about our latest releases and our monthly bargain books visit our website:
saperebooks.com

www.ingramcontent.com/pod-product-compliance
Lightning Source LLC
Chambersburg PA
CBHW060427180626
46817CB00007B/2698